Copyright

Making the King © 2024 B. Lybaek and Sarah JD

Cover Designer: Cruel Ink Design

This is a work of fiction. Names, places, characters and incidents are either the product of the author's imagination or are used fictitiously, and any resemblance to any actual persons, living or dead, organizations, events or locales is entirely coincidental.

Warning: the unauthorized reproduction or distribution of this copyrighted work is illegal. Criminal copyright infringement, including infringement without monetary gain, is investigated by the FBI and is punishable by up to 5 years in prison and a fine of $250,000.

ISBN: 978-1-7393922-6-0

Making the King

B. LYBAEK & SARAH JD

B. Cybaek

Sometimes you come across characters that worm their way into your heart. They stubbornly burrow into your brain, refusing to let go. That's exactly what happened with Cara and Rochus, AKA. Mama C and Rocco. So when Sarah suggested we write our anthology piece on them, it was a clear yes from me. (She has the best ideas, though she never remembers me telling her that ;-)

It's been an adventure learning how to co-write with another author, and I think what works for Bibi & I is that we really like to mess with our characters.
When writing the Cruz Kings MC series, we each added side characters not really knowing how much we would fall in love with them, so when trying to come up with the story for the anthology, I was drawn to Cara and Rocco's story, and where the Kings all began.
How did Rocco become so ruthless, and Cara so strong? We know that only comes from going through some dark shit, so here it is. Their dark and twisted story :-)

Acknowledgments

Thank you to

Our kick-ass alpha & beta ladies.
You guys are the absolute best.

Mr. Duncan and Mr. Lybaek... for the endless supply of
snacks and support. And for putting up with our plotting
calls at weird hours. (Making it work between UK and AU
time zones is no joke!)

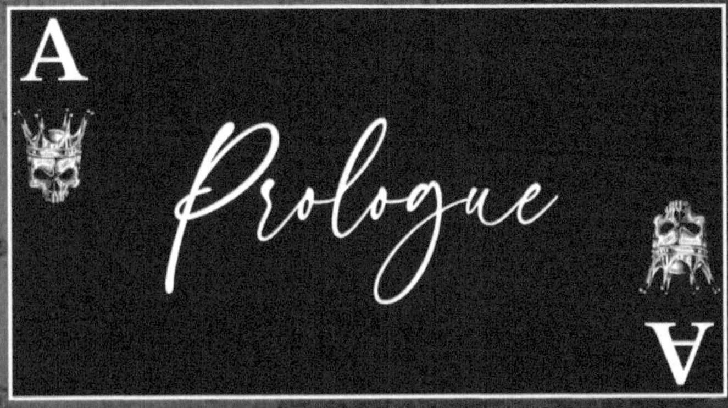

Cara

"Do you, Cara Rodríguez, take Rochus King as your lawfully wedded husband?"

Blinking, I look up from the floor and stare into the scared eyes of the spineless priest. Being here, wearing this dress, is making a mockery of my childhood.

The strapless dress is a complete replica of a dress I once saw on TV, and promptly told my bitch of a mother I wanted to get married in. Everything matches from the sweetheart neckline to the floor-length skirt. The bust is so tight my tits are threatening to spill out, not that it matters.

I'm not even sure why I'm dressed, and a part of me almost wishes I wasn't. Better naked than tainting one of the *few* good memories I had of my childhood.

"Cara," my dad prompts, digging the gun harder into my back. "Answer the priest."

I want to laugh at the fact he's threatening me with a gun. It just shows how little he really understands me if he thinks the gun is the bigger evil when I'm being married off to a stranger at sixteen.

For now, I have to play along and not give away that I'm not scared of him. But how can I be when he's lorded this very day over me for so long? I don't know when I stopped being scared, only that rage and a burning need to punish my parents for taking something from me is all I feel now. My childhood. My freewill. And at times, even my will to fucking live.

I run my hands down the skirt of the dress, smoothing an inconsequential wrinkle. The bottom of the skirt is covered in blood, but sadly, it's not the blood of my enemies. It's the blood of the couple who accidentally walked into the church half an hour ago. Needless to say, they won't be telling anyone what they stumbled upon.

Tossing my waist-long, dark hair with purple streaks—that I only got to piss him off—over my bare shoulder, I sneer, "If I must," answering the rhetorical question.

"Y-you have to say 'I do'," the priest says, his hands shaking so badly I absentmindedly wonder if he has arthritis or some shit.

"Why?" I challenge, my voice ringing out loud. "There's a gun fucking pointed at my back, and another at yours," I nod my head toward my twin brother, Mateo, who's standing behind the priest. "So tell me, Mr. Priest man, why the hell does the wording matter?"

I quickly look away from my twin. I can't fucking stand looking at the traitor I shared a womb with for eight months.

Next to me, my groom, Rochus King, coughs, and it sounds like he's trying to cover up a laugh. "Can we just get on with it?" he asks, trying to take my hand. "I want to move on so we can get to the part where I can finally consummate this holy matrimony, or whatever the fuck you call it."

I turn my head and look at him. If I force down my disgust, I can admit he's somewhat lucky in the looks department. Not that it matters. I might be a child bride, but I'll also make sure one of us is a widow before the night is over.

While my dad has a fucking boner for this marriage, it fills me with nothing but hatred. I knew it was coming, I've known that since I was twelve. That's how old I was when my mom sat me down and explained my purpose in life.

That was the day my childhood ended. With a few choice words, she changed my carefree existence into one where I had to... let's just say, knowing you'll be sold to the highest bidder when you're sixteen doesn't exactly make it easy to continue your life.

Not long after that talk, my parents dragged me to my sister Julietta's wedding because daddy dearest wanted me to know what was in store for me. It wasn't a joyous day, and I hated seeing my beautiful sister marrying the forty-something year-old guy. He reeked of sweat and alcohol, and I can still recall the offensive stench.

I've been told that Rochus King is nineteen, which I guess I should be happy about. Then again, if I don't take matters into my own hands, he might have a long life in front of him.

A snigger tries to burst free as I remember the vial inside me. The small see-through glass was brought to me by my sister, when she pretended to help me to the bathroom. According to her, it's a very strong sedative that she uses on her husband at least once a week.

Seeing as I have no pockets or anything to hide the vial, I saw no other option than to shove it inside me. I suppose it's almost poetic that the way to end my husband's life is in my vagina, a place he'll never touch. That's what I told my sister during our rushed time together, and it felt good to see her tentative smile before her horrid husband dragged her away.

As soon as I was in place, next to Rocco, they left. But not before Julietta's husband made sure to announce he'd only allowed my sister to come as a reward for her good behavior. Personally, I think he just wanted her to see me miserable.

I startle, realizing I've been lost in my head when Rochus whoops, "Fuck yeah I do." He nudges me with his shoulder.

"I mean, would you look at her? She's worth every fucking cent."

Swallowing down the disgust I feel at his words, I shoot him a smile I know is laced with innocence and not portraying my thoughts of how I want to make him scream in pain for buying me.

"D-do you have any vows?" the priest asks.

"No," my dad says, sternly.

At the same time, I say, "Yes."

"Cara," my mom scolds, speaking up for the first time.

I don't need to look at her to know she's scared, and I can't say I blame her. If I step out of line, my dad will make her pay for my transgressions. Maybe I should feel bad about that, but I don't. It's not my fault she married the devil, allowing him to sell her daughters. That's all on her, and as far as I'm concerned, she's as bad as he is.

Rochus smirks at me and nods. "Let's hear your vows."

Squaring my shoulders, I recite the practiced words. "I promise to give you everything you deserve. From today, and until our last day together."

There. It's vague, yet completely true. I'll fucking give Rochus what he deserves, and one way or another, it'll be tonight. When he wants to consummate the marriage, as he so eloquently put it.

Fucking pig.

As fucked up as it is, I'm glad my dad kept me a virgin. I guess he learned his lesson with Julietta. My fucked up parents didn't even try to mask their disappointment when my sister was sold for less than they expected, all because they started whoring her out at twelve. So, they went to great lengths to keep me a virgin, always making sure I knew it was so they could sell me for more at their creepy black market auction.

"Get on with it," my dad demands.

"Y-yes, of course," the priest stammers. "Do you umm... do you have rings?"

I look expectantly at the guy who bought me. I fully expect him to say I'm not worth it and move on, but to my surprise he fishes a black velvet box from his pocket. When he opens it, my eyes widen as the two gold bands come into view.

"Of course I fucking do," he says, smiling widely.

Taking my hand, he slides the gleaming ring onto my ring finger and winks at me. Then he hands me the other one, and I roll my eyes as I shove it onto his digit.

The priest clears his throat. "Rochus King, you may now kiss your bride."

Fuck. Me.

I don't want this man's lips on me. Though I've never been kissed, I've been forced to watch the men with Julietta enough times to know it's nothing like in the movies. The slobbering, foul smelling pigs she's had to...

"Do you mind?" Rochus asks, and I look up in confusion.

Surely he wasn't talking to me, was he? Because I mind a fucking lot. No, of course, he isn't asking me. If you're fucked up enough to buy a child bride, you don't ask permission.

"Mind what?" my dad barks, sounding as though he's being inconvenienced by the question.

Rochus sighs. "I don't want to kiss my wife at gunpoint. So, I ask again. Do you fucking mind?"

No one talks to my dad with so much disrespect, so I'm fully expecting him to punch Rochus. But he doesn't. To my astonishment, I feel the gun being removed from my back. Without meaning to, I straighten my spine, like I'm testing that the pressure is really gone.

Before I can contemplate doing anything, Rochus places his hands on my hips and turns me toward him. My gray eyes fly to his. They're the color of chocolate, and there's something hidden in the depths. Something that makes me feel...

"Relax," he breathes.

I don't get the chance to retort. Rochus' lips on mine silence me.

It's not the disgusting and brutal kisses I've seen my sister be subjected to. In fact, it's soft and slow. He isn't using his tongue, only pressing his lips to mine.

Rochus' hands move from my hips, slowly trailing up to my head. He winds his fingers through my locks, and I take his lead, moving mine to his shoulders. Before I know it, I instinctively open my mouth, but to my surprise, he doesn't deepen the kiss.

This is nothing like I was expecting it to be, and I'm completely caught off guard. Forceful and disgusting, that's what I'd prepared myself for. After seeing what my sister's husband did to her, I wouldn't even have been surprised if Rochus bent me over a pew and fucked me right here. But this...

"That's enough for now," Rochus murmurs. Just as I'm about to rethink my opinion of him, he lets go of my hair and slaps my ass. "The rest will come once we're out of here. Don't wanna desecrate this holy place, do we?"

I almost throw up in my mouth as he turns around and winks conspiratorially at my dad, who laughs boisterously.

"When the last payment goes through, you can fuck her bloody for all I care."

The lack of care for my well being no longer shocks me. All it does is cement the fact that one day I want to dance on this fucker's grave.

As soon as the words leave my dad's mouth, the door slams open and a dark-haired guy struts through. When he reaches the couple lying in a pool of their own blood, he jumps over them and does a fucking twirl.

What the actual fuck?

"Did someone ask for money?" he asks, nodding first at Rochus and then my dad. Walking straight up to me, he takes my hand and kisses the back of it. "Congratulations, Mrs. King."

My lips part and I want to hurl insults at him, yet no words come to mind. I can only stand there, gaping, as he pulls out his phone and shows the screen to my dad.

"There you go, Carlos. Cara no longer belongs to you."

For some reason, those words hit me, making me feel lighter. I no longer belong to the man who's put me and my sister through hell while doting on our brother. Where I resemble our bitch mom, Mateo's the spitting image of our dad—and just as vile and cruel as him.

But now... I'm free. From my dad, at least. And soon, if everything goes according to plan, from my husband as well.

"So we're all good?" Rochus asks, arching an eyebrow.

Dad takes his phone out of his pocket and taps on the screen. "Yep," he confirms with a nod. "The bitch is yours. Pleasure doing business with you, Rochus and Cain."

Rochus pulls me to his side and throws his arm around my shoulder. "Do you want to say goodbye to your family?" he asks.

"Yes," I snap, sarcastically. "There's nothing I want more than a tear-filled goodbye with the people who just fucking sold me. Estúpido." I didn't mean to voice the Spanish insult, but I don't regret it.

"I want to say goodbye to my daughter," my mom cries out.

Bitch even sounds like she means it.

"Let's go," I say to Rochus, completely ignoring her.

"No, Cara. Please. I want to hug you one last time."

I remain unmoved by her words. It's too little and much too fucking late.

"We should get going," Cain says, staring pointedly at the door he entered through. "Like, right fucking now." He adds the last part so low only me and Rochus can hear him.

Rochus nods and rushes me toward the exit. I can barely keep up with him, almost stumbling in the stupid high heels I was forced to wear.

As soon as we're outside, we come face-to-face with a group of masked strangers. Each one of them is wearing black from head to toe, the only thing standing out is the red diamond on their shoulders.

"Ready?" one of the men asks, and when Rochus nods, the stranger waves the others ahead.

"What's going on?" I ask, but I don't get an answer.

Without another word, the masked strangers, including my new husband, storm the church. It only takes seconds before gunshots ring out, and despite my mantra of staying strong, I lean against the church with my heart in my chest.

Who the hell are these people? And more importantly, why am I staying out here? I don't care if they're slaughtering my family, only that I'm left behind.

Resolutely, I sneak back inside, ignoring the men calling out for me to leave. I flip a few of them off, but other than that, I keep my focus ahead. Luckily for me, their attention is on the scene unfolding in front of them.

My dad's kneeling at the altar, and his right-hand man lies lifeless next to him. I knew Henry was lurking around somewhere. Years of being my dad's daughter have taught me that he never goes anywhere without his backup.

"Please," my dad begs, pathetically holding his hands up like in a prayer. "W-whatever you want."

Hearing my dad beg like this has excitement coursing through me as I move closer until I'm next to Rochus,

"You," my dad spits, no longer pleading for his life. "You did this, you useless cunt."

"Careful," Rochus warns. "You did this to yourself."

He kicks my dad square in the chest, sending him into the blood surrounding Henry's body.

"I want to kill him," I announce, my voice steady and devoid of all emotion.

"W-what?" Rochus asks, eyeing me like he isn't sure he heard me correctly.

"He's my fucking dad, and I want to be the one to end his miserable existence," I say, hating that I have to repeat myself.

I don't care who this Rochus is, or that he's now my husband. He's clearly not on my dad's team, and that's perfect for me. I'll even consider not lacing his drink with the sedative if he gives me this.

Before Rochus can make up his mind, my mom is unceremoniously pushed to the floor next to my dad.

"Mija," she sobs, looking up at me.

The endearment makes me flinch. She used to call me mija, meaning dear or darling, when I was a child. But she lost the right to call me anything like that years ago.

"Shut up," I hiss.

The noise in the background fades away as I look into the eyes of the woman who gave birth to me, and also ripped away any semblance of safety and happiness I might ever have had.

"You're as bad as he is."

I don't know I'm moving until I find myself ripping the gun from Rochus' hand. As soon as it's in my hand, I point it at my crying, pathetic mother.

"Cara!" Rochus warns.

Tuning him out, I bare my teeth. "Death is too good for you," I snarl, my hatred for her coating my words.

I'm absently aware that more people arrive, and a scuffle breaks out close to us. I know I should look, but I can't. I'm too transfixed by my dad kneeling on the floor, and the evil glint in his eye that's always present.

The sound of gunshots ricochets off the walls, and there's a thud from a body hitting the floor. People are shouting, and...

As soon as the sound registers, I make a snap decision. I only have seconds, and I use them to point the gun at my dad.

"May you rot in hell," I scream.

As soon as I make the decision to pull the trigger, all the other sounds in the church assault my ears. The roaring of police, and the demand for me to put down the gun. But I can't. Not until my dad is dead.

"Drop your fucking gun."

My hands shake as I clutch it harder.

"Drop the fucking gun and get on your knees with your hands above your head."

Tears stream down my face, blurring my vision.

"No," I whisper.

"Do it!" Rochus hisses.

Then he steps in front of me, putting himself between me and the police, holding his arms out to his side. I don't know if it's to shield me or to show them he's unarmed. Either way, I know an opportunity when I see one.

I look into the cold, dead eyes of my dad, the man I once loved. It seems so long ago that I hardly remember what it was like.

Then I pull the trigger, sealing my fate.

Rocco

The fuck is wrong with me? I'm anxious as hell, leaning against my truck, waiting for my child bride to exit the prison gates. Jesus, even thinking of her as a child bride turns my fucking gut. That day was never meant to end the way it did, with her locked up in prison.

The whine of the oversized gates opening draws my attention as the large metal barriers slowly start rolling open.

Fuck. How did things end up like this?

The job was meant to be simple. Well, as fucking simple as it can be when you're dealing with the sick cunts in the skin trade. There's always a chance that things will go south, but it's a risk we are willing to take if we can save as many of the innocent girls being sold to sick motherfuckers around the world as we can.

I was the fucking ruse this time, posing as a spoilt rich boy whose father purchased him a fucking virgin. The auction was done online, and finalizing the transaction happened a week later when I walked into that church and met Carlos Rodríguez, and his daughter Cara, only sixteen at the time, duressed to be my fucking wife.

I was only nineteen myself, but fuck, I'd been with the Diamond Crew for a while by that time, and had spent life on the streets for a number of years before that, so I knew how to bury my fear deep and only show the world a hard exterior. It's how I learned how to survive the cruelty of adults that thought their needs, their desires, meant more than a child's consent.

The large metal gates come to a clanging stop, the tall wire fencing built right up to them like a cage rattles as a gate further in opens.

Shit. How can one chick make me so fucking nervous?

The Cara Rodríguez I met when she was sixteen was a contradiction. Her features were everything soft, from her satin smooth cheeks and large doe eyes, and how fucking soft and plump her lips looked. And fuck, they felt it too, something which fucking pisses me off.

Not the fact that her lips were soft, but how it was nice kissing them.

Like what the fuck? She was sixteen. And while there are only three years between us, I was still classed as an adult that day, so I should never have liked how her lips felt against mine.

It was torture enough having to fake that I was excited about consummating the marriage, and fuck, even having to slap her ass felt so fucking wrong.

So why was she a contradiction?

Because as sweet as she looked with her long silky dark hair, big eyes, and those fucking kissable lips, she had the fire of a warrior princess inside her. A warrior princess who saw an opportunity to take matters into her own hands, and fucking killed her dad in front of everyone, including the cops.

Now, here I am, three years later despite the fact she refused to see me the entire time she was locked up. I kept trying for the first six months, but I eventually gave up. I turned my attention to helping our crew, while our Aussie associate, Baz Marx, worked tirelessly to get Cara's murder sentence reduced to manslaughter, and get her released early.

Yeah, we had to pay off a judge, a couple of cops, and even the prison warden to remove the murders Cara committed while inside, but we couldn't leave her in there when we were meant to save her.

A group of women start walking down the caged tunnel, and I hear some excited gasps around me from others who are waiting for their loved ones to be released.

I stand taller, pushing off my truck and rolling my shoulders back as I watch the women get closer to the exit.

I'm not even sure if Cara will recognize me. She wasn't present during the closed hearing last week where the judge ordered her to be released into my care as part of her parole terms. I've seen her though. Well, a picture of her. A prison headshot. I've studied it daily for the last few months, conjuring scenarios in my head as to where the innocent-looking girl that I met three years ago went, because staring back at me is a woman. A hard woman. A woman who, like me, has learned how to survive.

A couple of prison guards move to the wire gate at the end of the cage and unlock it, pushing it open where the first woman steps out toward her freedom.

There are some squeals from a few cars down, and then they run into each other's arms and hug.

I ignore the commotion and focus on the gate, watching as woman after woman steps out, but none are my wife.

Where the fuck is she?

Frowning, I take a few steps forward to get a better view into the cage and see a tall figure strutting down the path as she talks to a female prison guard. The closer they get I can see a cigarette being shared between them, before they hug each other.

The moment Cara Rodríguez steps out of the cage and into the parking lot, my lungs fucking forget how to function. That definitely is not a child. That is a woman, curvy in all the right places, holding herself tall and proud and so fucking full of confidence, the same confidence I got a brief glimpse of at our wedding.

She glances around the lot, her body stiffening when her dark gaze lands on me, and she takes one last drag of her smoke, before dropping it to the gravel, and using the toe of her shoe to stub it out.

Jesus, where did she even get those clothes? She went to juvie in a fucking wedding dress, and walks out of prison in booted heels, skintight leather looking pants, and a fucking cheetah print cropped tank.

If I thought Cara needed saving from prison, I'm getting the feeling that I was very fucking wrong.

Her heels click as she walks over to me, one foot in front of the other, her hips swaying in a way that reminds me of catwalk models doing their strut.

Fuck. Do they teach them that in prison?

"Who did you fuck up the ass to swindle this?" she asks, coming to a stop in front of me.

I'm speechless for a moment as I take her in. She's still there, that innocence from the child she once was. But either she's covering it up to appear stronger, or, she's been hardened in such a way that even though you can see signs of the nineteen-year-old in her features, her soul is ten years older.

Given the teardrop tattoo under her eye, something I know she got after committing murder while in prison, I'd say that I'm looking at the latter.

"Don't I get a thank you? You're free now."

She scoffs. "Hardly. I'm going from one prison to another."

"Living with me won't be like a prison." I snap, feeling the sting of her insult.

Her dark brows hitch. "I'm still your wife. That sounds like a prison to me."

She brushes past me, moving to the passenger door, getting in.

Fuck. She could be more grateful. I get that this isn't the best situation, but we've worked on getting her released for the entire time she was locked up, and this is what I get.

Rounding the truck, I climb in and start up the engine, acutely aware of her presence in the cabin. My knuckles turn white as I grip the steering wheel, my eyes trained straight ahead, not really seeing anything as her pissy attitude digs its claws into me.

Calm the fuck down, man.

She doesn't understand.

She thinks I bought her from an online black-market auction and married her underage.

Well yes, that is what happened, but she doesn't know that the marriage was a ruse to protect her. She doesn't know that we were there to save her.

She doesn't know me. She only knows the persona I was in that day as I performed the ruse.

Shifting next to me, Cara stretches her legs out, placing them on the dash of my truck, and my fucking blood boils.

"Get your fucking feet off the dash."

The low growl that comes from me causes her to shift a little, but her feet remain in place.

Slowly, I release the wheel and turn in my seat, glaring at her.

"I won't ask fucking twice, Cara. Get your feet off the dash."

A sinister smirk slowly spreads her lips, drawing my eyes to them and how fucking plump they still are.

"Too late. You already did."

"What?" I snap in confusion as I drag my gaze from her lips to her eyes that appear more gray than usual.

"You said you won't ask twice, but you already did. You asked the first time, and then right after you said you won't ask twice. So you did." She smirks. "Ask twice."

My lips part to argue with her, but she has a fucking point which I don't want to admit, so I lurch forward, grabbing her ankles and pull her feet down off my dash.

"Hey! Don't touch me!" She hisses, her fists balled like she is preparing to throw a punch.

I chuckle. "You're my wife. It's my right."

You fucking idiot. What sort of moronic caveman comment was that?

"Yeah? Well, I'm not opposed to becoming a widow. I hope you know how to sleep with one eye open." She shoves me back, her small hands stronger than they look.

I chuckle. She's kind of funny.

Even so, I'm not dumb enough not to take her threat seriously. I could always tell her the truth about that day. Explain to her why she's still my wife when the whole thing was a ruse, but this way seems more fun.

Let her be fucking scared of me.

What do I care?

As soon as the twelve months are up and we can file for a divorce, assuming I can keep her out of trouble from violating the terms of her parole, then she can walk the fuck away, and I can turn my focus back on saving more innocent children.

Turning my sights to the road, I pull out of the prison parking lot and turn the radio up to fill the cabin with music as we make the two-hour drive back to Santa Cruz.

She stays quiet for the trip, sitting mostly tense for the first half, but then relaxing back into the seat for the second half, putting her window down and letting her fingers dance in the wind as she dangles her hand out the window.

The more time that passes, the more I settle back to my old thoughts about wanting to help her, instead of slapping her for being such an ungrateful bitch. I need to remind myself that she's out of the loop with the details of that day. That she has been in survival mode for years and isn't going to trust anyone anytime soon.

As I slow the truck to suit the speed for inner Santa Cruz, Cara sits taller in her seat, looking out at our surroundings. I have no idea where she's originally from. Definitely California since we were tracking the movements of her father across the state for a while before the auction even took place. Though I get the feeling by how curious she is, that she isn't from Santa Cruz.

I look around, trying to see it through her eyes, and if she didn't know where she was, she does now by the Santa Cruz Warriors banner outside their office.

"Have you ever been to Santa Cruz before?" I ask, my words instantly making her stiffen.

"No."

"The beaches are nice. The wharf is cool. Some good places to eat. There's a deck that the sea lions lounge around on. The summer tourists love that."

I can see in my periphery, Cara turning from the window to look at me.

"Are we going to go for strolls on the beach, hand in hand, before going to the wharf where you'll hand feed me and look longingly into my eyes?" She makes a gagging noise before continuing. "If you think I'm going to be your well-behaved wife and bend to your will, then you better think again."

I know I shouldn't say it. I know it'll just make things worse. But I can't stop the words from falling from my lips.

"Oh, you'll be bending to my will alright."

"Un-fucking-likely!" she yells, and I shoot her a smirk.

"We'll see."

"You won't live long enough to try." She threatens and I chuckle.

"Again. We'll see."

"Ugh. You're impossible." She huffs, crossing her arms over her chest and sinking back into the seat.

I can't argue about that. I am being impossible, just to annoy her.

On the other side of town, I scan the front entrance of the adult entertainment club, Dirty Diamonds, as we approach, noticing it's quiet out on the street.

The club is open but doesn't get busy until night when most members have finished their nine to five, which gives us time to focus on the real business we do.

"That place there," I point as I slow the truck, "That's where you will work."

Her eyes scan the place before her head whips in my direction.

"I'm not fucking stripping for anyone!" Her declaration is loud in the cabin, and I smirk as we idle past the club.

"You won't be stripping there," I tell her, catching her mortified expression.

"I won't be a whore either!" she yells again and I nod.

"Good thing that's not a fucking brothel then."

"Then... what will I be doing there?"

I speed up now that we're past the club, turning the corner to take the street toward the waterfront, and my little beach shack.

"The books," I say, noticing her glance back out the windows as the buildings turn to houses.

"The books? Like, bookkeeping?" she asks, turning back to me, and I nod. "But I don't know anything about book-keeping."

"That's okay. I'll teach you."

She falls silent, so I sneak a glance at her to find those dark brows hitched again.

"What?"

"You'll teach me?" She scoffs. "Is it not enough that I have to stay under the same roof as you, but have to endure you at work as well?"

"Tough gig, I know, but I think you can handle it."

She huffs again, and I bite back my smirk. I can see she wants to rile me up. She wants to make me mad, and it's annoying her that I'm not biting this time.

As the ocean comes into view, out of the corner of my eye I see Cara sit taller in the seat. I love this place and my little patch of paradise. It's nothing grand. The complete opposite in fact, but it's mine, and it's right across from the water.

At the end of the street, I turn onto my road, and a couple of houses in, I turn into my small driveway.

My shack is small. One bedroom, one bathroom, a living room and kitchen. The laundry is out the back in the small courtyard, but that's the extent of my humble abode.

"Couldn't decide what color to paint it?" Cara remarks as she takes in the façade of my house. Her new home.

I smirk, knowing she's referring to the three different paint colors.

The timber cladding that surrounds my bedroom is a mint green, while the cladding that wraps around the front living area is yellow. The white trim is the only thing that ties it altogether, and the aqua front door is a statement piece.

No one but me has to like it, and since I do, I don't really care.

"It's unique." I comment and she fake laughs.

"You've got that right."

I try not to let her dig at my cozy shack annoy me, and climb out of my truck, hearing her do the same.

Opening the door to my home, I turn back to invite her in, but find her at the sidewalk, staring over the road to the mix of rocky banks and sandy beaches that stretch along this part of Santa Cruz.

"Beautiful, isn't it?" I say, coming up behind her, and she nods.

"There's something freeing about the ocean, so open and as far as you can see."

I nod, even though she can't see me. "Well, now you get to look at it every day," I remind her, and she turns to look over her shoulder at me. "Sometimes, I sit out here for hours staring at its beauty." I gesture to the chairs behind me that sit under the living room window, and her eyes follow, spotting them. "There's also a great view from my bed."

Her face falls, and she turns back to the ocean.

"What about my bed? Is there a view from my room?"

"Sure there is. It's the same view I get, since my bedroom is your bedroom."

"What!" She spins on her heel, but I'm already making my way back to my door, stepping into my house.

"You can't be serious?" she asks in a panic, stepping inside as well, and for a moment, she falls quiet as her eyes scan the small space.

"I'm very serious. You're meant to be my wife. Your parole officer said he might do spontaneous home visits to make sure you are abiding by your parole terms. And since my home only has one bedroom, I don't see where else you're gonna sleep."

Her mouth drops open before she storms through my little shack, going into my bedroom, and coming out the second door that leads to the only bathroom in the house. Then she steps into the kitchen, doing a spin before joining me back in the living room.

"This is it?" she asks, shocked, and I nod. "But there isn't even a laundry room."

"It's outside." I point to the back door, "in the little court-yard."

"No." She all but whispers, her face falling, her hard exterior vanishing for a beat before she puts her mask back into place.

"Yes. I'm sorry it's not a palace for you, but with time, I'm sure you'll come to love it as much as I do."

Shaking her head, she glares at me. "I'm not sharing a bed with you. I would rather die."

Rolling my eyes at her dramatics, I shrug. "Suit yourself. Enjoy the couch."

Tossing my keys on the bar top bench that divides the living room and kitchen, I reach back and pull my shirt off, draping it over the barstool.

"What are you doing?" Cara asks, and I try not to react to the slight edge of fear in her tone.

"It's hot, and I'm in my house." I shrug, turning my back on her and going to the fridge to grab a beer. "Want a drink?"

"No." She huffs, and I shrug, opening the bottle and drinking it down as I walk back into the living room.

Her dark gaze is on me, traveling over my bare torso, and when she notices that I've caught her checking me out, she quickly turns her back to me.

It's weird having her in my space. It's not like I haven't had women here before, but Cara is different. As small as she is, she seems to dwarf my living space by her presence alone.

"So what's it going to be?" I ask coming up behind her and she stiffens, moving quickly across the room so she can keep her eye on me. "You gonna sleep in our marital bed?"

"Sure. Once I've gutted you and buried the body."

Throwing my head back laughing, she just glares at me and waits for my response.

"Okay, Killer. If you say so." I tease before pointing to the bedroom.

"Inside the closet are some clothes for you. I had Alice and Sasha from the club go shopping for you. They got you some toiletries as well, but if there's anything you need, we can pick it up later after we've been to the club."

"We're going to the club?" she asks, looking a little worried.

"Yes, but only to grab a few things so I can show you the basics of your job, because tomorrow, you start working there."

Cara

The snores coming from Rochus are almost perfectly timed with the soft laps of the ocean. The few days I've been here, I've refused to join him on the bed, or take the couch. I'm sitting on the floor, hiding in the darkest corner of his house. Shack... whatever the hell it's called.

One thing I learned in prison was to never let your guard down. You're never more vulnerable than when you're sleeping, off in whatever nightmare your subconscious concocts for you. That's partly why I stay awake during the night, napping at odd times during the day when I can.

The other reason is my nightmares... the ones I've had since Julietta took her last breath. I can still hear the sounds she made as she choked on her own breath after she was stabbed to death. My beautiful, brave, and kind sister bled out on the dirty shower tiles.

She didn't deserve that. Julietta was the best person I've ever known, and nothing could ever be good enough for her. Let alone living her days out in prison after killing her husband not long after my wedding from hell.

If I allow myself, I can recall the feeling of her matted hair, and too thin body as she gasped for air she no longer needed. I knew she was dying, but I still held her and sang to her.

Twinkle, twinkle, little star,
How I wonder what you are.
Up above the world so high,
Like a diamond in the sky.

Esta noche allí estarás,
Cual diamante brillarás.

There isn't a perfect Spanish translation of the song, so toward the end, I was stringing words together from my memory. It's the song Julietta sang to me at night when I felt scared of the future. Even though she had to endure her own hell, she always found the strength to be there for me.

At least until she got married and had to leave our home in San Francisco to move in with her husband. The years after that were the hardest to endure. I missed her so much my soul fucking hurt.

I don't think about San Fran as my home, and I haven't since the day she moved out. Now, I guess I have no fucking home. A place to live, yes. But that doesn't make it a home.

Shaking the memories from my head, I look out the window. The sky is clear, making it all too easy to see the stars as they shine so brightly.

"Te amo mi corazón," I whisper into the night. "I love you so much your absence hurts."

So far, I've done a good job of avoiding certain things in my mind. Like, who am I without her? She was my heart, my conscience—everything that was good inside me died with her.

The price for Julietta's freedom was my soul, which is forever blackened.

I feel my eyes misting, but I don't allow any tears to escape. Julietta told me to be strong, to never bend to anyone, and to take control of my destiny.

"No one can keep someone like you down, Cara. Give them hell and then get the fuck out of there. Promise me you'll find a way to be happy."

"I promise," I murmur as I look up at the stars.

Unconsciously, I close my hand around the cross hanging from the necklace my sister gave me before she died. I still don't know how she managed to keep it in prison without anyone knowing.

A sinister smile stretches my lips as I recall the two women who tried to take it from me. Needless to say, one of them didn't live to tell the tale, and the other never bothered me again.

I reach for the cigarettes on the floor and light yet another one. The ashtray at my feet is already full, so much so the ashes I flick into it land on the floor. The dutiful daughter still living somewhere deep inside me wants to get up and empty it, but that's not happening. No way in hell am I risking waking my darling husband.

With a sneer on my lips, I look down at the laptop resting on my legs. When Rochus first mentioned I'd be doing book-keeping, I hoped there'd be an easy way to get my hands on some of their money so I can get the hell out of here. Sadly, I'm only given access to the fucking expenses, which is hella boring.

Since I've already completed the shit I'm expected to do, I take full advantage of having the laptop and start snooping through the other docs and sheets. It only takes me a few minutes of looking at the strip schedule to spot an error.

"Estúpido," I mumble to myself.

One of the girls—or Diamonds, as they call them—is listed for a shift on a day they've also given her time off.

"Do you ever fucking sleep?" I stiffen as Rochus turns to his side and switches on the bedside lamp.

Despite my best intentions of ignoring him, I look up from the laptop. The white sheet he clutches when he's deep in slumber is barely covering him, so his torso and one leg are on full display.

My heart skips a beat as I involuntarily take in his toned physique. He really isn't bad to look at. Such a shame all those muscles and enticing grooves are wasted on someone who was willing to buy and marry a child.

I don't actually care about my age, that's the least of his offenses as far as I'm concerned. Whether I was sixteen or twenty-five, he bought me, and that's something I can never forgive, let alone forget.

Rochus clears his throat, and as I look into his grinning face, I know he notices me checking him out.

Puta.

"None of your business," I sneer, finally remembering to answer his question. "And if you think I'm going to let my guard down around you, you're badly mistaken."

He nods like that's what he expected me to say. "Are you at least going to shower and change your clothes today?"

I want to shrink in on myself, embarrassed he's basically telling me I stink. He's probably right. It's been three days, and I've barely eaten or drank anything, trying to avoid the bathroom as much as possible.

It's not just that I can't look at bathroom tiles without remembering my sister, it's yet another time where I'd be vulnerable.

"Come on," Rochus says, sitting up on the bed. "Is there... I mean... do you need help to shower?"

When my expression turns murderous, he immediately holds his hands up.

"I didn't mean it like that," he rushes out.

Pretending not to notice the curious way he looks at me, I refocus on the laptop. I highlight the error in the schedule and leave a comment with a suggestion of who can fill in without it messing with the other schedules.

Within seconds, there's a reply to my comment from someone named Cain. Curious about who he is, I click on his profile picture. Though he looks a little older, it's clearly the guy who was at the church on my fucking wedding day, the one paying my dad.

Good catch, Cara. I owe you!

The six seemingly small words make me smile.

He's right... he owes me. Maybe if I help out, I can garner enough favors for my freedom.

I'm so engrossed in my thoughts I don't notice Rochus has moved until his hand closes around my upper arm, and he hauls me to my feet.

"Enough of this," he growls.

I kick out at him, but narrowly miss him when he moves to the side.

"Let go of me," I demand, outraged he's touching me.

I don't know why I'm surprised. On our wedding day, he did say he couldn't wait to fuck me, so this must be him reaching the end of his patience. Panic claws at my throat and I shake my arm, trying to dislodge his grip.

Rather than doing as I say, he moves until his body is flush against mine. Then he effortlessly throws me over his shoulder.

"Rochus!" I cry out, and slap his back, but he doesn't budge.

As he carries me over to the small bathroom, my breath quickens. No. I'm not going in there. I flail my arms and legs, doing my best to hurt him. Despite landing a few good punches, he doesn't react apart from a grunt or two.

"You're going to have to play nice eventually," he says as he puts me down on the bathroom floor.

My vision wavers, and it feels like the walls are closing in on me.

"I won't let you fuck me," I scream as I fight to keep my panic at bay.

Rochus chuckles. "I'm not in the habit of forcing anyone to have sex with me. But I don't want to smell you all day. So get in the fucking shower."

When I try to push past him, he quickly darts out the door, slamming it behind him. As I hear what sounds like furniture scraping against the floor, I jump into action and throw myself at the door.

It's too late.

Whatever he moved is barricading the door, preventing me from getting out. Not that it deters me from kicking and punching the fucking door.

"Let me out," I scream.

No answer.

"Rochus!" I snarl his name.

When that doesn't work, I spin around and look for anything I can use to help me escape my new prison. Of course, there's nothing. As I go through the cabinet and shower, I don't even find a razor. The motherfucker must be hiding it.

Swallowing, I try a different tactic. "Please let me out. I promise I'll be nice."

Still no answer.

My heart thunders in my chest, and I swear the damn walls are moving nearer. If I don't get out of here soon, they'll swallow me whole.

"P-please," I sob, not able to control my panic.

I can't be in here much longer. The walls are almost touching my arms, and the light is flickering. If it goes out, I'll... I can't... I have to get out.

I only have one thing left to bargain with. Rochus doesn't know I'm still a virgin, or maybe he does since I've been locked up since we got married. But unlike many other inmates, I didn't indulge in any kind of sexual activities. I'm as untouched as I was three years ago.

Fuck, I really don't want to give my body to him, but I will if it's my ticket out of this cursed room.

"I'll make you feel good if you let me out," I offer, my voice breaking off on a whimper as the light flickers again.

When he still doesn't let me out, I start kicking and punching again while screaming at the top of my lungs. I even ram my head against the door.

I scream until my throat hurts, and the light disappears. Falling to my knees, I wait for the room to swallow me. To...

"Jesus fuck!"

I barely hear the roar or feel my body being jostled as he lifts me up and carries me out of the bathroom.

"Cara?"

Gasping, I greedily inhale as much air as I can. Despite the oxygen in my lungs, it doesn't feel like enough, and I continue to take in as much as possible. It's like a vicious circle, though. The more I breathe, the more lightheaded I feel. Yet I can't stop. My brain keeps telling me to carry on, so I do.

"Stop it!"

With each exhale, it feels like I'm depleting my body of the much needed air. I don't even try to answer him, instead I fight to make the room stop spinning.

Closing my eyes, I sag in his hold on me. I'm vaguely aware I'm in his lap, my head resting against his chest. The hairs on his chest tickle my nose.

The longer we sit there, the less I battle to breathe. My body relaxes, and I force my breathing to match the rise and fall of his chest.

It's still dark outside, and the only light illuminating the room is the bedside lamp. Its yellow light creates an almost cozy atmosphere.

When I try to open my eyes, they feel heavy so I decide against it. Barely aware of my actions, I burrow my head into him and breathe in his scent. Rochus smells of citrus and the forest mi abuela took us to for a picnic once.

One of Rochus' hands runs up and down my back, warming me everywhere I feel cold. I shouldn't be cold. Not when I'm fully dressed. Though a part of me wants to punch him for touching me, I ignore it. For the first time since I was a kid, I allow someone to hold me.

I'm so tired and weak from denying myself more than the bare minimum of food and water that I'm honestly not even sure I could fight him if I wanted to. Rochus is big, and from his need to always remove his shirt when he's in the house, I know just how ripped he is.

Before long, I feel myself drifting off, and despite knowing I shouldn't sleep when he's around, I don't have it in me to fight it.

I'm back in the prison, my sister lying on the floor with her head in my lap.

"It's okay, Cara," she whispers, with a smile on her lips. "I'll be free soon."

"No," I cry. "Don't leave me. Por favor quédate."

Even though I know she can't, I beg for her to stay with me.

"No one can keep someone like you down, Cara. Give them hell and then get the fuck out of there. Promise me you'll find a way to be happy."

The shiv in my hand clanks as it falls onto the floor. It's covered in Julietta's blood.

"Cara!"

I dart my head around, looking for whomever called my name. There's no one else here, though. There never is.

"You must go to him," my sister whispers.

"Who?" I ask, bewildered. "We're all alone."

She laughs, but unlike the other nightmares, she doesn't sound like she's dying. She sounds happy. "To your husband, of course."

"I don't trust him," I say, confused.

This conversation is all wrong. That's not how my nightmares play out. Julietta dies over and over, and we never talk about anything else.

"For fuck's sake, Cara!"

I look around again, trying to figure out where the voice is coming from. Fisting the shiv, I hold it tightly in case someone is playing a trick on me.

"You need to wake up," my sister sing-songs. "And you need to stop living in the past."

Jerking awake, I shoot my leg out, instinct telling me to kick first and ascertain the situation later.

"Fuck!" Rochus grumbles.

Without wasting a second, I roll to the side and off the bed, positioning myself in a defensive crouch. As I narrow my eyes and look at Rochus who's sprawled on his back, I register the fact I was on the bed and he's only wearing his boxers.

"What did you do?" I snarl.

Realizing I'm still fully dressed, even wearing my heeled boots, I relax a little. It's enough to notice the red welt matching the toe of my boot spreading on his chest.

"What did I do?" he sputters as he gets to his feet. "You fucking kicked me, you psycho. I was only trying to wake you up."

I blink, feeling confused.

"Why did you take me to your bed? Trying to fuck me while I was asleep?" I spit. Even as I say it, that doesn't feel right.

No, wait. I fell asleep in his arms after he... he...

"You fucking locked me in the bathroom, you puta," I hiss. My Spanish accent is coming out heavier than usual.

During the three years in lockup, I've worked hard to rid myself of my accent, and it's gotten a lot better. Though, there are still times, like now, where it's hard to hide, especially when Spanish insults slip out as well.

Rochus runs a hand down his face, and to his credit, he looks shamefaced. "I'm sorry about that," he sighs. "I didn't know you were going to have a fucking panic attack."

Shit.

He knows my weakness now.

"So what?" I say, scathingly. "If you think I'm weak enough for you to take advantage of me, you're sorely mistaken."

His eyes twinkle with amusement as he runs his hand across the mark from my kick. "You're definitely not weak," he chuckles. Then he schools his features, removing all traces of amusement. "And just for the fucking record, I won't take advantage of you."

I roll my eyes because isn't that exactly what someone about to take advantage of me would say?

When he takes a few steps back, I finally get to my feet as well. Lord, even with the distance between us, he dwarfs me. At five-foot-nine I'm used to being amongst the tallest, but Rochus' six-foot-five makes me seem like a child. Which I suppose is apt since I'm his fucking child bride.

"What happened to Julietta? That's your sister, right?"

I glare at him. "Excuse me?"

Maybe I shouldn't be surprised that he knows that, but a part of me feels violated since he knows that about me when I know nothing about him. I suppose it's possible he came across her name when he purchased me, but that doesn't exactly make it better.

"You were screaming out her name in your sleep. Does she… I mean… is she okay?" He looks confused, but he sounds like he's worried.

Huh, maybe he does actually care.

"She's fine," I say, my voice almost cracking. "She's dead, so she's in a better place." I look upward, hoping what I'm saying is true.

"How did she die?" he asks.

A yawn escapes me, and I take my time stretching while I consider if I'm going to reply or not. It's not like I owe him an answer, yet I find that I want to give him one. At least part of the truth.

I look into his dark eyes, surprised I can see my own reflection. "A monster killed my sister," I croak.

"When?" he asks, taking a step closer to me.

Although I want to flinch away from his intensity, I stay in place. "Almost a year ago. It wasn't long after I got transferred out of juvie."

His brows furrow in confusion. "Who told you?"

I let out a humorless laugh. "No one had to tell me, Rochus. I was there, holding her as her life literally bled out of her."

"What?"

Rolling my eyes, I continue. "She was in prison for killing her husband, and we served our sentences together."

I watch as Rochus opens and closes his mouth several times. He shifts his weight from one foot to the other, still holding his hand over where I kicked him.

"Fuck. I should have kept an eye on her," he says, sounding like he feels… responsible.

Now I'm the one who's lost for words. Why does he even care? He only saw her once, when he married me.

"Whatever," I sniff disdainfully. "She wasn't yours to look after."

"Maybe not, but—"

"No buts," I hiss. "Just fucking drop it."

He runs a hand through his short, dark hair. "Fine," he spits back. "But I still want you to take a goddamn shower and put on some clean clothes."

At the mention of a shower, my hands begin to shake. I ball them into fists to stop it, which doesn't help. So I end up hiding them behind my back.

"Unless you want me to kick you again, you better rethink that," I hiss.

He holds his hands up. "Yeah, whatever. Look, I get you don't want to go into the bathroom, so I have an idea."

I arch my eyebrow, silently asking him to elaborate.

"Follow me." That's all he says before spinning around.

Doing as he says, I trail after him and follow him through the back door out into the laundry area and small garden.

Pointing at the hose attached to the tap in the wall, he says, "There. If you don't want to go into the bathroom, you need to shower out here."

"Absolutely not," I hiss. "I'm not going to—"

"Enough!" he barks. "I didn't fucking touch you while you were sleeping, and I'm not going to perv on you either. You can keep your underwear on for all I fucking care."

While I contemplate the compromise, he walks back inside. I'm still busy mulling the idea over when he returns with soap, shampoo, conditioner, a towel, and some clean clothes.

"Have at it," he grins, slamming the door after him as he disappears again.

I tentatively move over to the hose while trying to gauge if he can see me from the window, and if any of the neighbors can watch me. Since I can't be sure, I decide to take his advice and keep my bra and panties on.

Showering in your underwear isn't as easy as it sounds, and it doesn't even feel like I'm getting completely clean. It'll have to do though.

I swear I hear Rochus laugh as I switch on the tap, spraying myself in the ice cold water from the hose. It's not ideal, but it's better than going into the bathroom. In record time, I wash my hair and as much of my body as I can.

Afterward, I use the towel he left for me to dry, and then to hide my naked body as I strip out of the drenched underwear. Though it's awkward, I manage to put on the fresh bra and panties underneath the towel.

I get dressed in the black jeans and purple tee Rochus left for me. It fits like a glove, but is nowhere near as comfortable as my leather stuff. I need to get my hands on some money so I can buy more because that shit is all I want to wear.

Looking down at myself, I can't help smiling at the purple. It's so unlike me that it makes me want to laugh. The only time I've ever had purple anything was... oh, right. The highlights I had when we got married. Does he think I like purple? Or is this a coincidence?

Wait, didn't he say someone else had picked out my clothes? I know it shouldn't matter either way, yet I think I like the idea of him picking this specifically for me.

Rocco

The way Cara Rodríguez sways her hips when she walks should be fucking illegal. How does a nineteen-year-old know how to do that? Is it a natural progression into womanhood, to just instinctively know how to capture a man's attention with something as simple as walking?

Whatever it is, has my eyes lingering on the round globes of her ass as she walks in front of me as we enter Dirty Diamonds. I swear she's testing me. Waiting to see if I'll turn into the monster she thinks purchased her at the auction. Waiting to see if I'll throw her down and take what's owed to me as part of the marriage agreement.

Her virginity.

Fuck. I hate that she thinks I'm that person, and I also hate the way I'm so fucking drawn to her and eager to know if said virginity is still intact.

"I don't know why we are here. I already told you I finished all the book work." Cara's tone is laced with bitterness as she tosses a glare over her shoulder at me. "Jesus, were you just looking at my ass?"

Spinning to glare at me as she steps through the curtains into the main room of the club, I watch her fists clench like she is gearing up to punch me.

Fuck, I think I want her to punch me. I think I'd love to wrestle her to the ground and press my body into hers and...

"Rocco, my man." Cain claps me on my back, snapping me out of my lust daze. "To what do we owe the pleasure?"

I smirk at Cain. He knows exactly why I'm here. I sent him a text earlier making sure there weren't too many of his pretty Diamonds around in the hopes Cara would feel more comfortable.

"Are the showers empty?" I ask, darting my gaze to Cara whose steely eyes widen.

"They are as empty as my soul," Cain sing-songs, before throwing his head back and laughing.

Cara's glare softens as a frown takes its place, her eyes now studying Cain.

He's a crazy fucker. She will come to that realization quickly the more she comes into contact with him. As crazy as he is though, he's solid. Reliable and trustworthy, traits that are hard to come by in our world.

"I have arranged all the most beautifully scented products for you to shower with." Cain directs to Cara with a bow, and she jerks back like she's just been slapped.

"What do you mean? I don't need a shower." Her gray eyes turn to me filled with panic and I frown.

I haven't been able to establish why she doesn't like showering. I thought perhaps she has a problem with confined spaces, but the dancers' locker room has a large open shower space that allows multiple women to shower at once. I figured she'd feel more comfortable there, and since her last shower was a couple of days ago in my backyard after the whole bathroom screaming incident, I figured another shower was due.

"Come on, Cara. I'll show you. The showers here are in a large room that you can have all to yourself." I step up to her, taking her upper arm, but she shoves away from me, beelining for the exit.

"I showered a couple of days ago. I don't need another fucking shower."

It only takes me two strides to catch up to her before I wrap my arms around her waist and tug her back against me. She flails against my hold, but when I press my lips against her ear, she stops.

"Cara, just do me a favor and at least take a look at the showers they have here before dismissing it. I swear, if you don't want to use them, you don't have to."

Her chest is rising and falling rapidly under my hold, the fitted clothes she wore when she stepped out of the prison gates like a glove on her body again today. From this angle, I can see down the front of her top, the valley between her breasts squeezing together by the hint of the black lace bra she's wearing.

Shit.

Don't get fucking hard!

I will my dick to listen to my brain. Pressing a boner into her ass right now isn't how I want things to go down. I'm trying so fucking hard to hide how she affects me.

She may be my wife, but she didn't choose this, and technically neither did I. Not for the purpose of love or some sick and twisted craving to possess a minor. By marrying Cara, I then became her guardian, which meant her parents, the sick cunts, could no longer have a claim on her. It was an arrangement I agreed to at Dante's request. Being only nineteen at the time, I was closest in age to her, aside from Cain, but he would have scared her more than anything with his flighty personality, so I was the best option.

So as married as we are, I will not ask her to perform her marital duties, or even pretend to give a shit about me. Except maybe when we see her parole officer. But other than that, I want her to just be free and safe, and fuck, even though I want her to shower, she smells so damn good.

"Do you promise?" she asks quietly, her voice a little shaky. "Will you give me your word that you won't make me use the showers if I don't want to?"

"Yes," I breathe against her ear. "I promise."

For a moment, a brief millisecond, I feel her lean into me, tilting her head to press her ear closer to my mouth.

Fuck!

DON'T GET HARD!

Think of something gross.

Gangrene toes.

A bucket of vomit.

A cow giving birth.

Cara tugs at my arms around her waist before I can do anything else, so I release her and watch as she turns to face me.

"Show me."

Wait. Is she asking me to show her my hard dick?

When I don't speak, she rolls her eyes.

"Earth to Rochus. Show me the damn showers."

Oh damn. Yes, the showers.

Fuck, I need to get my head out of the gutter when I'm around her.

Maybe I should find a Diamond to take the edge off while she's showering. That should help me stop responding to her like a fucking dog in heat.

"Call me Rocco," I suggest, my voice sounding husky, so I clear my throat.

"Or, you can call him Mr. King." Cain's voice reminds me that he's still here, having witnessed me losing my fucking mind. "Or Master King. Or just Master. He'd like that too."

"Really?" I snap at him, and he shrugs like he's done nothing wrong.

"She's your wife. She should be prepared for how you like it." Cain shrugs and I roll my eyes, turning back to Cara.

She's eyeing both of us like we are freaks.

She's probably not wrong.

"Come on." I urge her to follow me, and she does, giving Cain a wide berth.

He gasps and slaps his hand to his chest like she's just stabbed him, the dramatics coercing a giggle to fall from Cara's lips.

Fuck, I like the sound of that. I haven't heard that from her until now, and fuck if I'm not going to make it my mission to make it happen again. And again. And again.

Weaving through the tables, I lead Cara to the back section of the building and down the long passage until we reach the dancers' locker room.

After a quick rap of my knuckles on the door, I ease it open, ducking my head in to make sure it's empty, before pushing it wide and gesturing for Cara to step in.

She does so slowly. Cautiously. Like she's ready for a fucking bear to jump out at any second.

I go with her, staying close to her side as she walks through the space, her eyes raking over the racks of skimpy costumes, and the lockers with each dancer's name drawn in lipstick on the front.

"The shower room is through there." I point toward the door at the far side, and she makes her way over to it by my side.

Her chest is heaving faster the closer we get, her hands trembling as her eyes widen with fear.

I have no fucking clue what happened to her. No idea why this is such a massive deal to her, and even though I have no right to know, I want to know the reason behind it.

Taking the lead, I push the door open, revealing the large, tiled room beyond.

Cara gasps, leaps back and shakes her head frantically. "No."

"No?" I ask, still holding the door open, and she stumbles backward, tripping on her own foot as she frantically shakes her head.

Lurching forward, I reach out and catch her just in time, saving her from falling back on her ass.

"No!" She cries out, shoving at me, her breathing rapidly nearing panic attack level.

"Shhh. It's okay. You don't have to." I remind her, holding her to me as I rub my hand up and down her back.

Looking down at her, I see her hands fisted in my shirt, her eyes wide with fear on the now closed door, like she can see through it to another realm where beasts roam the planet.

"Talk to me, Cara. Tell me why you can't step foot inside that room."

She shakes her head frantically, dragging her gaze from the door to press her forehead on my chest.

I'm not gonna lie. I fucking like having her this close. I just wish she wasn't so scared.

"Talk to me please. I thought the room would be big enough."

She nods this time, keeping her head pressed to my chest so I can't see her face.

"It's not the size."

"Okay, well it can't be water since you showered outside. So what is it?"

She shakes her head against my chest. "I can't."

My shoulders drop in defeat. Her fear. Whatever it is, runs deeper than I thought, which means until she knows she can trust me, she's not going to tell me her secrets.

"Okay. Let's go and grab a drink then. You can shower outside later when we get home."

My words have the right effect, making her relax, her fists releasing my shirt as she steps back, her breathing not so dire now.

Reaching out to take her hand, she snatches it away like I repulse her, and I try to remind myself that's not why she did that, but it still stings a little.

She has no reason to trust me, I get that, and I could tell her the real reason why I married her, but she's not ready to hear that yet. She'll just think it's a lie, so I need to wait until I know she'll truly hear me when I tell her.

Leading Cara back out to the main room, some Diamonds are there, watching each other rehearse, so I head to a table on the far side to give us a hint of privacy.

"Oh hey, Rocco," Mindy beams, doing a small, excited jump on the spot which makes her tits bounce. The patrons love that shit.

Me, not so much.

"Hi ladies," I offer them all, making sure I don't single one out and make them feel special, which is what Mindy wants.

A drunken night and a gang bang later and she somehow has it in her head that she's my girl. It's been that way for a couple of years. You'd think the fact I haven't touched her since would discourage her, but no, not Mindy. She's dedicated, if anything.

The women all call their hellos as we pass by and I watch Cara when she's not looking to see her annoyed frown as she looks at the women.

Ushering Cara to her seat, I excuse myself to get her a drink, and after I give it to her, I excuse myself again to find Cain.

"Is she enjoying the shower?" Cain asks as I pop my head in the supply room he's rummaging through.

"Nope. She couldn't even step foot in the room."

Cain's brows shoot up. "Damn. Any ideas what's triggering her?"

Sighing, I cross my arms over my chest as I lean against the door jamb. "Nope. It's not the confined space. And it's not the water. So, I have no fucking clue."

Nodding, Cain looks thoughtful as he straightens. "Maybe it's just the room itself. It sounds like she's had a bad experience inside a bathroom."

One of my brows lifts. "You think?"

"I think about a lot of things. Toadstools. Magic mushrooms. Vaginas. Lizards. Cockroaches."

I sigh at my friend. I shouldn't have expected any other answer.

I look back down to the mouth of the hallway, seeing Mindy walk past, heading for Cara.

"Dammit," I mumble, pushing off the wall. I don't want Mindy messing with her.

Just before I reach the end of the passage, I hear raised female voices before Cain grabs my arm and yanks me back, shoving me hard against the wall.

His body weight is suddenly on me, and I frown down at him, wondering what the fuck he's up to now.

"Wanna explain what the fuck—"

His hand slaps over my mouth, his eyes darting around sinisterly before he whispers. "Don't let them know you're here."

"Why?" I mumble against his palm, and he rolls his eyes as if the answer is too fucking obvious to speak out loud.

"So we can hear what they say about you. Duh."

I chuckle against his palm, but quickly forget about how close he is to me as Mindy's voice gets louder.

"I don't know why you're looking so smug. You're nothing but a child. You don't have what it takes to please a man like him," Mindy sneers and I hear Cara chuckle.

"Why don't you take your jelly tits and go and tell someone who cares."

Mindy gasps. "See. You don't even care about him. Why are you even here? He's married, you know."

"Oh, really?" Cara asks, sounding more amused than anything. "Where's his wife?"

"She's probably at their house, preparing herself for when he gets home. On her knees, waiting submissively. Just the way Rocco likes his women."

"And you would know, I guess?" Cara asks.

Fuck, does she sound annoyed?

Maybe I'm hearing things.

"Oh yes. I know." Mindy purrs. "I know exactly how he likes it. Hard. Brutal. Controlling."

"Tell me something," Cara asks, "have you been with him since he's been married?"

Mindy giggles. "Well, I mean, it was only that once, and well, everyone had a sample of everyone that night. If his wife had been brave enough to show up and join in, then I'm sure she would have loved it too."

I struggle against Cain's hold, but he shoves me back against the wall, shaking his head. "Uh-uh. Let's see if she's a mouse or a snake."

I roll my eyes at him, ready to argue when I hear Cara's voice again.

"So the answer is yes. You've fucked him since he's been married."

"What she doesn't know won't hurt her."

"And what if she found out? What do you think she'd do?"

Mindy giggles. "She won't find out. No one here is dumb enough to open their mouths about that if we ever get to meet her."

"Oh, I don't know. You seem pretty dumb to me."

Mindy gasps, and then there's a loud slap, and I can't hold back anymore, shoving Cain back hard and rounding the corner.

Mindy screams as Cara fists her hair and spins her, slamming her back against the wall with an oomph. As Mindy gasps for breath, eyes wide, Cara grabs the neck of my beer bottle and smashes it on the edge of the table before pressing the jagged glass to Mindy's neck.

I try to lurch forward, but Cain wraps his arms around me and grunts in my ear.

"Let her work it out."

"She'll kill her." I grunt back but Cain chuckles quietly.

"If she kills her, then we'll clean it up."

"I guess you really don't know who I am," Cara hisses in Mindy's face, who is now sobbing, trembling with fear. "I am Mrs. King."

All the tension leaves my body at her words.

"I am Mrs. King."

Fuck. Why do I like the sound of her saying that so much?

"Y-you're h-his w-wife?" Mindy stutters through her tears and I watch a slow, sinister smirk spread across Cara's face.

Fuck. She's beautiful.

"I am," she agrees. "Tell me why I shouldn't kill you for touching what's *mine?*"

"Oh man. She just claimed you," Cain mutters in my ear, and I snap back to reality and shove him off me, again.

"I-I-I..."

"Cara." I rasp, stepping up to her side, but she doesn't take her eyes off Mindy. "Forget her. Let's go home where you can punish me for my transgression."

Mindy's eyes widen, which is exactly the reaction I want.

What's going on with her and Cara is a power play. Mindy has lost, but I want to make sure she knows she never had a chance of winning.

This time, Cara's steely gaze flicks to me.

Good. I have her attention.

"Forget her. She means nothing. She is nothing to me. Let's go."

Cara stares at me for a few long beats, her eyes a tornado of fury, and I know it's not really about being jealous. It's about respect.

Slowly, Cara eases back, dropping the broken neck of the bottle to the floor leaving a trail of blood on Mindy's neck where it nicked her.

"Go near him again and see what happens," Cara snarls before stepping away and turning her back on a distraught Mindy.

"Rocco?" Mindy whimpers, which pisses me off. What the fuck does she think I'm going to do? Stick up for her? Un-fucking-likely.

"Next time you, or anyone else, disrespects my wife, I won't stop her from following through." Then I lean in closer. "And don't ever presume to fucking know me. You know fucking nothing."

Cain chuckles and claps behind me as I step up to my wife and link our fingers. I expect her to snatch her hand away, but she doesn't. Instead, she holds my hand tight and walks out of the club by my side.

I should probably be concerned that Cara may actually want to punish me for my transgression, like I offered her. The dominant part of me is furious at the thought, but there's a part of me that would gladly kneel for her if that's what she needed. I'd give her that, at least once, as long as she knew that if she steps over that line with me, there's no turning back.

Cara

On our way back to the beach shack Rochus—Rocco—lovingly calls home, we stop at a drive thru and get some food. Despite my insistence that I don't need my own meal, Rocco ignores me. And maybe he's right to because putting Mindy in her place has made me hungry.

"I'm not fucking discussing this again," he snaps. "You need to eat more."

Scowling, I turn around and look at him. I don't like being told what to do, especially not when he's right and I'm wrong. I know I can't keep myself going like this, especially not if I'm going to keep my promise to Julietta.

"Okay," I say, trying not to giggle at the shocked expression on Rocco's face. "But I don't like banana shakes, and I want extra large fries."

I don't know whether I like banana shakes or not, I've never had one. I've never even been to a drive thru. While we wait in the line of cars, I use the time to study the menu placed between the lanes.

The options are overwhelming. How do I know if I like pickles on my burger? Or if the chicken nuggets are good?

"Do you know what you want?" Rocco asks when there are only two cars in front of us.

"Umm..." Hesitating, I skim the menu again. "I'll take the large cheeseburger meal, a vanilla shake, and... five cookies."

My stomach rumbles in agreement.

"Anything else?"

I turn my head to look at Rocco, unsure why he's asking me. Then I look back at the sign, pondering what else I might want to try. "Mozzarella sticks," I say. "And maybe an ice cream."

"Is that all?" Rocco chuckles.

Feeling self conscious, I wring my hands in my lap. Did I order too much? I did, didn't I. "Maybe I don't need the mozzarella sticks," I sigh. "Or the cookies."

Damn, I really wanted the chocolate chip cookies. They look so delicious in the picture, and so does everything else.

"You can have whatever you want," Rocco says. "Personally, I'm a big fan of their curly fries and shakes."

Rocco drives up to the window and places the order. Not only is he ordering everything I asked for, he's also ordering other things and different flavors.

A knot forms in my stomach as I realize I don't have any money to pay for my food. So far, Rocco's been keeping me fed, and even bought me new clothes. But I can't keep taking his money. Okay, so technically I am working for it by doing the books for Dirty Diamonds.

That reminds me...

"Cain owes me a favor," I rush out once he's paid and driven to the next window, where we wait for our food. "He wrote that in a comment after I corrected the shift schedule."

Huh, I never knew there's so much waiting involved.

Rocco turns his head and looks at me. "Is that so?"

I nod eagerly. "Yes. Do you think I can use it to pay for my share of the food?"

His eyes twinkle with mirth, but he doesn't answer me until we've received our food and are heading back to the beach shack.

"Look," Rocco says, breaking the silence. "If Cain owes you a favor, that shit is priceless. He doesn't give out favors easily. So I'd save it for something you really want."

Without meaning to, I stare longingly at the bags of food resting in my lap.

"Cara."

Stupid tears gather in my eyes because I know he's about to tell me I can't have any of the delicious smelling food.

"Look at me."

Refusing to let him see my shiny eyes, I keep my gaze fixed on the paper bags for the rest of the drive. I even hold on to them when we're back at the shack, refusing to part with the food just yet.

My stomach hurts, it feels like it's gnawing on itself as pangs of hunger make me feel lightheaded and like I might collapse.

Once we're inside the cozy house, Rocco tells me to place the bags on the coffee table in front of the couch. I discreetly hide one behind my back, the one with the ice cream and cookies.

After getting some plates from the small kitchen, Rocco sits down on the couch and pats the space next to him.

"Come sit," he says.

Shaking my head, I take a step back. I look at the back door, wondering if I can get away with sprinting out there.

Rocco sighs. "Look, I get that I don't know half the shit you've been through. But it's getting real fucking hard not to take your attitude personally."

Looking at him, I furrow my brows in confusion. I don't get why he's taking it personally. He hasn't done anything wrong, I have. I'm the one who's meant to cater to him, submit to him. That's what my mom taught me, and Mindy said that's what he wants.

"Can we just fucking eat in peace and... I don't know... talk or some shit?" When I don't move, he adds, "You know your ice cream is going to melt, right?"

My eyes widen as I realize he knows I'm hiding it from him. "You can't have it," I warn, lifting my chin.

I know I'm behaving like a kid, but it's so hard to navigate my new reality. I never wanted to be here, let alone to be married. But I've never had a choice in these matters. No matter how brutal prison was, it strengthened me. In there, I didn't let anyone walk all over me and take my food, and I won't allow it on the outside either.

Even as a kid, I never allowed anyone to touch what I perceived as mine. I think that's the real reason I got so pissed with Mindy at the club. Rocco's my husband, and that should mean something. Even if it's not a love marriage, I'm not okay with him getting his rocks off while I was locked up.

"I'm not interested in your fucking ice cream," Rocco laughs. "All I want is to share a meal and have just two minutes where you don't look like you're contemplating killing me."

Tilting my head to the side, I look at him from beneath my lashes. He sounds sincere, and he doesn't look threatening. Maybe it's okay to let my guard down while we eat.

Moving over to the couch, I slowly sit down as far away from him as possible. I prefer to watch him closely, so I adjust my position on the couch by pulling my legs up and leaning back on the armrest. I even place the ice cream on the table with the rest of the food.

"What do you want to try first?" Rocco asks as he shoves some fries into his mouth.

I point at the burger, and when he hands it to me, I unwrap it right away. The first bite is so good I moan in pleasure. The meat is full of flavor, and the lettuce, tomato, and bun taste so much better than the prison food.

"That good?" Rocco laughs, and I nod eagerly. "Try a curly fry."

He shakes them in front of my face, not stopping until I take one. "Oh my God!" I exclaim with my mouth full. "They're great."

As my gaze collides with Rocco's, I'm surprised how dark his eyes are. I mean, yeah, they're always dark. Yet, right now, they're almost black. But instead of making him look menacing, he looks like a forbidden treat that I... I shake my head because it doesn't matter how he looks.

Rocco continues to push food on me, not stopping until I've tried every single thing on the table and slurped the last of my shake.

"Do you want your ice cream now?" he asks, arching a brow like he's daring me to consume more food.

"Absolutely," I say eagerly.

Reaching for the tub, I scoop some onto the spoon that came with it. Once again, I moan. The caramel and chocolate flavors exploding on my tongue are too fucking much. This is the stuff of dreams.

"Can I try some?" he asks.

Despite the teasing lilt to his tone, I shake my head vehemently. "No."

Rocco snorts and bends down to kick off his shoes. I know what comes next, and yep, like clockwork, his shirt is the next to go.

"Why do you always do that?" I ask, genuinely curious.

"Do what?"

Rolling my eyes, I take another bite of the heavenly ice cream. "Walk around shirtless."

He shrugs like it's no big deal. "I'm in my home, what's more natural than being as comfortable as possible?"

I take a moment to mull over his words. I guess it makes sense. Not everyone comes from a fucked up home where there was never enough food, or where being dressed was a luxury.

Putting down the now empty tub of ice cream, I unzip my boots and pull them off before getting up from the couch, placing them neatly by the door. It's awkward, but I walk backwards, refusing to take my eyes off Rocco. He might have had my back at the club, but that doesn't mean he won't pounce when I'm not looking.

As soon as I'm back on the couch, Rocco says, "I want to talk about what happened with Mindy."

Here we go. He'll probably tell me off for attacking her.

"I'm not sorry for what I did," I snap, defensively.

"You shouldn't be."

My lips part, but I can't think of any words to say. This isn't the reaction I was expecting.

"You and I aren't together, Cara. So I can do whatever the fuck I want. But—"

I jump off the couch and place my hands on my hips, my temper getting the better of me. "Is that so, husband?" I sneer. "Can I fuck around as well, then?"

Fuck me. I shouldn't antagonize him or remind him that I legally belong to him.

"You can try," Rocco snarls, getting to his feet. "But it won't end well for whoever you give your virginity to."

His nostrils flare as he crosses his tattooed arms over his chest. I'm momentarily distracted by the ink on his chest.

"Cara!"

The way he snaps my name has my hackles rising. "I'm not a fucking virgin anymore," I lie. "You're about three years too late."

Horror creeps over his features, and he takes a step toward me. "What?" Although I don't want to give him any ground,

I take a step back. "You weren't a virgin when we got married?"

I force out a laugh. "Sure I was. But I took care of that within the first week in juvie."

Bullshit, that's what it is. Rocco doesn't need to know that, though.

A low growl emanates from his throat as he clenches and unclenches his fists. He looks scary, so I'm not sure why I don't feel any fear. He could easily pick me up and do whatever the hell he wants, and maybe that's why I can't stop pushing him.

So far, he's been... nice, something I don't trust. I need to see what's underneath the surface. When Mindy antagonized me, I got a small glimpse of Rocco's monster. Which reminds me...

"You want me to punish you?" I ask, completely changing the subject.

"Say fucking what?"

I nod. "You said I could punish you."

Palming his chin, he runs his thumb up and down the scruff. "I didn't say that for you."

"But you deserve to be punished," I exclaim.

I have no idea how I could do that, only that it feels right. In prison I punished everyone who disrespected me. Usually with my fists or feet, which was enough for them to learn their lesson and leave me the fuck alone.

Rocco's different, and to truly punish someone, you need to know what they either fear or hold dear. With him, I don't know enough to even take a guess.

"Take your best shot," he smirks.

I nod. "I will. Eventually."

"We'll see."

Without another word, Rocco disappears into the bathroom, and within minutes I hear the water from the shower running.

This is our routine. He showers before bed, and I half suspect it's partly to give me privacy to change into the leggings and tee I sleep in. Well, sleep is much too generous. I still can't relax enough to let myself go completely, so it's more like I'm resting.

After tidying the empty containers and all traces of our food orgy, I brush my teeth at the kitchen sink and quickly get changed. It feels weird to be out of my leather, and I still haven't decided if that's good or bad.

Lying down on the couch, I pull the laptop on top of my stomach and begin rifling through the files. It's mostly to have something to do since I already know there isn't any new work for me to keep myself occupied.

My eyes grow heavy, and I swallow down a yawn as I quickly reply to some of Cain's comments on my last notes. Once that's done, I'm blurry-eyed from exhaustion and the battle to stay awake is becoming harder.

Rocco might be as long as another half hour in the shower. I never know with him. So I make the snap decision of catching a speed nap while he's getting ready for bed.

I turn to my side so I'm facing the room and close my eyes, letting the waves crashing on the rocks across the road, and the water from Rocco's shower lull me to sleep.

"Cara."

I groan, annoyed to be woken up, and blink to get used to the darkness.

"Be quiet and don't fucking move." Rocco hisses, his mouth so close to my ear I can feel his hot breath on my skin.

I open my mouth to answer, and stiffen when I realize his hand is clamped around my mouth and his weight is crushing me to the couch.

That motherfucker. I let my guard down, and now... and now... I buck, trying to get him off me, but he doesn't budge.

"Whatever you think I'm doing, this is not it. Listen," Rocco whispers urgently.

That's when I hear it, someone is jiggling the door handle and it sounds like they're trying to get inside. As soon as the realization hits me, I stop fighting him and become completely still."

"Mija, I know you're in there!"

I stiffen as I hear the endearment only my mom has ever used. It's not a woman's voice, though, and I already know who it belongs to.

"Don't be a coward, Cara. Come out and play."

Fuck. Mateo. My twin.

"You know who it is?"

I nod.

"Your family?" Rocco whispers directly into my ear.

I nod again.

He curses low enough that my brother shouldn't be able to hear him, and then he reaches for his phone. The light is so harsh I close my eyes, shielding my irises.

Why the hell is Mateo here? I don't belong to him. Rocco bought me, so my family doesn't have a claim on me anymore.

"Caraaaaa," Mateo shouts gleefully. "Why are you hiding from me, sister? Is it because your husband hasn't claimed you yet?"

His words bring forth a memory of a conversation I overheard between my dad and Julietta's husband. Basically, dad was saying that until the buyer fucked my sister, the deal wasn't complete even if money had changed hands.

Fuck.

Rocco hasn't done... that. Does he know about this? Is he wanting me to go back to my family?

Sweat coats my forehead as I struggle to breathe.

I can't go back, not after killing my dad. I'd sooner fucking die myself.

"Are you okay?" Rocco murmurs. "Gray and Gunner are on their way. Don't worry, no one's going to lay a hand on you."

Right now, I'm glad for the darkness. With how perceptive Rocco is, he'd see the panic written all over my face within seconds.

"Nod if you're okay," Rocco urges, so I do. "Okay. Just hang in there."

Just as the words leave his mouth, a window shatters and I scream into his hand. Rocco curses, but doesn't move off me. If anything, he presses his hand harder against my mouth as we listen to the footsteps from somewhere outside.

I lose track of how much time passes until the sound of a vehicle approaching reaches us.

"That's them," he says, no longer whispering. "I'll be right back."

Rocco gets off me and throws open the door just as there's a knock. A young guy with dark wavy hair stands in the doorway.

"Gray," Rocco snaps.

"Gunner's looking around, but I didn't see anyone," Gray says.

"I'll check the back," Rocco snaps. "Stay with Cara."

"We already checked. Gunner dropped me off a few houses away and gave me a head start so the engine didn't tip them off to our arrival. There's no one here."

Rocco ignores him and walks over to the back door, keeping one hand at the small of his back as he kicks it open. Holy shit, does he have a weapon hidden?

I don't know why it never occurred to me that he'd be packing. It seems so obvious, and obviously a factor I've overlooked.

"Hey," Gray says sheepishly. "We haven't been formally introduced. I'm Gray."

I slowly get to my feet, my legs still shaking. "Hola," I greet him.

With no idea what else to say, I just stare at him. Unlike Cain and the few other people Rocco hangs around, Gray looks homeless. His clothes don't fit him properly, and he just has an aura of being lost.

"Are you okay?" he asks, sounding uncomfortable.

I shrug. "Sure. Why wouldn't I be?"

He chuckles, which makes him look younger than I first thought he was.

"All good," Rocco says as he comes back inside. "This is Gunner." He points at the guy with sandy blond hair behind him.

"Sup," Gunner says, looking anywhere but at me.

"Hi," I say. Then I look at Rocco. "Is he gone?"

Something in my tone makes him pinch his lips together as he nods. "Yeah, no traces of anyone." I wish he'd look away instead of studying me like I'm a rare specimen. "Are you sure you're okay?"

"Sure," I say, trying—and failing—at sounding chipper.

Knowing that Mateo so easily found me has me on edge, especially since he's right. Rocco hasn't claimed me, but now I need him to. And fast.

"What did he want?" Gray asks, looking between us.

Rocco looks deep in thought as he says, "I'm not sure. I don't even know who it was."

I breathe a sigh of relief and plaster a smile on my lips. "It was my brother," I say sweetly. Then I move to Rocco's side, and place my hand on his bicep. "You saved me."

His gaze snaps to mine, uncertainty swimming in his dark eyes. "Umm..." Palming the back of his head, he trails off.

"Thank you," I say sincerely.

I might have a role to play, but my gratitude is still heart-felt.

Rocco takes my hand, and I allow him to intertwine our fingers while he talks with Gray and Gunner. Since I have to up my game if I want to make sure our marriage is con-summated so my family can't claim me, I lean against him and wrap my arm around his waist. At first he stiffens, but he quickly relaxes and returns my affection by moving me in front of him so he can hold me from behind.

Too preoccupied with breathing and mentally talking my-self into doing what needs to be done, I barely hear their conversation.

"Okay, we'll patrol tonight," Gunner says, though he doesn't sound happy about it.

"For sure," Gray adds.

After saying goodbye, they leave and I have a plan that I'm pretty sure will work.

While Rocco closes and locks the doors, I slowly move over to the bedroom. I turn to him and bat my eyelashes. "Can I sleep with you tonight? I don't want to be on my own in case he comes back."

Despite the nod I get in return, I can feel his suspicion.

"Do we need to board up the window?" I ask as I suddenly remember hearing one shatter earlier.

"No, it wasn't one of ours," he says curtly.

I watch as he gets back into bed, and I quietly climb in and make myself comfortable. We don't speak, we just lie there as a heavy silence stretches around us.

To keep my mind busy so I don't fall asleep, I try to remember the tips my sister gave me on my wedding day. Too determined to never let it happen, I didn't pay much attention back then. And now, I wish I had.

I smile as Rocco's breathing deepens and eventually his snores echo in the quiet room. Game time.

As quietly as possible, I shimmy my leggings down and kick them off. Then I move around on the bed, testing to see how deeply Rocco's sleeping. His snoring doesn't change, which means he's far gone. That's good since we're both sticking to our side of the bed, and I need to be much closer for what I have in mind.

Swallowing down my guilt, I move closer until our bodies touch. I cautiously lift the sheet, needing to get a better look at what I'm dealing with here. Unlike the men my sister had to fuck, Rocco doesn't have a beer gut hiding his crotch, which makes it a lot easier.

I move my hand to his crotch, but when I connect with his dick, it's soft. How the hell am I meant to make him hard and get his boxers off without waking him up?

Needing more time to form a new plan, I turn to my back and stare up at the dark ceiling like the answers to my problem are written there. They aren't. And the more I think about it, the more impossible it seems.

As the room brightens and the sun shines through the windows, I realize I'm out of time. I can't keep stalling. Throwing caution to the wind, I move back to my side and, once again, I reach for him. This time, he's hard, and when I touch the bulge in his boxers, it jerks under my touch.

While dragging the sheet down, I keep my eyes on Rocco's face, needing to make sure he's still sleeping. Luckily for me, he doesn't stir and his breathing stays the same.

Now that I can see his boxers more clearly, I notice they have a slit in them. I snake my hand into the gap, and gently ease his cock through.

Rocco's dick is very different from the previous ones I've seen. It's huge, and there's a vein running along the length. The tip is angry looking and wet, something shines from the tip.

With jerky movements, I straddle Rocco and slide my panties to the side. I wrap my hand fully around his large cock, giving it a few strokes before I line the head up with my opening.

What I'm about to do is wrong on so many levels, and I wish there was another way. But having Mateo show up like that changes everything.

I can't go back. There's just no way.

Three!

Fuck, I don't even know if he'll fit...

Two!

I shouldn't be doing this...

One!

I *have* to do it.

Needing to get it over with, I slam down and take him all the way inside me in one move.

Fuck!

Pain flares to life, nearly blinding me as it feels like he's ripping my vagina apart. My eyes water, and I bite down on my hand to stop my whimpers from escaping.

Shit, this really hurts.

Rocco's lids fly open, and he gasps my name.

Despite the need to get away from him, I force myself to move up and down.

"What are you doing?" he rasps, but I ignore him.

The pain doesn't matter, only that I lose my virginity. Which I guess I've technically done now. I can't believe how much it hurts. Every move makes it feel like my insides are being stabbed.

I'm so focused on the task at hand that I don't notice Rocco's hands on my hips at first.

"Don't touch me," I hiss, slapping his hands away.

"W-what?"

He looks so confused I almost feel bad for him.

"This isn't what you think," I admit. "I... we... this had to be done."

"Had to be done?" Rocco echoes. "If you wanted me, all you had to do was say so." His voice is husky with remnants of sleep.

When he tries to touch me again, I leap off him and the bed. That's when I see it, the blood coating his hard dick.

Fuck.

Rocco looks down at himself, and I want to shrink under the death glare he sends my way when he notices the blood.

"What the fuck did you do?" he roars, sitting up.

I startle, and a part of me wants to cower and beg for his forgiveness. That's when the perfect excuse hits me.

"You had to be punished!" I shout back. "I told you I'd get you, and now I have."

Rocco

Cara has been outside under the cold shower for way too long. I need her to get the fuck back inside so I can find out why the fuck she did that. Why would she tell me she wasn't a virgin if she was, and then impale herself on me while I was sleeping?

That's not how she should have lost her virginity, and fuck, perhaps she shouldn't have lost it to me, but here we fucking are. Even though I didn't come inside her, I've never been happier to know she's on birth control. I think the record Baz and Dante showed me said something about hormone control or some shit like that.

Inside my bathroom, I kick off my boxers and sit my junk in the sink, quickly washing Cara's blood off. My cock is a bit raw. She was barely wet which is why I was so fucking confused about what she was doing when I woke up. She literally impaled herself. She wasn't ready, and even though I was hard, neither was I. Why the fuck didn't she let me touch her? I could have worked over her clit and made her slick for me in seconds, but instead, she slapped my hands away.

Fuck, I have no idea what's going through her head, something that I need to fucking resolve now. I'll shower later when I've had a fucking discussion with my wife.

A knock at the front door of my house makes me still, and I check the time on my watch. It's only 8am. Who the fuck is here at this time of day?

Remembering we had a prowler last night, I quickly shuck on a pair of shorts and a t-shirt and snatch up my gun as I hurry to the door.

"Who is it?" I snap, my gun pointed at the timber separating us.

"Officer Dudley," the gruff male voice says. "I'm Mrs. King's parole officer."

I relax momentarily until I realize what this means.

Shit. The parole board believes this to be a real marriage. They stated that they will visit to confirm we are actually living as a married couple, as I am now responsible for Cara during her parole term.

We are definitely married. Just not happily or with Cara's consent.

Quickly shoving my gun in the drawer by the door, I pull open the door to see a short man, round in the belly wearing a crisp navy suit and glasses sitting at the end of his nose.

"Hi," I say, cracking the door.

"Oh. Mr. King, I presume?"

"Yes. You're here to see Cara?" I ask dumbly, because obviously that's why he's here.

"Yes. I thought a surprise visit nice and early would be the best time to catch you both before you start your day."

"Ah... Yes. Of course," I mutter, looking briefly over my shoulder to the back door that Cara is still behind, showering. "My wife is currently showering. Would it be possible for you to come back later?"

"Oh, there's no need for that." He smiles, stepping forward and pushing against the door. "I can come in and wait."

I want to punch him. Get my gun out and introduce him to that.

I can't though. In order to ensure Cara follows her parole terms, she has to remain out of trouble, and therefore, so do I.

"Come on in." I sweep my hand out, gesturing for him to enter even though he already fucking is. "Take a seat on the couch if you like. I'll just let her know that you're here."

"Thank you." He nods, moving to the couch while I make my way to the back door and duck outside.

My eyes immediately land on Cara's shivering naked back as she stands under the stream of water.

Shit. She's gonna freak when she knows I'm looking at her like this.

Glancing down, I see the towel draped over the back of the wicker chair and scoop it up before stepping up behind her.

"Don't freak out and scream," I say quietly, and she gasps, spinning wide eyed as she tries to cover her tits and cunt with her hands. I don't look. I have the towel held out in front of me, ready to wrap her in.

"What are you—"

"Shhh." I hush, moving closer to wrap the towel around her front. "Your parole officer is inside."

"What?" she whisper-yells, and I nod, keeping my eyes on hers.

"He's here. Wanted to catch the married couple before we start our day."

Her mouth drops open as if she's going to say something, but then she snaps it back shut.

"It's okay." I offer, leaning over to turn the cold water off at the tap. "I told him you were showering. I'll say you went across to the water for a morning swim and you're showering out here, so you don't track sand through the house."

She nods, her body still trembling from being so damn cold.

"Dammit, Cara. Why won't you just use the shower inside where the water is hot?" My concern for her must surprise her, although I don't know why, but her brows shoot high as her lips quiver.

"I-I like the c-cold."

"You're a terrible fucking liar," I say quietly, reaching forward to brush a strand of her hair back, but she jerks away like I'm going to burn her if we touch.

"Jesus, woman. This guy needs to think we are married. When you step foot inside, you'd better turn into a good fucking actress."

With that, I turn my back on her and go inside to entertain Mr. fucking Dudley while we wait.

"I thought you said Mrs. King was having a shower?" The man in question asks and I nod, moving to the cupboard to take down three mugs.

"Yes. She went for a swim over the road. She showers out back when she does that to avoid tracking sand through the house. That shit gets everywhere."

Risking a glance at Mr. Dudley, I see him nod, happy with my answer.

"Coffee?" I ask, and he nods again.

"Black. No sugar."

I set to work, putting the mugs in the microwave to heat before uncapping the lid on the coffee jar.

When the back door opens, both Mr. Dudley and I look up to find Cara walking in, fully dressed bar her bare feet, as she towel dries her hair.

"Oh. Mrs. King. Bruce Dudley. Your parole officer." He moves into the kitchen, holding out his hand, and Cara just stares at it for a moment before she reluctantly takes it, like she'd rather touch anything else but him.

"Hi," is all she says, and his lips thin.

Meanwhile, I try to focus on the task of making the coffee now that the water is heated.

I don't know why Bruce tries to be so formal. He deals with ex-cons all the time and I'm sure the majority aren't welcoming people.

"Let's take a seat." I gesture to the small two-seater table by the wall, and Bruce nods, making his way back out of my tiny kitchen.

"Can't you make him leave?" Cara hisses at me quietly, and I shake my head.

"Nope. He's your parole officer. Not mine." I pick up a mug and hand it to her.

She takes it absentmindedly as she glares daggers in the back of Bruce's head as he pulls out a chair and sits at the little table.

"Don't forget to pretend to like me." I grin, handing her the second cup.

She frowns now, her eyes dropping to the two mugs she holds while I pick up the third one.

I don't know why I do it, but when I pass by her, I give her ass a light tap, and she goes to jerk out of the way, but remembers she's holding two steamy hot cups of coffee, so she can't go anywhere.

I chuckle as I pass by, but then her whispered words pull me up short.

"I could just expose you for the creepy dick that purchased a child bride. Then I won't have to act and I won't have to be your wife anymore."

Slowly I turn back to peer at my wife, taking in her heated cheeks and tense pouty lips.

"Go for it, Killer."

"I'll do it." She bares her teeth as she hisses at me, and I chuckle quietly.

"Even if Bruce believes you, he's not the one pulling the strings. But go ahead. Waste my day and his. I'll just end up back here by the end of the day, ready to take you to our marital bed to finish what you fucking started this morning."

Dark eyes broadening wide, Cara goes to step past me, her nostrils flaring in anger, but I grip her biceps, pulling her up short and whisper in her ear.

"You don't fucking know the hoops I had to jump through to get you released, but I can tell you, your only options are staying here with me, or going back to prison. Make the right choice, Cara."

Knowing that the Bruce guy is staring at us, I lean forward and press my lips to her cheek, feeling how hot her skin burns under my touch.

Brushing past her, I walk over to Bruce and hand him his black coffee before taking the only other seat at the table.

Standing with a cup in each hand, Cara looks at me like she expects me to stand up and give her the seat.

I don't.

I push the chair back a little more to make room and pat my leg.

"Come here, hun."

Bruce beams across the table, and I tug Cara's shirt, dragging her closer until she has no choice but to sit as she places the cups on the table in front of us.

"It's always nice to see a couple reunited." Bruce grins before taking a sip of his coffee.

"Relax," I whisper against Cara's ear, and when Bruce looks up, I give her ear a little nip.

I don't really need to go to all this effort to put on a show for Bruce, but Cara doesn't know that, and by the way a shiver runs down her spine and she sinks a little more into me, I'm fucking glad I'm overdoing it.

"Now, Cara. My records show you have gained employment at a place called Dirty Diamonds. Is that correct?"

"Yes." Cara nods and Bruce writes something on the notepad in front of him.

"What is Dirty Diamonds' main business activity?" he asks, and Cara stiffens.

"Entertainment." I answer for her, and Bruce nods, writing that down too.

"And what sort of entertainment?" he asks, his expression all business and no fucking fun.

"It's a strip club." Cara responds this time, and a small smirk tugs at the corner of her lips as she watches Bruce's brows hitch.

"A strip club?"

"Yes. Amongst other things." She answers, and Bruce reaches up and tugs his glasses off.

"What is your job role there?"

I can see the glint in Cara's eye as I peer around at her. She's trying to cause trouble. And I just fucking know she's about to announce that she's a dancer.

"Cara does the book work." I butt in, giving her thigh a pinch under the table, and Cara frowns, but doesn't bother looking at me.

"Oh, good. You're good with numbers then?" he asks Cara and she shrugs.

"It's not hard."

"Yes, it is," I whisper against her ear, and she stiffens, shooting me a wide-eyed glare.

Luckily, Bruce is busy writing something and isn't focusing on us, so I keep fucking going. Making sure to torment my darling wife.

"Can you feel it?" I whisper before giving my hips a minuscule thrust under her.

It's not a lie. I am hard. My dick has been fluctuating between flax and hard ever since I woke up to have her riding my cock. It doesn't fucking care that I'm a little tender there.

Fuck, she was so damn tight. I'm aching to squeeze my dick into her again. Next time, I'll make sure she's slick.

Bruce asks more questions, and for the most part, Cara behaves, answering what she can without hinting to the ruse and how we became husband and wife.

As Bruce goes over the appointments he's booked for Cara to attend at his office in the coming weeks, I press my nose to her neck and inhale her sweet scent until I'm unable to hold back, and I press my lips to her neck.

"Insecto del amor," Cara says sweetly, which sounds ridiculous falling from her lips. "Behave while we have a guest."

What the hell does insecto del amor mean?

Fuck, that annoys me. Why haven't I tried to learn some Spanish? She could have called me a dickless monkey for all I know.

Chuckling fakely along with Bruce, I'm fucking ecstatic when he puts his notepad away and stands.

"Well, thank you both. I'm glad to see you readjusting to life. You both seem very happy together."

Cara gives a nervous laugh while I smile and nod, easing Cara off my lap so I can stand.

We say our goodbyes, and the moment I shut the door, a pillow from the couch slams into my head.

"Ouch," I say even though it didn't hurt.

"Eres un idiota," she sneers, glaring at me.

Fuck, I like it when she's angry.

"Did you just call me an idiot?"

"Yes!" she yells, grabbing another pillow and tossing it my way.

Dodging it, I charge for her, and I expect her to squeal and run, but she doesn't.

No. Cara Rodríguez is not a scaredy cat, and if I were a smarter man, I'd be afraid.

Luckily I'm not smart.

"We need to talk." I growl standing over her as she holds her chin high, not backing down.

"We have nothing to talk about." She declares and goes to spin away from me, but I circle my hand around her bicep and hold her in place.

"You fucking know we do, Killer. You told me you weren't a virgin. Then you took advantage of me, and I don't believe your bullshit that it was a punishment for getting laid while you were locked up."

"I'm on my period. That's why there was blood. Don't flatter yourself to think I would give someone like you my virginity. You're a monster!"

Gripping both her arms now, I tug her flush with me and press my nose to hers until we are breathing the same fucking air.

"That wasn't period blood, Cara. I felt the moment I broke your hymen. Why did you do that? If you wanted me, I could have made you feel fucking good."

"I don't want you!" she shouts. "Let me go!"

"No," I hiss, leaning forward and hoisting her over my shoulder before she can run off.

"What are you doing? Let me down!"

I slap her ass for good fucking measure and walk us into the bedroom before tossing her on the bed with a bounce.

"Why wouldn't you let me touch you?" I ask, and her lip curls as she hisses like a snake at me. "Goddammit, Cara. Just fucking answer me!"

"Because you don't need to touch me to do the act!" she yells back, and I fall still.

What?

"The act?" I ask, my anger vanishing.

"Sex, you imbecile!"

What the fuck?

"What about foreplay?" I ask, and she frowns.

"What?"

"Foreplay. You know. Kissing. Cuddling. Touching."

She just stares at me, her anger falling from her face.

"Cara, have you ever had an orgasm before?"

"What? I... Isn't that for men?"

Holy fucking shit. Is she serious?

"Who told you an orgasm was just for men?"

For the first time since picking her up from prison, she looks as young as her nineteen years as her eyes drop to her outstretched legs.

"Mom said a wife's duty is to please her husband and make sure that he is hard and feels good, and has an orgasm every time he wants one. Otherwise I'm not doing my job properly. She said there was no pleasure for me to have, and suffering through the pain of it every time was how I would get my satisfaction."

"Fuck, Cara. She lied to you. That's not how it's meant to be."

Her gray eyes dart up to meet mine again, and her lower lip trembles and tears well in her eyes.

She's never looked more vulnerable than in this moment.

"It's not?" she asks quietly, and I shake my head.

"Fuck, no. Yes, the first time or two will hurt for you, but if the man is doing his job properly, the pain will subside and be replaced with pleasure. Ecstasy."

She shakes her head, confusion contorting her beautiful features.

"But my sister... she never felt good. It was always so... brutal."

What the fuck!

"Cara, is that why you hurt yourself on me this morning?" I ask, not able to hide the concern in my voice.

"Well... Yes. It had to be done. You're my husband, and I..." She trails off, and I can see that there's more she wants to say, but she's not ready to reveal it to me.

"If you had let me know what you were doing instead of just... doing it, I could have shown you how it's meant to be. Especially for your first time. You must be so sore."

Her cheeks flush crimson, and her eyes drop so I can't see them, telling me without even saying the words that she is.

"I'm a little sore too." I admit, hoping it will make her feel better.

Her gray gaze shoots back up through the fan of her dark lashes.

"You are?"

"Yes. Even though you think you were ready to take my cock, you weren't. I could have helped with that. Made you feel good so your... insides were ready."

Fuck, right now I feel like I'm talking to the sixteen-year-old girl that I married three years ago. How has she not learned this stuff, even in prison?

"But isn't it wrong for me to feel good? Isn't it meant to hurt?" she asks on a whisper and my heart fucking aches for her. For the lies she's been told by her own fucking parents.

"Fuck no." I rush out, quickly kneeling on the end of the bed at her feet. "Let me show you that it can be the complete opposite."

"W-what? How?"

"Let me touch you. Give me permission to pleasure you."

Shaking her head frantically, Cara shuffles up the bed more until her back hits the headboard.

"Okay," I say, holding my hands up. "Let's try something different. How about you touch yourself?"

Her eyes widen. "No. I can't. That's not allowed. It's dirty."

"You can. It's normal. Trust me, everyone masturbates. It's as natural as the act of sex itself."

Still, she shakes her head.

"Okay, then. Just watch," I say, standing from the bed and tugging off my shirt. Her eyes widen but she doesn't say anything, so I toss my shirt aside and tug down my shorts.

My hard cock springs free, the fucker already geared up to please her, and part of me hates that I'm so hard given the situation. But it's her. The way she looks at me with those big eyes, so innocent yet curious. She's fucking trusting me right now, and apparently, my dick likes that.

"Oh. Wait. What are you doing?" She looks panicked, but I hold up my hands and turn my naked body from side to side, hoping it will distract her.

"Let me show you how I get myself off. What I do in the shower each morning and night while I think about you."

Wrapping my hand around my shaft, I keep my eyes trained on Cara's as she stares at my engorged cock, and absentmindedly licks her lips.

"You think about me?" she asks, quietly, and I nod.

"Yes, I do. And doing this feels so good." I tell her, pumping my cock, slowly turning to the side so she can get a better look at what I'm doing. "I imagine it's your hand. I imagine you on your knees sucking my dick into your mouth, your cheeks hollowing as you suck me down as far as you can go. I imagine thrusting into your mouth, hearing you gag a little as I watch you watching me. Your eyes will water, but it's so fucking beautiful, that I can barely hold back."

Sucking her lips into her mouth, Cara shifts on the bed, pressing her thighs together.

"Do you feel it, Killer? Deep down in your cunt. A flutter. A hot gush. The need that you want something more."

"Yes." She breathes, and fuck, pre-cum rolls from my tip at her words.

Climbing on the end of the bed, I kneel in front of her, running my thumb over the bead of pre-cum.

"See this? It's my cock telling me that it's ready for more." I hold up my thumb. "You want a taste?"

She shakes her head, but her breathing deepens, and her eyes don't leave my cock and she presses her thighs together again.

"Just touch yourself." I suggest, and she shakes her head, even as she squeezes her legs tight.

"I promise it will feel good. Just pull your pants down and press your fingers to your clit."

Her dark eyes meet mine again now, and I nod. "It's okay. I promise I won't touch you. I won't do anything to you that you don't want me to do."

I jerk my dick faster, and that seems to spur her on. She quickly shuffles around until her panties and leggings are at her ankles, and then she toes them off, kicking them over the side of the bed, but she keeps her knees squeezed tight.

"Do you like looking at me like this?" I ask, pumping my cock. "Do you like watching what you do to me?"

She nods quickly, and I grin. Finally, I'm getting through to her. Connecting without getting into a sneering match.

"Open your legs, Killer. Let me see how wet you are."

Slowly, as she bites her lip, she pries her knees apart to reveal the satin of her cunt, and it's fucking glistening.

"Oh Cara. You are already so wet. So slick. I can see it."

"Is that... wrong?"

I shake my head. "Fuck no. That's perfect." I start panting as my dick fights to take over, but I need to hold back. I can't fucking come yet. Not until she has. "Press your fingers to your clit." I urge, and when she looks indecisive, I wonder if she's going to do it. I'm surprised when she follows my order, grazing her fingers over the area.

"Oh!" She cries out at the first contact, and I nearly lose my load.

"That's it. Press into it. Or move your fingers in a circle over it." I urge and again, she follows.

Her breathing is rapid now, and I hope like hell she can come, because she deserves to feel this pleasure.

"How does it feel?" I ask, my voice raspy.

"It... It feels sooo... Oh." Her lids fall shut momentarily. "Like I need something... I don't know what."

"Fuck, Killer. It needs to come. Your body needs to come."

She nods, even as her face contorts into pleasured pain.

"I can't... I don't..." She cries in frustration, and I release my dick, shifting closer.

"Let me help you. Let me take over and make you feel the best you've ever fucking felt."

"B-but how?" she asks, glaring at my cock like it offends her all of a sudden.

"Let me show you how a simple kiss can give you what you need."

"A kiss? I don't understand. You want to kiss me?" she asks, her fingers still pressing into her swollen clit.

"Yes, Cara. I want to kiss you here." I reach forward and only when I know she isn't going to flinch away do I close the distance and press the tip of my finger to her lips, which part as she releases a breath. "And I want to kiss you here." I slowly graze my finger down her neck, trailing over her top to circle the tip of her fabric covered breast.

The action causes her chest to push forward into my touch, and a whimper escapes her, but I keep going.

"And I want to kiss all the way down here." I graze my finger over her abs to her bare flesh just above her mound. "And then, when I kiss you here," I ease my finger under hers and press it to her clit, "I won't stop until you come on my face."

A whimper mixed with a growl escapes her, and before I know what's happening, she's pressing her lips to mine.

I fist my hands in her hair, taking control, forcing her to slow down, and she follows quickly, allowing me to nibble on her lips, and slip my tongue into her mouth, until she's moaning.

She's writhing against me, and I know I can make her come now, so I don't waste any more time, peeling her top off, and unclasping her bra as we kiss, and when it falls free, I begin my journey down.

My lips brush over raised skin between her breasts, and without trying to make it obvious my eyes travel over her skin there to find scars. Burn scars, like from a cigarette or something.

Fuck, I want to kill someone. I want to find out who would do such a thing.

Did she have these when I married her or did she come by them in prison?

Something to find out a different time. I need to focus on her. On pleasuring her, so I turn my attention to her dark nipples.

They are pebbled into hard peaks, large and fucking succulent. My cock jerks as I lave at her nipples. First one and then the other, and I fucking love how responsive she is, moaning for me, her fingers delving into my hair.

Continuing down, I leave her nipples to head to paradise, shifting back on the bed so I can get in a good position to start my meal.

"Lay back a bit." I order, glancing up at Cara to see her gray eyes filled with lust and want as she watches on. "I'm going to kiss you here now, beautiful. And I want you to just let yourself feel everything. Just let yourself go. Let your body take you where it wants to go."

She nods eagerly, and I shoot her a grin and a wink before turning my sights on the dark lips of her cunt.

The first lick causes her to jolt, so I grip her hips, keeping my eyes locked with hers as I give it another lick.

She moans and relaxes a little more, so I proceed with what I said I'd do, and I make her feel good with my kiss.

I kiss the folds of her cunt like it's her sweet mouth, and fuck it tastes just as good, if not better. As I flatten my tongue up her center and over her nub, she starts writhing under my hold accepting the building pleasure.

I could insert a finger, but it's not needed and since she's still sore, I want to avoid causing her more pain. I can feel how close she is, I can taste the slickness oozing from her entrance as she lets go and accepts what her body needs.

Her cries come rushing out as her body tenses, and I fucking love how loud she is, probably unaware of it herself.

Flicking my tongue faster, I grip her hips tight, and she explodes against my lips in a pulsating convulsion, and my balls tighten before I shoot cum all over the sheet underneath me.

"Fuck me." I pant as I draw back once she melts into a boneless heap on the bed. "That was fucking transcending."

A lazy smirk tugs at her lips as her lids flutter open and our gazes lock.

"You're telling me. When can we do it again?"

Cara

My body still sings with pleasure as Rocco pulls me closer, my back to his front. He palms my hip, his thumb stroking the skin as I do my best to relax.

"I hate to bring it up again, because you obviously don't want to talk about it, but fuck, Cara, I want to understand."

Rocco's words make me stiffen and his arm snakes around me, holding me tight to him like he's worried I'll flee.

"Why did you impale yourself on my cock like that?"

Squeezing my eyes shut, I ponder whether I should tell him the truth. So far, he's been honest with me, and he looked devastated when he saw my virginity blood coating his cock.

"I had to," I mumble.

"But why?"

I shudder in his arms, and he moves his hand to my stomach, spreading it so he's covering more of me. It feels good. Strange, but good.

"Because you hadn't claimed me," I admit in a small voice.

Rocco's chest rises and falls rapidly, and his fingers dig into the skin on my stomach. "What the fuck does that matter?" he growls.

I don't know why, but his reaction makes my heart skip a beat, and a smile I'm glad he can't see, stretches across my lips. Warmth spreads in my chest, something I've never felt before so I don't know what to call it.

"When dad sold Julietta, he told her husband-to-be that the sale wasn't complete until he'd fucked her."

I shudder again as I remember how my sister's husband abused her while we all watched. That's how I always thought it would be.

When I was in prison, I heard women moan with pleasure, but I always thought that was fake. Something they did because they had to. I'm sure some of them did because not everything that went down was consensual, just like not all of it was forced.

Rocco shifts behind me and moves his hand again. At first I think he's going to touch me like earlier, and I'm not sure if I'm disappointed when he moves the tips of his fingers across my stomach. It tickles, but not in a way that makes me want to laugh. It's more like fire trails in the wake of his gentle touch.

"I understand why you did it." He nuzzles into the crook of my neck, and I arch my back as his lips graze my skin. "But if you ever do something like that to me again, I'll make you fucking regret it."

"W-what?" I stammer, not liking the harshness of his tone.

"Did it ever fucking occur to you that I didn't want to do something like that?"

I furrow my brows in confusion. "No," I answer honestly. "You're a guy. Guys expect sex, and you were hard so I thought you would like it."

When he doesn't answer, I ramble on.

"Besides, Mindy made it clear you like hard, brutal fucking."

As soon as the words leave me, I wonder if he's angry because he wasn't in control. She said that's what he wanted, and I took it from him.

"So fucking what? I might be a guy, but I've already made it clear I don't force anyone to have sex with me. I never thought I had to fucking explain I don't want to be used either."

Used... yes, I used him.

"I don't understand," I say softly. "Explain it to me."

He sighs, and the air tickles my skin. "Mindy should never have fucking run her mouth like that. But yes, I like fucking. And yes, I like it hard."

"So you're upset with me because I did it wrong?"

I feel him shake his head. "No, I'm upset because you took my fucking choice away, and hurt yourself instead of talking to me."

Silence stretches around us as I contemplate his words. I hear them, yet I can't make sense of them.

"And because your pleasure is important to me."

There it is again, the mention of pleasure I never even knew existed.

"Why?" I ask.

"Because when you fuck me dry like last night, it hurts both of us. If you're wet, it'll feel amazing for us both. Sex with me is about pleasure. I'm not claiming to be a good guy, and I like pushing boundaries. But consent is important to me." His solemn tone portrays just how serious he takes it, and it makes me feel bad for what I did.

"I didn't know," I whisper.

Should I apologize? I don't want to because what I did had to be done, and even if it wasn't intended as punishment, it kind of worked. Though a true punishment should be served in public, that's what my family did and it worked.

When Mateo and I turned twelve, dad put him in charge of my punishment. I still have the burn marks from the many times he used my skin to put out his cigarettes. Sly as he is, he always aimed for places that would be hidden by my clothes.

After undressing me earlier, I know Rocco's seen the scars between my tits, and maybe even on my inner thighs. I'm not ashamed of them, they prove I'm strong and that I learned from my mistakes.

"You had a fucked up childhood," Rocco says. It's not a question, so I don't answer. "Sex can be a way to love someone with your body, but it can also just be about pleasure. Wanting to feel good. Do you understand?"

"I-I think so."

Honestly, I'm not sure I do. But I want to, and I want to feel good again. I experimentally arch my back again, pushing my ass back against him.

"Cara," he warns on a low growl. "You don't have to do this."

"I want to feel good," I say. "You said it could just be about the pleasure. That's what I want."

Rocco rolls his hips against me, and I feel his hardness slide between my thighs. We're still naked from earlier, which makes it feel even more intense.

"One last question," he says. "Then I promise I'll make you come again."

Not liking the way it sounds like a trade, I ask, "And if I don't want to answer?"

"I'll still make you come."

"Okay," I agree. "Ask away."

"Who hurt you?"

Fuck, he did notice the scars on my body.

The decision to open up isn't a conscious one, my mouth just won't stay shut. "Mostly it was Mateo. When I did something wrong, he had to discipline me in front of our sister and parents."

Rocco makes an angry sound in the back of his throat. "That's why you want to punish me, isn't it? Because I did something wrong."

"I did punish you," I remind him. "Even if that wasn't why I did what I did, it doubled as that. So we're even."

"You're so fucked up," he grumbles.

He's not wrong.

I'm just about to remind him of his promise to make me come again when Rocco moves his hands to my tits, palming them before he pinches my hardened nipples. When he thrusts his hips against me again, I moan. The tip of his cock slides through my folds and hits my clit, the touch making my pussy throb with want.

"Again," I moan. "Please."

He continues to move his cock between my thighs, and I feel myself get wetter with each roll of his hips. Fuck, this is what I wanted.

"Does it feel good, Killer?" he groans, and I eagerly nod.

"Y-yes," I cry out. "I need more."

The primal sound coming from deep within his throat stirs something awake inside of me, causing my core to ache. Rocco burrows his face into the crook of my neck. His lips and teeth graze my skin in a way that makes my inner muscles tighten.

Rocco slides one hand down my stomach and all the way to the apex of my thighs. As his fingers skim my clit, I moan his name.

"That's it, Killer. Fucking say my name."

"Rocco," I half-scream as he adds more pressure to my clit. "Yes, that's it. Don't stop." I barely recognize my own voice, it's throaty with need.

"Does it feel good?"

I barely hear him over the thundering beats of my heart. I'm too far gone to be able to form coherent words. Instead, I move my hips backward as he moves between my thighs, moaning unashamedly when he hits just the right spot over and over again.

"C-can I touch you?" I ask, desperate to know what he feels like but unsure if it's okay or not.

"Of course," Rocco groans. "Roll to your back."

Doing as he says, I roll over, immediately spreading my legs, welcoming him as he moves between them. The tip of his cock nudges against my opening, but he doesn't move inside.

"Wrap your hand around my cock," he commands huskily. "And rub me against your clit."

"Oh!" I cry out as I do just that, and it feels fucking amazing.

When I had him in my hand earlier, I didn't take the time to really get a feel for him. But now I do. The skin is smooth, except for the vein running along the length. Is it supposed to be this hot? To throb in my hand? It feels heavy, and... and... fuck, I don't know. It's hard to focus on anything other than the way he feels against my pussy.

Groaning, Rocco commands, "Squeeze me tighter." I don't admit that I'm afraid to hurt him. "Here, let me help you."

He places his hand on top of mine and adds pressure until I'm holding him how he wants it. He's so big I have no idea how he fit inside me earlier, and my hand can't even close around his girth.

"Now rub yourself."

I lift my hips and angle them so he's hitting me in a way that has pleasure coursing through my veins. I can't stop moaning, every touch sends me higher, and I feel my toes curl.

"Rocco." I cry out his name, unsure how to get us both where we want to be.

"I got you, Killer," he groans as though he's reading my thoughts.

He thrusts into my hand, hitting my clit with each movement and before long my legs are shaking and my free hand clutches the sheet beneath me.

"I-I'm going to... I can't... Rocco!"

"Oh fuck," he groans as he picks up the pace. "Yes. I'm going to paint your cunt in my cum."

Unable to form words, I cry out as I come apart. This is nothing like before, it's much more intense, and I can barely catch my breath.

Once I'm no longer shaking, I push myself up on my elbows. "What was that?" I ask curiously.

Rocco falls down next to me, a lazy grin on his lips. "What was what?"

"That," I repeat, gesturing between us.

"An orgasm, Killer," he says, rolling his eyes like I'm not making sense.

I shake my head. "Nuh-uh. This was nothing like earlier. It was... more."

With a chuckle, he pulls me into his embrace, and I rest my head on his chest. "They're not always the same," he explains patiently. "Some are better than others."

Huh, I never knew that. Then again, why would I when I never even knew a woman is able to feel good during sex.

Rocco's phone vibrates on the nightstand, and he reaches for it, cursing as he answers.

"What?" he snaps into the microphone.

I can't hear what's being said on the other end, but whatever it is has Rocco getting out of bed, reaching for his clothes.

"Fine." Silence. "Yeah, we'll be there soon."

I watch as he finishes getting dressed, unashamedly enjoying the show.

"We need to leave?" I ask, unable to hide the excitement in my voice.

Although this has been the longest day in some ways, I don't feel tired. I feel reinvigorated, and like I need to do something other than lie here.

"Yeah," he confirms. "Cain wants to go over something at Dirty Diamonds."

Wrapping the sheet around me, I head toward the back door for a quick shower.

"Where do you think you're going?" Rocco sounds amused.

Turning around, I face him. "To clean myself," I explain, confused when he shakes his head.

"No way, Killer. I want to know your cunt is painted in my cum."

I feel my cheeks heat at his words, and a refusal is on the tip of my tongue. But then I take a second to ponder it, and... I think I want that too.

"Okay," I relent.

Ignoring his satisfied smirk, I get dressed in the leggings and top from earlier. It's not as impressive as my leather outfits, but paired with the boots it's not half-bad. Plus, without heels I feel too small next to Rocco.

We get into his truck, and he quickly drives us to Dirty Diamonds where Cain's waiting outside. He's leaning against the wall, one leg propped up as he blows smoke into the night.

"My, my, my. If it isn't Mr. and Mrs. King," he says as a way of greeting. "How are you doing, Cara?"

"Better than some, worse than others," I say with a shrug, making sure to turn each S into a hiss.

Cain's brows shoot up. "You heard me," he laughs, and I nod. "Well played, snake."

Rocco shakes his head and takes my hand. "Let's get on with whatever's the reason you dragged me down here," he says as we follow Cain inside.

"Oh, I'm sorry," Cain retorts. "Did I disturb your sex-a-thon?"

"His what?" I ask.

With a wink, Cain elaborates. "You see, some people turn sex into a marathon, or as I call it, a sex-a-thon. Wait, are you two having sex?"

"None of your damn business," Rocco growls.

At the same time, I say, "Yes."

When Rocco looks at me, I just shrug. I'm not embarrassed by what we're doing, and I'd rather that the word spreads than having Mateo show up again. Or bitches like Mindy think they can take what's mine.

As we reach the bar, Cain points at the guy behind it. "That's Tex. Make good friends with him, Cara. He holds the keys to the liquor cabinet, so to speak. And if he likes you, he won't mind making you some fancy cocktails despite your age."

I wave awkwardly at Tex who nods back at me.

"Right, I'm going to borrow your hubby," Cain says, turning toward Rocco.

"Give me a sec," my husband says, not taking his eyes off mine. "Try not to get into any more fights, Killer."

I grin. "I can't promise that."

He chuckles, closing the distance between us. "Just know that it makes me fucking hard to see you stand up for yourself. So unless you want me to make you come here, don't tempt me."

Bending down, he fuses his lips to mine. His tongue licks at the seam of my mouth until I open for him, and snake my tongue around his.

Kissing Rocco is the sweetest addiction, and I almost forget where we are as he tilts my head back and deepens the kiss.

"Behave," he rasps as he pulls back, shooting me a wink before he leaves with Cain.

I walk over to the bar, greeting Tex as I sit down on one of the tall barstools. "Hi."

"You're the wife?" he asks as he looks up from the glass in his hand.

"That's me," I confirm.

Without asking what I want he starts to mix me a cocktail. I don't know what it's called, but it's pink and fucking delicious.

I quickly learn that Tex isn't one for small talk, and that suits me just fine. Turning on the chair I watch the strippers on stage. There are five of them, and while some interact, others do their own thing.

The room isn't as full as I had thought it would be on a Saturday, but with how many people who come up to the bar it looks like business is booming. Maybe it's because it's late. I don't know when the club's prime time is, but I suppose it's possible it's earlier in the evening.

"Are you Cara?" a woman asks as she comes up to me.

"Alana," Tex says, greeting her.

I nod at her. "That's me."

"There's someone here to see you."

At first, I don't understand. But then I remember that young homeless looking guy, Gray mentioning he might see me around here, and I assume it's him. If it is, I'll offer him a fucking haircut, so he doesn't look as unkempt as he did last night... err... this morning. Shit, it's all blurring together, making today the longest day.

When I get off the stool, Tex says, "Stay nearby so I can keep an eye on you."

"He's just right over there," Alana says, pointing toward the nearest alcove.

I follow her over, and as she pushes through some of the guests, my blood runs cold. "Mateo," I gasp. "What the fuck are you doing here?"

My twin looks more haggard than the last time I saw him. His eyes are wild, and there's a welt on his arm.

"I came to see you, of course." The smile on his face sends chills down my spine. "How are you doing, dear sister?"

Taking a step back, I eye him cautiously. "You have no right to check up on me," I hiss. "You need to leave. Now. Before Rocco sees you."

Mentioning the man who bought me doesn't deter my brother in the slightest. He shrugs like it's of no consequence to him. "You're family," Mateo insists. "Why can't I just come and see you? I've missed you. We should catch up."

As I scrutinize him, I can't decide if he's lying or not. Mateo has never been sentimental, which would suggest he isn't being honest. But... what if he is?

"I-I..."

"Come on, Cara. Me and mom are the only family you have left, and we want to start over."

The words pluck at my heartstrings.

Family...

How often have I wished mine was different? That I was loved rather than used. This could be my opportunity to get what I've always wanted.

Just as I think that, Julietta's face pops into my mind. It's too late. The family I wanted included her, and she's gone. Killed by a cold-blooded fucking monster.

"No," I snap.

"Please, Cara," Mateo begs, something I never thought I'd hear.

I straighten my spine and take another step backward. "Do you honestly think—"

Before I can finish speaking, Mateo gets in my face. Fury rolls off of him as he slaps me. "You stupid fucking cunt," he snarls. "You never did learn your place."

My hand shoots up to my cheek, it's burning. "W-what?" I stutter, confused by his outburst.

Everything happens so quickly I barely have time to react.

Mateo lunges, swinging his fist at me, and I don't lift my arm quickly enough to block him. His fist connects with my chin, causing my head to snap to the side as I stumble backwards.

No!

Not to-fucking-day.

In prison, I took up kickboxing in the gym, and unofficially I learned to throw knives. Since I don't have my own blade, the latter won't help me.

"Is that all you've got?" I sneer.

Then I kick out, aiming for his stomach. But Mateo manages to move to the side, avoiding me.

"You bitch," he shouts.

Rolling my shoulders back, I stand as tall as possible, refusing to show any weakness. "At least I'm not some pathetic mama's boy," I taunt. "Unlike you, I don't hide behind our parents."

A sinister smile spreads across his lips. "And unlike you, dear twin, I'm fucking worthy. All you were good for was being sold. Tell me, did your pathetic husband finally fuck you?"

There's something in his voice that causes me to really look at him. They say that all twins have a special bond, and right now, that feels true, even though it's not a good one.

"It was a warning," I say. "Coming to Rocco's house last night was a warning, wasn't it?"

He shrugs, pretending to look indifferent but I see the relief in his eyes. "So what if it was?"

Yeah... so what if it was? I don't know. But surely it has to mean something.

"I don't know," I almost whisper. "Why would you do that?"

As if he's angered by my question, Mateo clenches and un-clenches his fists at his sides. "Don't start asking questions, Cara. You and I were pitted against each other since we were kids, and that's how it will always be."

Tears form in my eyes, and a single one escapes, trailing down my cheek. "Okay," I choke out.

I'm not going to attempt to change his mind, because he's right. We haven't been close since we were kids, and one somewhat kind act isn't changing that.

I see the second he decides to attack me, and I swiftly kick out at him again. This time, I hit him square in the chest, and it's his turn to stumble backwards.

"You cunt," he seethes.

Rolling my eyes, I volley, "I'm getting so sick and fucking tired of people using that word against me."

Without pausing, he comes at me. Or, he tries to. But before he reaches me, Rocco steps in front of me, a gun in his hand.

Rocco

"You lay one more hand on her and it's the last thing you'll fucking do." I seethe, my whole body vibrating with rage as I stare down who I assume is Cara's twin brother given the same gray eyes staring back at me.

"This is not your concern." The gutless prick glares at me even as I feel Cara's dainty hand on the back of my shoulder.

"You're wrong about that," I hiss. "Cara is my wife and therefore my only fucking concern. The only reason I haven't pulled the trigger yet is out of courtesy for her, but please, give me a reason to ignore her."

"Rocco. Don't."

Mateo chuckles in front of me, holding his hands up and taking a step back.

"Okay, okay. I won't lay another hand on her. For now."

I growl right as Cain's voice joins the fucking party.

"You know, I have no such fucking obligations to Mrs. King, other than keeping her safe, so I'm more than happy to paint the room with your fucking blood."

"Cain." Cara warns, and he chuckles.

"I'm almost tempted to do it just to have your wrath aimed at me, Señora. You fight like a badass."

"And if Cain doesn't do it," Tex's voice comes from the other side of where we stand, low and menacing, "I'll fucking shoot you simply for disrupting business."

I smirk, believing both my friends' words. Cain is a crazy fucker, and Mateo's lucky he even got a fucking warning, and Tex, the quiet guy behind the bar, well he's there for a reason, and it's not just because he knows how to make those fucking fruity drinks the Diamonds love so much. The Diamond Crew only recruits the best, after all.

"I hear you loud and clear." Mateo still grins, and I wonder if he's a match for Cain's energy. Something we shouldn't take lightly.

Straightening his clothes, he leans to the side, his eyes traveling past me to where I assume he's looking at his sister.

"Always a pleasure, sis."

He shoots her a fucking wink as he steps over an upturned chair and makes his way to the exit. Keeping my gun trained on him, I watch Cain and Tex follow behind him as they make sure he leaves the premises.

As soon as they disappear through the curtain, I lower my gun and spin to Cara.

"Are you okay?"

My eyes dance over her face as I tuck my piece into the back of my jeans, before I run my hands down her arms, searching for injuries.

"I'm fine," she says quietly, her attention shifting to the exit, which is when I see her swelling jaw and red cheek where I saw the fucker slap her from the security cameras I was watching her on while I spoke with Cain.

Pressing my fingers to the other side of her jaw, I tilt her face so I can get a better look.

"Jesus." I mutter, hating to see her marked like that. I should have killed that fucker, if not for this, but for the way he left her scarred after the punishments he gave her as they grew up.

"Alana! Sasha!" I call, not taking my eyes off Cara's inflamed skin, even as she tries to jerk away from my touch.

"Yes?" Sasha's voice gets closer, but I don't bother looking at her. "Can you get an ice pack for Cara, please?"

"Yes. Of course." She agrees just as Cain and Tex re-enter the club.

"Is he gone?" I ask, and Cain beams, strutting toward us like a fucking king that just won a war.

"He's gone, but he'll be back. He's as excited at the idea of playing as I am."

"This isn't a game." Cara snaps, shooting Cain a glare, and he rolls his eyes.

"Everything is a game, mi pequeño salvaje."

Shaking her head, a grin tugs at Cara's lips as Cain struts by, and I frown, trying to figure out what the fuck he just said to her.

"What did you say?" I ask Cain, who shrugs before disappearing down the hall and I turn my gaze back to Cara. "What did he say?"

"I don't know what you mean." She shrugs before stepping around me and moving to the bar to take a seat.

"Yes, you do. It was something in Spanish." I interject, moving to her side as I hear Tex chuckle to himself while he re-stashes his shotgun under the counter.

"I must have missed it." Cara shrugs but the smirk on her face tells me fucking otherwise and I growl.

"Dammit, woman. Just fucking tell me what he said."

Turning in her chair to face me, she shoots me a glare. "Why? Why must you know everything?"

"Because I'm your fucking husband."

Her lips thin. "Not a good enough reason." She turns back to face the bar right as Sasha places the ice pack on the counter.

"This should help." She offers Cara, giving her a soft smile before retreating, and Cara picks up the ice pack and the thin towel and gently presses it to her cheek and jaw.

"Look, I'm trying here," I tell her, sitting my ass in the seat next to her. "And the fact that you keep speaking in Spanish to me, doesn't seem very fucking fair because I don't understand it."

"I wasn't the one who spoke Spanish that time." She points out, and I grit my teeth.

"I'm just trying to understand you. He said something that made you grin, and I want to know what it fucking was." She shrugs, even as Tex speaks.

"He said, my little savage."

My gaze darts to Tex, who grins past his mustache before shrugging and I grumble.

"Why the fuck does everyone but me know Spanish?"

Cara rolls her eyes. "I think the real question is, why didn't you learn Spanish at school? In prison, I was told it's an option for most schools that offer learning a foreign language."

My mouth goes dry as I feel the familiarity of my uneducated past slam into me, making me feel like the dumb street kid I was ten years ago.

Without meaning to, I shoot Cara a glare, but try to hide any other response I have to it by facing the bar and knocking the counter.

Tex gets to work pouring me a whiskey on the rocks, and my eyes catch Cara's reflection in the mirror behind the bar as she looks at me, a puzzled frown tugging at her brows.

Shit. She noticed my reaction.

I hadn't meant for that to happen. It's not something I've fucking given a shit about for years, but for some reason, now with Cara in the picture, I feel like my past will just show her how fucking unworthy I am to declare her as mine.

"Rocco?" Cara asks quietly, but Cain fucking saves the day, leaping in to burst our bubble with his larger-than-life energy.

"Tell me Mrs. King. Who taught you how to fight like that?"

My brows lift with interest, and I turn to see Cara's attention on Cain now.

"Prison. There's a lot of free time."

Cain nods. "I bet you ruled that place. Cara the Queen." He holds his hands up like he's framing a sign that has the words spelled out in lights.

Cara giggles.

Fuck, I love hearing that.

"Mr. King. Our fair ruler called me back." Cain bows like he's talking to fucking royalty. I wonder what pills he pops to live in the delusional world he lives in. Maybe I should ask him for some?

"And?" I ask, remembering back to the conversation I was having with Cain in the office before Cara's twin decided to show up.

"No location found as of yet, but Dante has people working on it. They are trying to track the most recent visitor as we speak."

I nod, ignoring Cara's curious eyes as she looks between us and tries to piece the information together.

I'd asked Cain to find out if Dante's sources had a lead on Cara's mom's location yet. After knowing it was her brother that came to taunt her at my house last night, or should I say, our house, I knew her mom mustn't have been too far away, but so far, she's been a ghost ever since she and her evil son got away after our wedding. I was hoping since Mateo showed up that perhaps they could get a new lead, and hopefully now with what I decipher from Cain, they will since they must be following Mateo after leaving here.

"Now who's keeping secrets," Cara mutters and I bite back a smirk.

"I'll fill you in at home." I toss back the whiskey I haven't touched, before standing. "Let's go."

Even though she shoots daggers at me, Cara stands and offers a wave to Tex and Cain as she holds the ice pack to her face. The moment she is standing, I link our fingers and ignore the eyes following us as we leave and head back to my little house.

"Are you ever going to tell me what you and Cain were just talking about?" Cara asks as I unlock the front door.

"I don't see why I should since you didn't think you needed to share what Cain said to you with me."

I know I'm being petty, but if anything, I'm doing it to rile her up a little.

I like seeing the fire in her eyes. Seeing the spark of passion to not let anyone rule over her. It's the only way I know how to keep her motivated to keep fighting.

"Tex told you what he said." She complains, stepping inside with me, and I shut the door, locking it before shaking my head.

"Tex told me. Not you. I asked *you* what Cain said." I point out, and her shoulders slump.

"Whatever."

Sometimes I forget that she's still in her teens. I know I'm not that much older, so I probably shouldn't think like that, but it's hard not to when there is a part of her that seems so much older than her nineteen years, and then there are parts that make her seem like she's newly a teenager.

I fucking hate her parents for raising her with such twist-ed beliefs.

A knock behind me at the door makes us still, and Cara's eyes go wide in panic.

Reaching for my gun, I whisper to my wife. "Hide." Before calling out. "Who is it?"

"It's Martina. Martina Rodríguez."

As Cara dashes into my bedroom to hide, I move to open the door, making sure Martina can see the gun in my hand.

"What do you want?"

"I-I want to see Cara." She stutters, her dark hair shorter than it was three years ago, her curls barely long enough to touch her shoulders.

"No." I snap, glaring at the woman who told Cara obscene lies about sex and her duty as a wife.

"But she's my daughter. I miss her."

I chuckle darkly. "She may be your biological daughter, Mrs. Rodríguez, but you're no mother."

"You know nothing. Please, I'm here to help you. Take her off your hands. She can be so troublesome."

I hear the faint hiss from my bedroom, confirming that Cara must be right behind the door, listening.

"Spare me your lies and fuck off. Cara is my wife, and I will not hand her over to you."

"You say that now, but you see, Mr. King, you will eventu-ally regret saying that. Cara was born a little different. She's not so smart. Needs a stern hand. She has a lot to learn."

"If she needs a stern hand, then rest assured, I will deliver it."

I move to shut the door, but she puts her booted foot in the way.

"Fine. How much? I'll buy her back."

"She's not for fucking sale!" I hiss, raising my gun to point it directly in her face, but she doesn't even flinch.

"Of course she's for sale. What's your price?" Martina ignores my words, her expression holding too much fucking confidence for my liking.

"Why do you want her?" I ask instead, and she rounds her eyes, trying to appear innocent.

"Because she's my daughter and I love her."

I scoff, right as Cara flies from the bedroom and tugs the door open.

"You don't love me! How could you? When you love someone, you don't do the things you did to me. To Julietta."

For the first time, I see Martina flinch, and even though Cara is inside the house with me, I still position myself a little more between them.

"That was your dad forcing my hand," Martina cries. "Things are different now."

Cara laughs but there's no humor in it. "Things are not different now. Mateo spoke with me and tried to coax me as well, but you know what? He can't hide his true colors. I know you don't have good intentions either. What do you have planned for me if you get me back?" Cara sneers. "You gonna sell me again? I'll fight. No one will get near me. I'll kill them."

Martina falls quiet, her expression turning from devastated to sinister.

"When we get you," she snickers, leaning in a little, "and we will get you, my darling girl. I'll make sure you are so hooked on coke that you'll do the most depraved things for your next hit."

In an instant, the barrel of my gun is pressed against her forehead.

"Give me one good reason why I shouldn't just shoot you here?"

"Rocco," Cara whisper-yells, rushing forward to drag my hand down so I'm no longer pressing the gun to her mother's head. "Company."

It takes me a second to figure out Cara's meaning, but then my eyes move past her evil mother to the police cruiser slowly idling by.

"And on that note," Martina mutters before turning her back on us and quickly darting toward the waiting black car in the driveway.

"Fuck," I hiss, keeping my gun low so the cops, who are carefully watching as they move slowly past, don't see me packing.

We both stand in the door waiting for the cops to move on as the black car reverses and speeds off in the opposite direction, before I urge Cara back and slam the door, locking it once again.

"Do you think that's why she really wants you?" I ask Cara, who is still staring at the door like she can see through the solid wood. "Cara?"

Slowly, she blinks, before directing her gaze to me. "I'm not a virgin anymore, so the only thing I'm useful for is turning me into one of their whores."

"Jesus." Not able to hold back, I step forward and pull her to my chest, wrapping one hand around her to hold her to me, while I use the other hand to take out my phone and call Dante.

He's in the UK with his family, so I hope it's not like three in the morning there, because I have no fucking clue about all that shit.

"Hello?" His deep voice is loud in my ear, and Cara must hear it, because she pulls back to look at me.

"Dante, I've just had a visit from Martina Rodríguez. She was in a black car. Get your tech team to hack into my security cameras and get her plates."

"Why would she be dumb enough to visit you?" Dante asks in confusion, because it's not the typical MO in this sort of situation.

"She thought she could buy her back, and that I'd fucking say yes."

"She's either really stupid, or she has a back-up plan." Dante points out before he turns his attention to something going on in the background. "Come on, give her back the glue. You both need to learn to share. Fucking girls are relentless today." The last part is muttered so low I think I'm the only one to hear it.

"I'm leaning toward the latter." I admit after he apologizes and turns his attention back to me before cursing.

"Okay. I'll put more men on the streets. Someone has to know where they are hiding."

"Thanks. Let me know if you find anything." I suggest and Dante agrees.

"Of course. You'll be the first person I call."

Ending the call, Cara moves away from me and starts pacing.

She's angry.

I can see it in the way her shoulders tense, and how her hands open and close into fists, over and over.

"Hit me," I say, placing my gun on the table by the door.

"What?" she asks, stopping abruptly to frown at me. "No."

"Fucking hit me," I urge again, slapping a hand to my chest, asking her to use my body to take out her frustrations.

Slowly, she shakes her head, but the way she bites the corner of her mouth, tells me she's considering it.

"Come on, Killer. It'll help with your anger." I slap my cheek this time. "Hit me."

And she does. I barely see the punch coming before her fist slams into my jaw, rattling my teeth.

"Shit," I hiss, eyes flaring wide. "You're strong. Do it again."

She does, this time the blow coming to my chest, causing me to cough a little as the wind flies from me.

"Again, Killer!" I yell, feeling the blood in my veins ignite.

This punch slams into my gut, bending me at the middle, and I don't get the chance to tell her to go again before she swings, but this time, I catch her fist and shove her hard against the wall by the door.

"Fuck me," I demand, staring into her furious gray eyes as her nostrils flare. "Fuck this anger out of your system. Use me, Cara. Take what you need and fuck me."

"I don't know how." She breathes, even though I can see how much she wants this by the scorching heat in her eyes.

"Then give me permission and let me fuck you until you can't fucking think anymore," I demand and fuck, she nods.

"Yes."

I'm on her in an instant, my lips claiming hers even as I palm her tit through the fabric of her top.

"Get this off," I growl, moving back as I drop to my knees, happy to see her hurrying to do as I ask.

Working her leggings down, I drag her panties with them exposing her flesh, and my heated gaze travels up her body as she flings her bra to the side.

"Look how filthy you still are." I press my nose to her exposed cunt and inhale audibly. "My dry cum makes your cunt look like a delectable treat."

Her heated gaze widens even as her lips part as she watches me close the distance and lick over her seam.

Instantly, her hands fist in my hair, and I love this about her. How she likes to hold on. Make sure I stay there until the job is done.

I wonder if she even realizes she does it.

Flattening my tongue, I press it into her clit as I drag it, and she widens her stance, giving me better access.

"Fuck, Killer. You're already so wet."

"I-is that bad? Should I be embarrassed?"

I growl against her mound, gliding my fingers up her inner thigh before pressing two fingers to her opening.

"Fuck no. Wet is good, remember. Wet tells me you want me. Just like a man has an erection, a woman's slick cunt is her version of a stiffy."

"Oh." She cries out, when I sink the fingers into her tight hot heat, stretching her.

As I start working my fingers into the spongy wall of her g-spot, I watch her face transform into a lust crazed expression.

"Tell me how to say beautiful in Spanish," I ask her, and she presses her head back against the wall as she starts to move her hips, chasing her high.

"Hermosa." She pants, and I grin, pressing my lips to her clit and kissing her passionately there.

Lost to the pleasure, she starts grinding against my face while I mash my fingers harder and faster, helping her get closer to ecstasy.

The moment she starts clamping around my fingers, I free my cock with my free hand, and when her cries slowly die off from riding her high, I stand quickly, hitch her legs up, and ease my cock inside her.

She tenses, but my lips find hers as I kiss her, letting her taste herself on my tongue, and I use my free hand to circle her clit, building her pleasure again to mask any discomfort she feels at my invasion.

I slowly thrust a few times, feeling how easy my dick moves inside her with each motion, and then her hips are pressing into mine too, wanting more.

Lifting her legs, I wrap them around my waist and walk us awkwardly, with my jeans around my fucking ankles, to the side and through my bedroom door before falling us onto my bed.

I don't stop moving. I continue pumping into her, faster and faster, loving her panted cries as she claws at my shoulders, holding on.

Breaking our kiss again, I push up, getting better momentum and pounding harder, watching how her tits jiggle with each thrust.

"Am I hurting you?" I grunt out, and she shakes her head.

"Yes. No. Don't stop."

I fucking grin. I knew she'd be a good student.

"Does it feel good?" I ask, before biting my lip and willing myself not to fucking come yet. I want to wait and ride that high with her.

"Yes. Oh yes." She cries, arching back and squeezing her eyes tight.

"Eyes on me," I demand, and her lids fly open, her steely gaze locking with mine.

"Hermosa," I tell her in her native language, and she smiles, like she appreciates that I remember the word I asked her for a few minutes earlier.

"I want you to come for me, Killer." I rasp, pistoning inside her. "Squeeze my cock. Milk me."

Even as I say this, I press my thumb to her clit and after only a few strokes, I send her soaring again with a loud cry.

The moment she starts clamping around me, my nuts draw up before pleasure erupts, shooting hot cum from my cock and filling her, deep inside.

I swear my hearing fucking vanishes with how hard I come, but after a few moments, Cara's panting breaths come back to me, and I blink myself out of my orgasmic daze to look down at her.

"Now that is how it's done," I tell her, and she giggles.

"That was... so much more than earlier. Will it keep getting better and better each time?"

"My cock aims to please. I'll be sure to try to bring you to new heights each time."

"Damn. Don't let me stop you."

Slowly a wide toothy smile spreads her lips wide and with the way her cheeks are flushed red, and her lips are puffy and well kissed, I fucking know I'm never going to get enough of her.

Of my wife.

Cara

"**S**o what's the deal with you and Rocco?"

I press the cold water bottle harder against the side of my face, feeling the plastic bend under my grip. Luckily, Mateo's punch didn't leave much of a bruise, so I don't even know why I keep cooling the skin down. Since it's been a few days since he hit me, the bruising would have already appeared.

"Why do you want to know?" I shoot back at Alana, tossing my long hair over my shoulder and narrowing my eyes at her.

She grins wider. "Because I'm so fucking curious. We all heard the stories of your marriage, but I don't think any of us expected you to become a real couple."

I'm not sure there's a label for what Rocco and I are. Yes, we're married, and we live together. We also do all the stuff married people do. So maybe that's my answer.

"Come on, mamacita," Sasha adds, playfully wiggling her eyebrows. "Give us something."

The word hits me right in the heart. I know that mamacita has become a slang word that can be used for all women. But it means little mom or hot mom. Something I never want to be... a mom, hot or otherwise.

"Wait." I turn around just as Cain comes sauntering up to the bar. "I want to know as well. Like, is my bro good in the sack? Does he—"

"Fuck off, Cain," Alana giggles as she picks up a coaster and throws it at him. "This is girl talk."

"Yeah, but Sasha is asking questions she already knows the answer to," Cain gripes.

My back stiffens, and I turn to the Diamond in question. "You've fucked Rocco?" Since that much is already clear, I ask what I really want to know. "While we were married?" I'm unable to hide the malice tinting my tone.

Sasha immediately holds her hands up. "Hang the fuck on. I don't fuck married men," she rushes out.

"We all have a past," Alana says. She shoots a glare in Cain's direction. "And some of us should stop fucking antagonizing the rest of us."

"But where's the fun in that?" Cain chuckles as he reaches for the glass of whiskey Tex's holding out to him. "It's much better once everything's out in the open. I'd hate for any nasty secrets to come back and bite any of your lovely asses later."

He has a point, and after how I behaved with Mindy, I can't exactly blame him for forcing the issue.

"I don't care," I say to no one in particular. "Whatever Rocco did before me is none of my concern."

The words are pretty, but the way I'm now looking at Sasha isn't. It's not her fault, and I'm rational enough to know I need to keep my inner bitch locked down tight. Because unlike with Mindy, Sasha isn't throwing it in my face, and I had no claim on Rocco then.

"None of your concern, ehh?" Rocco asks, as he comes up to the bar.

"Double Gs," Cain grins and nods at Gray and Gunner as they trail in behind Rocco.

While Gunner is all smiles, his pal looks like he wants to be anywhere but here.

Honestly, why does Gray look so... homeless?

I've never asked Rocco about his finances, and I never will. But as I look around at Dirty Diamonds, and all the people here, money doesn't seem to be a concern.

It's not like anyone is brimming with wealth, but no one looks as rugged as Gray. I mean, his clothes don't even fit him, and he's in dire need of a haircut. And don't even get me started on his lack of shaving. Unlike Rocco's scruff, which looks intentional, Gray's patchy stubble looks like it's from not caring.

"Nope," I quip, popping the p. "But I should warn you that if you fuck around on me, I'll fucking castrate you."

Sasha and Alana gasp while Cain and Tex chuckle. Rocco, though, he just smiles widely.

"And if you fuck around on me, Killer, I'll kill the guy in front of you and lock you up," he growls.

Considering my past, that warning shouldn't make my body ignite with desire. There's no helping it, though. Especially not when he comes up behind me and wraps his arms around my middle, definitely not as he licks and nibbles on the shell of my ear.

"Make no mistake, Killer. You're mine."

"Prove it," I shoot back.

With a playful smile grazing his lips, Rocco lifts me off the barstool and easily turns me around in his hold. I instinctively wrap my legs around his waist and my hands rest on his shoulders.

As Rocco's lips descend on mine in a bruising kiss, the rest of the room fades away. I can no longer hear their laughter, teasing jabs, or anything else. They become inconsequential and forgotten as I stroke Rocco's tongue with mine.

When he moves his hands to my ass, squeezing the globes, I moan into his mouth. My hips move of their own accord, and I rock against the hardness growing between us.

"Not here, hermosa," he rasps into my mouth.

"Then where?" I moan impatiently.

I'm vaguely aware of Cain mentioning his office, but I don't pay much attention. Instead, I pepper Rocco's jaw and neck with kisses, licks, and soft bites as he carries me away from the bar.

"Are you sure?" Rocco asks as he sits me down on what I assume is Cain's desk.

Rather than answering him, I undo the button and zipper on his jeans. My movements are hurried, jerky. I want him—my husband—inside me right the fuck now.

"Answer me, Killer," he demands.

I look up at him from beneath my long, dark lashes. "I'm sure," I confirm.

I barely recognize the person I've become as I shove his jeans and boxers down his muscular legs. The lust pulsating inside me stirs my action, and all I can think about is the way it feels when he moves inside me.

Letting go of me, Rocco pulls his shirt over his head, and kicks his shoes and socks off. I lick my lips expectantly as he stands in front of me, completely naked.

Damn, this man is as sculpted as they come. His cheekbones could cut diamonds, and his muscles call to me in a way I've never considered before. But I want to touch them, lick them, make sure I've tasted every inch of his skin.

"Stop looking at me like that, Killer," he rasps.

I frown. "Like what?"

He chuckles and holds his hand out for me to take, which I do. I let him pull me off the table and to my feet, and as soon as I'm standing, he rids me of my crop-top and bra.

"Like you want to devour me," he smirks. Then he palms my tits and pinches my nipples. "Like you want to own every part of me."

My mom's training kicks in, and I immediately avert my gaze. "I'm s-sorry. I didn't m-mean to."

Rocco's growl makes me flinch, and for the first time, I feel scared of him. My eyes widen and my breath comes out in pants as he bends until his face is right in front of mine.

"Rocco—"

"Don't," he says. The velvet smooth tone is such a stark contrast to the anger marring his face. "Ever fucking apologize for looking at me like that."

"But I—"

He cups my face, bringing our faces so close his breath fans across my lips. "Do you know what it does to me when you look at me like that?"

I shake my head.

"It brings me to my fucking knees, Killer. It's humbling to have a woman like you look at me like I'm a treat you can't wait to fucking dig your teeth into."

Looking into his dark eyes, I relax. I can't explain what it is about Rocco, but he has the power to bring me to my knees as well. With him, I don't feel ruined, or like the monster I really am. He makes me feel treasured and wanted.

Rocco has shown me a side of life I never even knew existed, one I'm wanting more of. It's still unbelievable to me that I'm feeling like this, and I'm not sure I know what it means. But maybe I don't need to. Perhaps I just need to accept it, and ride the wave for as long as possible.

"You do that to me, too," I admit softly. "Thank you for being so patient with me."

To my surprise, Rocco lets out a booming laugh. "I'm not patient, Killer. I'm selfish."

"Selfish?" I ask, confused about his choice of words. "No. You're generous."

Rocco moves his hands to my pants, practically tearing them off me along with my thong. Both pool around my feet, and I step out of my stilettos so I can kick the clothes off.

I'm now standing just as naked as Rocco, and despite the blinds not being closed so anyone can look in, I don't feel ashamed. How can I, when my husband is looking at me with barely contained lust?

"Yes," Rocco says, his hand cupping my pussy. "I'm very selfish when it comes to you. But I don't think I care anymore."

I don't understand what he's trying to say, so I ask, "What do you mean?"

He slides a finger through my folds, and I'm surprised I'm already wet. "I want you, hermosa. And I'm not sure I could give you up even if you wanted me to."

"Why would I want you to?" I ask. "You're my husband."

Fuck, I can barely believe my words. How I feel about him now is such a stark contrast to the day I got released from prison.

"Yes I am," he rasps as he rubs the heel of his hand across my clit. "But do you want me to be? You don't even know me, or what I do."

I moan when he slowly pushes a finger inside me, and before I know it, my hips gyrate to get more of his addictive touch.

Reaching for his cock, I squeeze it just like he's shown me he likes. I stroke it from tip to base, fascinated by the wetness that glistens at the engorged head. Without thinking, I run my finger through it and bring it to my mouth.

"Fuck. Cara," Rocco growls as my tongue darts out and I lick my digit clean.

"What is that?" I ask as my eyes flutter closed and I savor the taste.

Rocco chuckles. "It's called pre-cum."

Right.

Now I feel stupid for not realizing that. This is the effect Rocco, and a fucked up upbringing, have on me. It reduces me to an unthinking, insecure mess.

I'm surprised that the flavor doesn't repulse me. My sister's told me horror stories of having to drink cum from a jar, so if this is that, it's not bad. A bit salty, but I don't mind it at all.

"You taste good," I purr. Then I let the tip of my tongue dance around my finger pad again, greedily licking it completely clean. "Really good."

"Cara."

I like the way he growls my name.

"Get your ass on the desk. Now."

Pouting, I let go of his cock. "You didn't say please," I remind him with a wink.

I yelp when he playfully slaps my ass with a growl. "And I'm not going to."

This is a completely different side of Rocco, one I haven't seen before. The other times we've had sex, he's made sure to ask if he could touch me. While I appreciated that, I think I like this side of him. The one that doesn't ask permission, but tells me what he wants.

As I climb onto the desk, I have a moment of hesitancy since I don't know how he wants me. I ignore the part of me that wants to ask him and instead do what I want, which is sit on the edge with my legs spread wide.

Remembering how he taught me to touch myself, I slowly circle my clit. Now that he's done it to me countless times, I have a better idea of what I like, which makes it easier. It's not the same as having him touch me, though.

"Are you just going to stand there and watch?" I sass.

"Tempting," he rasps, fisting his cock. "Your cunt is so fucking pretty. I don't think I'll ever get enough of looking at it."

I moan. "What if I want you to come over here and touch me instead?"

Rocco arches a brow. "Is that what you want?"

I don't answer him right away. The way he fucks his hand is mesmerizing, and I can't get enough of watching him as he unashamedly jerks off for my viewing pleasure. And what a pleasure it is.

"Yes," I whimper.

Rocco squeezes his eyes shut and clenches his free hand. "Tell me, Killer."

"I-I..." My eyes turn heavenward as I struggle to get the words out. "I want you to touch me. Please touch me, Rocco."

"Where?"

Gulping, I spread my legs wider. My finger is still on my clit, though I'm not moving it anymore. "Here."

Rocco chuckles and looks at me. Shit, the lust in his eyes is almost too much.

"Not good enough, Killer. I want to hear you say what you want. Or better yet, demand it."

I clear my throat and swallow thickly. "I want you to touch my p-pussy. Use your finger to rub my clit while you fuck me with your cock."

Fuck me, I didn't know if I'd be able to get the words out. But there they are, hanging between us. I said it, despite my voice wavering.

"Fuck!" Rocco growls. Then he closes the distance between us. "Do you still not care if people can see us?"

I bite down on my bottom lip and shake my head. "Not at all."

Until her marriage, my sister didn't have sex behind closed doors so it's never been an expectation for me. And that aside, I want the horny Diamonds—especially Mindy—to see me please Rocco. They need to know once and for all that he's taken.

"Are you wet enough for me?" Rocco asks as he steps between my spread legs, and I nod. "I'm trusting you, Killer. Remember, it'll hurt us both if you're not."

Yeah, I don't need a reminder.

"I'm wet for you," I whisper.

Rocco growls. "Good. I'm going to fuck you now." I pant as he lines the head of his cock against my entrance. "Hold on to my arms, Killer."

I place my hands on his arms at the same time as he moves his to my hips, and when he roughly thrusts into me, I dig my nails into his skin for better leverage.

"Rocco," I cry out as he pounds into me. "It feels so good."

My tits jiggle with the force from Rocco's fucking, and my pussy clenches around him as my orgasm builds.

"Cara," Rocco growls, and my name sounds absolutely sinful on his lips.

Rocco bends, fusing his lips to mine. My eyes flutter closed as his tongue slides into my mouth, and I can't help grazing the organ with my teeth, which elicits a rumble from him.

I break the kiss and look up into his eyes. "Touch my tits," I demand, feeling brazen.

He stills between my legs, and I'm just about to ask if what I did was wrong. But then he rasps, "Lean back on your arms."

Once again, I do as he says. Moving my arms behind me so I can rest on them as I lower myself. "Like this?" I question.

Rocco groans in approval. "Just like that, Killer."

As he thrusts into me again, he captures my nipple between his teeth while palming both my tits. I cry out, and I think I call his name as pleasure shoots through my veins.

"Don't stop," I moan.

My cunt squeezes his cock so tight I know I'm hovering on the precipice, ready to fall with the next few thrusts.

Rocco picks up his pace, slamming into me so hard the desk moves with each piston of his hips. I wrap my legs around him, and push my heels into his hard ass in an attempt to get him deeper inside me.

Just as my orgasm crests, I sense eyes on me, and I look toward the window. On the other side of the glass is Mindy, the home wrecking bitch who tried to tell me I wasn't enough for Rocco. If I wasn't in the middle of the ultimate pleasure, I'd flip her off. But instead, I shoot her a shit-eating grin.

Take that, bitch!

My nipple falls from Rocco's mouth with a pop. "Fuck. Killer. I'm going to... I—" Rocco's words turn into a guttural groan as he slams into me once more.

I feel him spilling his hot seed into my pussy, that's still holding him in a vise.

"That's it, mi rey," I moan.

Feeling too boneless to hold myself up any longer I move my hands to his broad shoulders as I lie all the way down on the desk. Slowly, I slide my hands around his neck and pull him toward me.

"What does mi rey mean?" he asks as soon as both our breathing has returned to normal.

I try to hide my laughter. "That's for me to know and you to dot dot dot," I say.

"One of these days," he says, but he doesn't complete the sentence.

Even though I want to ask, I don't. I already know he won't answer me until I tell him what I just called him. My king. That's what Rocco King is. *Mine.*

Rocco stands and pulls me up with him. He hands me my discarded clothes, and we get dressed together in silence. It's not awkward, it's actually nice that we can be together without feeling a need to talk non-stop.

When we're both dressed, Rocco hovers near the door, and I get the feeling he's struggling to say whatever's on his mind.

"What is it?" I ask, deciding to help him along.

"I need to ask you a favor."

Exhaling slowly, I say, "Okay."

"Me and Gunner have some shit to do today, but I don't want to take Gray with us. He's in a bad fucking mood and needs to get out of his own head."

"And he needs a fucking haircut," I mumble like that's important right now.

Rocco chuckles. "He does. But he doesn't have his parents, and he's... well—"

"Gray needs help," I finish for him. "Okay, I'll help him."

The gratitude I expect doesn't come. Instead, Rocco furrows his brows. "Yes, but I just need you to keep an eye on him. Make sure he doesn't start a fight or something."

"Sure," I agree.

I already know there's more to the story than what I've just been told. But I'm not going to ask Rocco to betray Gray's trust. Plus, I know a little about what it's like to be your own worst enemy. And if my hunch is right, that's exactly what the homeless looking boy is.

Cara

After Rocco and Gunner take off to do God only knows what, I walk back inside Dirty Diamonds to find Tex and Gray at each other's throats.

"It's just one fucking beer," Gray fumes, balling his hands into fists.

"And it was just one fucking no," Tex smirks. "You're not old enough to drink, boy. And I'm not fucking serving you."

Sasha and Alana are still hanging out at the bar, and judging by their cackles they've had quite a few drinks.

"Are you fucking kidding me?" Gray roars, taking a step closer to Tex.

The bartender shakes his head. "Don't even think about it, boy. It won't end well for you."

As I look at Gray, like really look at him, it hits me what he needs, and it's definitely not alcohol. He needs an outlet, a place where he can let out the angsty and toxic energy inside him. I should know. That's how I felt when I was locked up, and it's the reason I took up kickboxing.

Rounding the bar, I hip-bump Tex out of the way, and glare at Gray. "That's no way to speak to people," I dutifully say.

"What's it to you?" Gray spits, glaring back.

Rolling my eyes, I point at the door. "Let's go." When he just stands there, I add. "You can come with me willingly, or I'll drag your ass out of here. It's your choice, but believe me, you're no match for me."

Predictably, he laughs mockingly at me, which is what I was hoping for.

"I don't think so. I like Rocco, and he'd never forgive me if I hurt you," he smarts.

Tex looks at Gray and bursts into laughter. "Oh, that's right. You haven't seen her fight. Believe me, boy. You're no match for her."

Gray straightens and puffs out his chest. "Make me," he challenges.

I smile sweetly at him. "And here I thought you'd never ask." Before he can retort, I jump onto the bar. "Let's dance."

Angling my leg so the nose of my shoe connects, and not the point of the heel, I kick Gray in the arm. I don't use all my power since I'm not actually trying to hurt him, only provoke him into letting go.

"You fucking bitch!" he shouts as I leap off the bar and onto the floor next to him. Then he shakes his head. "I'm not going to fucking fight you."

"Why not?" I argue. "Scared to lose to a woman?"

I'm absentmindedly aware that Cain's joined us, and that he, Sasha, Alana, and Tex are all placing bets on who's going to win. I hope Gray hears it, just as I hope it's going to rile him up.

He lets out an angry growl, and raises his fist, sending it in my direction. I quickly lift my arm to block him, which I manage just in time. But fuck me, he has a mean right hook.

"Again," I encourage him. "Hit me like you really fucking mean it."

He does, and I block all but one punch. That one lands on my tit.

"That's dirty," Sasha calls out.

"Foul play," Alana agrees, laughter palpable in her voice. "No tit punching."

After kicking Gray back, I quickly look over at the women and grin at them. But since I can't afford to remain distracted, I turn back to Gray and discreetly force him toward the door as I keep moving closer to him.

It takes a few more kicks and punches, but we eventually reach the door that's being held open by the bouncer.

"I win," I declare as I force him to move one foot out the door. "So now you're coming with me."

Without waiting for his reply, I push him all the way out and slam the door behind us with the bouncer inside. We don't need prying eyes for what I have in mind.

"Got a smoke?" I ask, only a little surprised when he pulls a pack and a lighter from his jeans pocket. "Thanks."

I take it and light it, inhaling deeply as I watch him fumble to light one for himself. Damn, his hands are shaking badly, and I know it's anger that's at the forefront of his mind. He's probably angry with me, but more importantly, he seems angry at the world.

"So what's your damage?" I ask as I purse my lips and create a circle of the smoke I'm exhaling.

"My damage?" he barks, looking at me like I'm out of my mind.

I nod. "Why are you so angry? And honestly, why do you look homeless? Have they not given you a place to stay?"

Gray spits on the ground. "What's your fucking damage? And why do you walk around looking like a trashy whore?"

Though his words sting, I shrug. I had a dig at him first and fair is fair. "My damage is my family," I admit. "They raised me to be the perfect cum dumpster, and then they sold me to Rocco."

"W-what?" he stutters, his eyes wide like he either can't believe my words or that I'm telling him.

I don't know why, but I feel an odd kinship to Gray. I recognize his anger, and that damaging attitude. But I don't want him to end up doing something he can't take back, something he'll regret for the rest of his life.

"Why are you telling me that?"

Shrugging, I admit, "I asked you first, but that hardly seems fair if I don't want to answer myself."

He looks at me so long I'm close to giving up. Then he lights up another cigarette and leans back against the wall.

"I killed my dad," he admits.

"Me too," I offer. "But you don't sound like you enjoyed it as much as I did."

He lets out a humorless laugh. "It was an accident, and I guess I didn't really kill him. I just... it was my actions that got him killed."

"Was he a good man?" I ask.

Gray nods. "I think so. I mean," he gestures to the building we're leaning against. "No one here is a good person. And my dad was mixed up with Dante. But they don't kill innocent people."

"Only buy them and marry them," I spit before I can stop myself.

Shit! I didn't mean for that to come out.

Hmm, so maybe Gray isn't the only one in desperate need of a heart-to-heart. As much as I'm warming up to Rocco, that's still a sore spot. I'm not trying to rewrite the past, what's done is done, and a part of me likes that he's my husband. But I've yet to understand it, and maybe that's something I really need.

"How much do you know about what's going on here?" Gray asks.

While he throws the butt of his cigarette on the ground and uses his shoe to stub it out, I consider his question. Fact is that I barely know anything, and that's partly my fault. I haven't asked any questions.

"That's a topic for another day," I say, wanting us to stay on track. "Where's your mom?"

He barks out another laugh. "Busy turning tricks, spreading her legs for any man who'll pay her."

I recognize the bitterness in his tone, and it makes me even more adamant that I need to help him before it becomes a toxin running so deep it infiltrates his bloodstream.

"At least she's doing it herself and not selling you for her own selfish gain," I say flippantly. "But tell me something, Gray. Do you think the people here are... I don't know... good people?"

He rolls his eyes. "I already told you they're not good people," he snaps.

Okay, yes, he did say that. But that's not what I mean, and I explain that. "Are they good to you? Do they take care of you and keep you safe?"

"I'm sixteen, I don't need anyone to fucking take care of me."

I arch my brow. "Is that so? Then I ask you again, why do you look homeless instead of taking pride in your appearance?"

"What's it to you?" Gray sneers. "You're not my mom."

His words remind me of my mom's visit a few days ago. The side of my face throbs as I recall seeing Mateo earlier that evening as well.

Both of them threatened me, but it's my mom's threat that makes me shudder. I don't know how to describe the look in her eyes. It was evil, sure. But it was also so much more. Like she believed every word she spoke.

The woman that came to Rocco's house is so different from the sniveling, pathetic mess I spared on the church floor three years ago. I didn't pull the trigger back then, because she wasn't the bigger evil. And, if I'm honest, I wanted her to live with her mistakes. But that woman wasn't the same one who came to buy me back.

With a shake of my head, I will my mind to stay on track instead of thinking about my deceitful mom.

I repeat my question to Gray, not looking.

He kicks off the wall and turns toward me, stabbing a finger in my direction. "Because it doesn't fucking matter," he roars. "I failed my dad, and you don't know what that feels like. Rumor has it you willingly pulled the trigger, and someone did that to my dad because of me. Do you have any idea what that's like?"

"No," I say as I shake my head. "I don't. But I know what it's like to be so angry with the world you'd rather burn it down than be in it. And I know what it's like to make yourself a victim."

"I am a fucking victim," he shouts.

Snorting, I throw my hands out to the side. "We're all fucking victims," I bite. "We don't have to act like it. We can become stronger and get to a place where we're living instead of just surviving."

I don't need to know everyone's story to know my words are true. Whether it's big or small, we're all victims of one thing or another.

The door swings open, stopping Gray from saying whatever he was going to, and the bouncer comes back out.

"You two need to move it along," he says as he attaches the door to the wall so it's wide open. "I need to get back to my post."

I look up at the sky that's darkened with thunder clouds. None of them have broken yet, so I'll take that as a sign to stay outside for as long as it takes.

With a nod, I drag Gray around to the back entrance where we sit down on the pavement.

"You know," I say when it becomes clear he's not going to speak. "My mom once told me that my only option in life was to 'fake it until you make it'." I make air quotes around the six damning words. "And as much as I hate her, I think that's true."

To my surprise, Gray nods thoughtfully, like he's actually considering my words. "I don't know where to start," he admits. "I'm so fucking angry at her, at myself, and my dad. But mostly at myself."

"Do you ever start fights just to blow off steam?" I ask, and when he confirms my suspicion, I carry on. "I did that a lot my first six months in juvie. Everyone assumes I did it to be the top bitch, and sure, that was the result. But mostly I needed to hurt someone else so my own pain felt less."

He runs a hand through his messy waves and tilts his head back. "So how the fuck do I fake it?"

"That's easy!" I exclaim. "Get your fucking appearance under control. That's step one. Because if you look better, people will assume you feel better. It's basically step one in the fake-it-until-you-make-it program."

The sound of rumbling engines reaches us, and I turn to look as several bikes drive around the building, presumably to park near the entrance. None of the riders spare us any glances, they're all looking ahead.

"Know who they are?" I ask.

As Gray looks at the bikers, he tenses. "Trouble," he sneers. "They're nomads who have banded together and created their own club."

He barely manages to finish his sentence before his phone rings, and I watch as he answers.

"Rocco," he says as a way of greeting.

There's some chatter on the other end, but I can't hear it.

"Yeah, she's here with me. Why?"

Gray's dark eyes find mine, and he says, "Rocco wants me to get you out of here."

I scrunch my face in confusion, but before I can answer, there's a loud scream and I leap to my feet.

"Gotta go, man. Hurry up." With those words, Gray ends the call.

I'm not aware I'm throwing open the back door until Gray wraps his arm around me and pulls me back.

"Sorry, can't let you in there. Rocco wants you far away."

Stomping on his foot, I spin around and bare my teeth. "Don't fucking touch me," I hiss. "And I'm not leaving."

"Cara!"

I know from the urgency in his voice that he's trying to do the right thing, and I appreciate that. Not that it'll change my mind.

"We'll tell Rocco you tried," I say. "But I'm not leaving when someone needs help."

I've never been a do-gooder, so I don't know why it's so important for me to stay. Maybe it's because a small part of me likes it here. With no time to stand around and self reflect, I continue down the dark passage.

As we reach the end of the dark hallway, we're greeted by bottles being thrown, and I narrowly miss one being thrown in our direction.

"Fuck!" Gray hisses.

We both duck in time, but one of the Diamonds isn't as lucky and a bottle hits her right in the face.

I watch from the shadows as Sasha storms to her defense, helping her up from the floor and over toward the door leading into the shower and changing rooms.

"Hey!" one of the nomads calls out. "Where the fuck's the rest of your pussy? We didn't come here for bitches who whine about being touched."

His fingers dig into the round ass of one of the dancers, who winces like he's hurting her.

Motherfucker.

"Keep your hands to yourself!" Tex's voice rings out, and the rowdy laughter from the nomads isn't enough to drown out the sound of his shotgun being loaded. "Now!"

"Where's Cain?" I whisper to Gray.

I don't understand why the man in charge isn't out there trying to get rid of the scum.

"Dunno," Gray replied. "He could be digging his way to China, or getting ready to burn the building down with them inside."

Huh? Neither of those options ring true, but I get the point Gray's making. And the fact that Tex is alone with the Diamonds out there does make it seem like Cain's up to something.

"Well, what if we want a specific Diamond?" A mean-looking nomad asks. "Do you fuckers take requests?"

One of the Diamonds clears her throat. "Of course we do. What's your pleasure?"

"Not you," he sneers as he backhands her. "We want the one with a teardrop tattoo."

The room falls silent.

I look at Gray, who's looking at me, and I can see the cogs turning in his head. Right now he has to be thinking the same thing as me; why would they want me?

"Not happening," Tex snaps. "Get the fuck out of here. Now."

The nomads shake their heads, menacing grins splitting their faces.

"We like it here," a big, burly guy sneers.

As soon as the words are out of his mouth, the stage light changes to an eerie red, and smoke erupts from the stage. There's so much it only takes seconds until it's enveloping most of the room, making it impossible to see through it.

"Welcome to the party!" Cain's voice rings out from every corner of the room.

A gunshot sounds and a body falls to the ground.

"Get down," Gray hisses.

Even though he can't see me, I shake my head. Narrowing my eyes, I try to see through the smoke, and I'm pretty sure I see some of the women run scared.

Another gunshot, and this time it's followed by high-pitched screams.

"Cara!" My head jerks in the direction of the deep, booming voice. "We have a message for you from your mom."

"What is it?" I shout back, unable to help myself.

"For every day you refuse to return to her, someone from your new life will die."

I see red as a woman lets out a bloodcurdling scream. Before Gray can stop me, I run into the room, not stopping until I collide with a body. Up close it's easy to see it isn't someone I've seen before, meaning it must be one of the nomads.

"Estás muerto," I scream as I kick him in the gut.

"You can't kill me little girl," he wheezes, doubling over as I kick him a second time.

Someone tackles me to the ground, and I flail my arms and buck as his crushing weight descends on me. He tangles his fingers into my hair and slams my head against the floor. I cry out, but don't stop struggling despite my vision swimming.

More screaming, and at least one more body hits the ground. The smoke is still too thick to see properly, but I have a feeling the Diamonds aren't fairing well. Feeling an unfamiliar need to help, or maybe it's punishment I want to dole out, I continue to try to land punches, but none of them stop the guy on top of me.

Luckily, someone barges into him, and the second he's unfocused, I buck again, unseating him. Using all my strength and training, I roll to my side and wrap my legs around him. Reaching for my shoe, I slip it off and use it as a weapon.

The guy laughs, not even realizing his end is fucking near.

"I told you what would happen," I hiss at the same time as I ram the stiletto heel into his neck.

I try not to cringe at the sound, but really, it's disgusting. So is the way he gasps, unable to form words.

Not wasting time, I leap off the ground and make my way toward the area I think the women are hiding. On my way I come across Cain, who's laughing victoriously as he swings his bat into the head of one of the nomads.

"Fancy seeing you here," he says to me.

"Fucking loco," I mumble. But then I remember where I'm headed. "Are the Diamonds okay?"

Cain shrugs. "No idea. But I fucking hope so."

The murderous glint in his eyes is downright psychopathic when paired with the joker-like smile he's sporting.

Before I can move again, Cain holds his hand out to stop me. "Here," he hands me a knife. "Something tells me you're good with one of those. So give them hell and don't let them fucking capture you. I'd hate to kill you for doing something as stupid as getting yourself womannapped."

Taking the blade, I nod. "Later, loco," I say.

Leaving Cain, I continue my search for the Diamonds. By now, their screams are coming from all directions, and I'm unsure where to go.

More gunshots ring out, but this time no one falls to the floor.

I narrowly manage to escape a fist swinging in my direction, but I'm not quick enough to see the second hand coming out, wrapping around my throat.

"Gotcha!"

Rocco

The screech of my tires is loud as my truck slides sideways into the parking lot of Dirty Diamonds. Gunner holds on for dear life, but he should know better than to be scared of my fucking driving. I've become an expert over the years, and the pelting rain only adds to the maneuverability.

"Gun ready," I hiss, and I slam on the brakes, my eyes scanning the parking lot past the windshield wipers to make out the numerous figures running out from the club entrance.

"There!" Gunner yells, pointing out the windshield, but I don't need his direction. My eyes have already honed in on the fucker dragging my wife by her hair as she kicks out, trying to get away.

He's a fucking dead man walking!

Throwing my door open, I tug my automatic shotgun from under my seat and leap from my truck, aiming at a leather cut wearing motherfucker who aims his handgun at me, and I pull the trigger.

The boom is loud, and I ignore the vision of the gaping hole in his chest as he flies backward, thumping to the drenched asphalt, before I step over him.

I continue shooting as I go, hitting a few of the nomad gang before my aim is off, missing another fucker as he charges out of the club doors.

A loud crack pierces the air before the asshole's back arches and he's thrown forward right before Tex steps out of the club entrance with his shotgun.

Grinning at my friend, he gives me a nod before we both turn our sights on my cursing wife, her insults not for the fainthearted as the cunt-faced prick manages to drag her up to a bike.

A war cry sounds as Gray comes charging from the back of the building toward my woman, but a nomad steps in his path, stopping him, and they start swinging fists.

My target is clear as I elbow an asshole that comes at me from the side, and as he stumbles back, I aim and shoot.

I grin at his stunned expression as the bullet practically eviscerates his throat.

Cara's insults draw me back to her, and as I storm across the lot, I watch my warrior queen as she fights back as best she can, kicking her attacker in the shin before she slips on the wet ground, losing her momentum.

The motherfucker still has her by her long dark hair and it pisses me the fuck off.

That is my hair to fucking fist! Not his!

"Hey!" I boom, and his head jerks up in time to see the barrel of my gun, only three feet away. I pull the trigger.

Cara squeals in fright at the sound as blood and brain matter rain over her. Panicked, she shuffles back on her hands trying to get away from the carnage.

Standing over her, I look down and admire how much of a fucking warrior she is. Not just a warrior but a queen, with blood coating her face as the rain washes through it, running down her neck and down between her tits.

"Cara." She's trembling, her eyes locked on the fucker who was trying to take her, his body now a slumped heap on the asphalt, half his face blown off.

"Cara!" I demand, and she snaps out of it, her shocked steel gaze darting to mine. "Let's go." I reach out a hand, and her trembling one takes it, letting me pull her to her feet.

Engulfing her in my arms, I turn in time to see another nomad charging for me, and I get my shotgun raised just in time to blow his head clean off his shoulders.

Cara squeals again, and flinches into me, not used to the loud crack of guns, but it's a sound she needs to get used to. She's in my world now, and shit like this is inevitable.

Pulling my handgun from the back of my jeans, I nudge her back and offer it to her.

"Here. You know the drill, Killer. Point and shoot."

Even though she trembles, she takes the gun and nods, her gaze locking with mine.

"No one touches what's mine," I tell her and it's like my words are a blanket of courage for her as she stands taller and rolls her shoulders back, giving me a nod.

There she is.

"No one touches what's mine either." She rasps huskily, and pride fills my fucking chest.

Fuck, I want to kiss her, but not with that fucker's blood all over her face. That will have to wait.

Side by side, we turn and face the foray, stepping into it together as we help my crew put an end to this.

By the time we are done, everyone is dead except for the one asshole Grayson is pummeling over and over, and Gunner has to wrestle Gray off the guy so we can get some answers.

"Start talking asshole," I snap just as Cain appears wearing a grin.

Jesus, he loves this stuff way too much.

"They were here for the Diamond with a teardrop tattoo." He tells me and I see fucking red.

My fucking wife.

What the actual fuck.

The nomad on the ground peers up through his swelling eyelids, blinking against the rain with a groan.

"What club are you from?"

Since they are on motorcycles, and wearing cuts, although no logo is displayed, they are clearly from an MC.

"Fuck you," he hisses, and Gray leans down, bitch slapping him before pulling back his cut and tugging down the torn neck of his shirt.

"I saw that he had ink," Gray mutters as he shows us the tattoo.

It's a skull, with the name, Cali Reapers, above it.

Fuck. I've heard about them. Causing havoc all up the coast.

"Why are you in Santa Cruz?" I hiss and the fucker chuckles and then coughs.

"Haven't you heard?" he wheezes. "We are bidding for this territory."

Frowning, my eyes meet Cain's who shrugs.

"What do you mean?" I ask the Reaper. "This territory is already claimed."

Slowly, the Reaper laughs like he's about to tell a fucking joke. But nothing about this is a joke.

"The territory is getting divided up, and Santa Cruz is up for grabs." He sneers before jabbing a finger toward me. "And when it becomes *ours*, you fuckers are through."

"Here's what we think of that." Aiming my shotgun at his knee, I blow it to shreds.

The Reaper briefly screams before passing the fuck out.

"Make sure he doesn't bleed out and make sure he gets back to his leader." I point down at him directing the order to Gunner and Grayson. "I want to make sure this message is loud and fucking clear. They come for my wife, or fuck with our people, then they fucking die."

Gray and Gunner get to work on stopping the bleeding and I turn to Cain.

"What do you need me to do?"

He waves me off. "Get your wife home and cleaned up. We got this."

Nodding, I step in closer, speaking quietly. "Cara's mom has obviously outsourced to try to steal her daughter back. Can you let Dante know?"

Cain nods, and we clap each other's shoulders before I turn to Cara and sweep her up in my arms.

The drive home is quick, since I only live down the road from the club, and I hurry since all I can hear is Cara shivering and her teeth chattering.

Skidding to a stop in my driveway, I leap from my truck, rounding it to open her door and sweep her into my arms again.

Like me, she is absolutely saturated, both with water and blood.

"I need to shower you." I rush out as I swing the door open, stepping inside the house. "I need to get you cleaned and warmed up."

Still trembling in my arms, mainly from the cold rain, she stiffens and starts to struggle in my hold when she realizes that I'm carrying her toward my bathroom.

"N-no." She chatters and I growl.

"Cara, there's no debate about this. The outside shower is freezing. You need to warm up in a hot shower."

"No," she says with demand laced in her tone, but I ignore it, shoving the bathroom door open, but I don't go in.

No. I need to wait for her to agree. I won't force this on her.

"Yes, Cara. Come on now." I insist. "Trust me, please. Just close your eyes if you must and trust that I will keep you safe in there."

"But."

"No buts. You know I need to get you into a hot shower. Please don't fight me on this."

She's quiet for a long beat, shivering in my arms as we both drip pink stained rain onto the floor in the hallway.

"I can shut my eyes?" she asks and I nod.

"Yes. Shut them and let me tend to you."

Slowly she nods.

Fuck. I know it must have taken a lot for her to agree with this. To trust me.

Waiting until she squeezes her eyes shut, I step inside my bathroom to my tub, and awkwardly lean over to turn on the shower stream, trying not to drop her.

"I need you to put your feet down." I start guiding her feet down, but she recoils, holding her feet up, her hands gripping my shoulders.

"Not on the tiles." She whimpers, and I frown. Maybe she doesn't want to feel the cold from the tiles?

"Okay, Killer. Not on the tiles. On the bathmat." I scoot the bathmat in place with the toe of my boot and ease her feet down to rest on the fluffy mat, happy that she lets me do that.

Keeping an arm around her and her trembling body pressed to my chest, I lean in and test the water, making sure it's not too hot, before I start peeling her clothes off, and then work on mine.

"Okay. I'm going to lift you over the edge of the tub." I explain, and she nods into my chest, her eyes still shut tight as I lift her in and follow behind her.

Slowly, I guide her under the spray, and watch as she keeps her lids shut, completely trusting me to make sure she's safe.

Fuck, that does something to me.

Inside my chest, the cold organ that beats starts to warm. It's like her trust is thawing it, and for the first time, I feel the impact of its beat.

This is what she does to me. Cara King. My wife.

Feeling unusually emotional, I'm glad she can't see me right now, and I turn my focus to her as I start my task at washing the blood from her skin.

The convulsing trembles from the cold slowly ease as my hands glide over her warming skin, and I will my dick not to get hard, because now isn't the time. Now it's the time for me to show her that I am trustworthy. That she can rely on me to take care of her. Of us.

After my hands run gently over her skin to make sure it's completely clean, I shampoo her hair, and then wash down her body with soap.

I've never done this to another person before, so I'm a bit fumbly, but she looks at ease as I wash her hair, her head tilting into the touch of my fingers like she enjoys my touch.

"You like that?" I ask quietly, and she nods against my fingers, grazing against her scalp.

"So much."

Jesus. Her voice has that husk to it again. It's a fucking turn on, and my dick stirs a little.

Down, boy.

"Let's rinse it out." I suggest, turning her a little as I take the handheld showerhead off and start rinsing the suds from her long hair.

Fuck, the way the water and suds stream down over her nipples is a temptation of its own, and I force my gaze away and focus on her hair only until it's completely rinsed and then I rehang the showerhead.

Chicks use conditioner, something I've never had to worry about, so not only have I never conditioned someone's hair before, but I've never used the product before.

Trying to avoid looking like a dumb prick, I quickly read the fine print instructions on the back of the bottle, glad I stocked up with different brands before she came to live with me, not knowing which one she would prefer, so not only is my shower stocked, but so is the outside shower.

"Sorry, I'm new to this part." I admit as I squirt some into my palm, and a small smile spreads across her face.

"Just concentrate most of the conditioner to the mid-lengths and ends and comb it through with your fingers."

"Okay," I rasp quietly near her ear, and I love the way it makes a shiver run down her spine.

Doing as she instructed, I lather the ends of her hair, working the slimy product up higher before using my fingers as a comb. I do this for a minute or so before rinsing it out and quickly washing myself while she stands waiting with her eyes closed.

Once I'm done, I pull her to my chest, looking down at her as she angles her head up but keeps her eyes closed.

"Can you tell me why bathrooms are such an issue for you?" I ask, and she frowns, her lids still sealed.

"I..." she shakes her head. "I'm not ready."

"Okay. How about my truth for yours?" I ask, and the moment I do, anxiety twists my gut. Maybe I'm not ready either.

Slowly, Cara cracks one lid slightly to look up at me.

"Will you tell me why you got so pissy about me asking why you didn't learn Spanish in school?"

I nod. "I will if you tell me your issue with bathrooms right after."

Grinning, she nods, and closes her eyes tight again. "Deal."

Shit. Where do I start?

"Uh..." I say feeling clueless on how to explain myself. I'm not used to talking about my feelings like this, but I want her to trust me, so I need to level the playing field. "I guess your question made me feel dumb, because I... uhhh..."

She cracks her lid open again. "You can tell me. I promise I'll never use it against you or think any less of you."

I'm meant to be this big bad tough guy, yet all I am is a street thug pretending to be more. She says she won't think less of me, but it's inevitable. The truth will show her exactly who I am.

The question is, does it matter? Do I think she'll look at me differently?

Even as I think it, I don't believe it. Cara is not a trivial person. She doesn't care for social standards or norms. The only thing she was raised to do is support her husband, so let's hope she still has that part inside her.

Shit. I need to tell her. It's the only way to move things forward.

"Can you look at me while I tell you?" I ask as she peers up through the minuscule crack of her lid. "With both eyes."

Slowly she nods. "I'll look at you and nothing else." She breathes and I feel pride bloom inside me.

She's so strong.

Prying both lids open wider, she looks up at me as droplets of the shower spray around us.

"I... uh... never learned any languages because I didn't go to school much after my tenth birthday."

Her brows shoot up. "Homeschool?" she asks and I shake my head.

"No, I... lived on the streets."

Her eyes round with pity, but she doesn't insult me by telling me how sorry she is or saying you poor thing. No. She keeps asking questions.

"So you were homeless?" When I nod, she asks. "Were you alone on the streets or with a parent?"

"It was just me. I don't have parents." I sigh, feeling a little more at ease with telling her this now that I'm finally doing it. "I'm an orphan."

She nods. "Foster carers?"

"Only abusive ones." I admit, and her brows hitch high. "I managed to get away eventually, and I never went back. For most of those years after, the other street kids knew me only as Rocco. No one knew my full name, and it wasn't until I was fourteen that I came across Dante, Luke, and Baz. At the time they were living it up as surfers, and they made sure I never went hungry. When Dante was twenty-one Luke got killed, and he transformed into a vigilante who stuck up for those who couldn't stick up for themselves. That's when he formed the Diamond Crew, and I never looked back."

She nods, her steel gaze roaming my face like she's making sure every inch is locked in her memory.

"What sort of abuse did you suffer?"

I tense at her words. I never expected her to ask that. I'm not sure why. She is a curious woman. Probably because she has so much to learn since her background was a lie.

Cara has been through some horrific abuses of her own. Her scars tell that story. But I've never spoken the words of my abuse out loud to anyone.

I can never...

I shake my head, flashes of a time I want to forget bombarding my brain.

"I can't," I whisper and her eyes turn glassy.

"Were you... Did they..." She struggles to finish, but that doesn't matter because I know what she's trying to ask.

"Please don't ask me to say the words out loud, hermosa." I plead, because if I do, I think I will break. And if I break, I don't think I'll ever be able to be put back together.

The burning at the back of my eyes is an unfamiliar sensation. I've not felt it since the day I ran, and never looked back.

Cara's gentle hand comes up to cup my cheek, "Rocco. I won't ask you to say it, but it will help me if I can confirm it."

I gulp, the lump in my throat the size of a melon, as I struggle to stay put and not pull away.

"I think I understand. They took something from you. Something they had no right to take. They raped you, didn't they?"

My breathing is rapid and my skin prickles with humiliation at admitting this, for the first time, and then, I slowly move my head in a nod.

"Shit." She cringes, shaking her head like she is disgusted, but not at me. At herself.

"What is it?" I ask as she squeezes her lids shut again.

"I... feel worse now about what I did to you. Forcing myself on you without your consent."

"No, Killer." I cup her face right back. "Look at me." When her gray eyes lock with mine again, I continue. "That's different. Please don't compare what we have with the monsters from my past."

A fat tear tumbles from one of her eyes as she stares up at me. "Are they still alive? The people who abused you."

I shake my head. "No. Dante and I made sure they were dead years later. He never knew exactly what happened, but he understood enough to know they were scum abusing children."

"Damn. I wanted to kill them for you," she says, her tone laced with disappointment. "Their entrails would make for a beautiful trophy."

I smile at that.

"I have no doubt they would have suffered immensely by your hand."

She nods in my hands. "Too fucking right."

I chuckle.

"Your turn, Killer." I urge, hoping she will open up to me. "Please tell me why you can't bear to enter a bathroom?"

Her smile drops, and her gray stare falls to my chest.

"Blood," she whispers, and I release her face and run my hands through the spray of water, down her back.

"Blood?"

She nods. "There was so much."

"Whose blood?"

"J-Julietta's."

My brows shoot up. "Your sister's blood?"

She nods. "Sometimes, I can still smell it. Feel it as my feet slipped in its thickness on the..."

"On the what, Cara?" I ask, pressing my fingers under her chin to tilt her head up to me.

"On the tiled floor," she whispers, before squeezing her eyes tight.

Frowning, I run her words through my head before my eyes dart to the tiled floor of my bathroom, and then my mind wanders to the shower room at Dirty Diamonds. Shit. The floor was tiled there, too.

"Do you see it? The blood, every time you look at the tiles on a bathroom floor?"

She nods frantically before burying her head into my bare chest.

Damn. It all makes sense now.

"I don't want to be like this. But I can't stop the images flashing before my eyes." She admits, and I nod as I press my lips to her wet hair, knowing exactly what she means.

An idea comes to my mind as I remember how she didn't want to put her feet on the tiled floor before. She doesn't have a problem in my shower, most likely because it's a smooth bathtub, so I ease her back and notice her eyes are squeezed tight again.

"Cara, I need you to stay right here for a minute or two so I can do something. Okay?"

Slowly she nods, reaching her hand out blindly to find the metal shelf that holds the soap, shampoo and conditioner.

Once I know she's steady, I climb out of the tub and dart from the room, dripping water onto the carpet of the hall as I rummage through the linen closet. I get every towel I can, and hurry back into the bathroom before laying out the towels on the floor, making sure there is no sign of the tiles underneath.

Once done, I step back into the tub, reaching out to my wife.

"I'm back."

"Where did you go?" she asks, still with closed eyes.

"Open your eyes again for me," I ask, and she reaches out, running her hands over my pecks until she's pressed to my front, and only then does she crack her lids.

"I need you to trust me, Cara. Trust that I have your back. That I will keep you safe. That I am here to care for and protect you." I give her a little squeeze. "I need you to look at the bathroom floor."

Immediately, she shakes her head and squeezes her eyes tight.

"Cara please. I promise it's okay. Just take a look for me, please."

Honestly, I have no idea if this will work, but I need to at least try.

If it works, then great. I know what I have to do to make her feel comfortable in my home. Our home. And if it doesn't work, then I will think of a new solution. I'll think of a thousand until one sticks.

"I'm not sure if I can," she whispers, and I give her a reassuring squeeze.

"You can. You're the bravest person I know. You can do it."

Slowly, she nods and cracks her lids again to look at me. "Good girl."

Her eyes widen before a repulsed expression crosses her face. "Seriously? Good girl? Say that again and I'll cut you."

A laugh bubbles up my throat, and I throw my head back as I let it take over, welcoming its lightness.

"I have no fucking doubt you'll cut me. And noted." I grin, trying to compose myself.

It makes sense that she's not into praise kink. Not that she necessarily knows what that is. She's finally free of the rules her family tried to brainwash her with, and given she was forced into submission, I can see that Cara will probably never be a submissive woman. Sure, she's submitted to me a few times, giving me the control, but that was her trusting me to teach her how sex should be. I don't doubt that in the future we are going to butt heads in the bedroom. I can already see her dominant nature coming through.

"Good. Don't forget." She snaps sternly and I chuckle even as I draw a promise cross over my heart.

"Now, Killer. Stop stalling and take a look at the floor."

She blinks a few times, and I can see she's fighting against her instincts, but then slowly, she turns her head and eyes the floor.

Even though she's stiff in my arms and her breathing quickens, she keeps her eyes trained on the toweled floor.

"Talk to me. Is it better? Worse?"

"Better," she whispers before turning back to me. "Thank you."

My smile is small as I take her in, brushing my thumb over the teardrop tattoo just under her eye.

"When your twelve-month parole period is up, and you have the right to decide how your future looks, I really hope you'll consider staying here with me. As my wife."

For a moment I'm looking back into the eyes of the six-teen-year-old girl that was given no choice. She was just as scared as the woman is in front of me now, but both versions never let anyone see. But I do. I feel like I can see into her soul.

"I'll consider it," she whispers, and fuck. That's all I can ask for at this point.

I want her to stay, but I won't force her. I won't take her decisions away from her.

"That's all I ask."

Cara

Like most nights, I'm back in the prison, my sister lying on the floor with her head in my lap.

"It's okay, Cara," she whispers, with a smile on her lips. "I'll be free soon."

"No," I cry. "Don't leave me. Quédate por favor."

Even though I know she can't, I beg for her to stay with me.

"No one can keep someone like you down, Cara. Give them hell and then get the fuck out of there. Promise me you'll find a way to be happy."

The shiv in my hand clanks as it falls onto the floor. It's covered in Julietta's blood, and her body is covered in stab wounds.

Her beautiful eyes are bloodshot, and her breathing is garbled wheezing.

"Forgive me," I beg. "Please say you forgive me."

She takes a shuddering breath. "T-there's nothing to f-forgive."

Fat tears roll down my cheeks, but I swallow down the sob lodged in my throat. I need to be strong for Julietta.

Using her last strength, Julietta places her hand on top of mine. "I-I f-forgive Mateo, t-too," she stutters as tremors tear through her. "W-we'll all m-meet again."

Her hands fall limp, and despite knowing she's dead, I shake her and cry out her name. "Julietta!"

I'm ripped from the nightmare so suddenly I feel my head spin.

"Shh," Rocco coos. "You're safe, hermosa. Please wake up."

I blink, and it takes me a moment to realize I'm safely in Rocco's bed, and not sitting on the dirty, tiled floor from my nightmare. As my eyes get used to the darkness in the bedroom, his concerned face comes into view.

"Rocco?" I gasp his name, not quite able to believe he's here. "You're here..."

As he shifts, I realize he's learned his lesson about waking me up from a nightmare. He isn't anywhere near my legs. Instead of being behind me like he was when we fell asleep, he's crouching on the floor, next to my side of the bed.

Can't say I blame him. I've kicked him at least four times, and he's still carrying the marks to prove it.

"Of course I'm here," he rasps. "I'll always be here."

His words cause sobs to tear through me, and I'm unable to stop them. I drag my knees up, curling in on myself as I cry into the pillow.

It's been almost a week since he told me what he suffered when he lived on the street, and the condemning words broke something inside me. Opened the floodgates, and I don't know how to stop them. Every night it's the same nightmare, and every night he wakes me. Then comes the uncontrollable sobbing.

"Fuck. Tell me how I can help you," Rocco pleads.

It cuts me to hear him sounding so helpless, but I don't think there's anything he can do. My tears aren't just for me and Julietta, they're for him as well. For what he went through, and the shame I saw in his eyes when he told me his secret.

And... and if I'm being completely honest, they're also for Mateo. Once upon a time, my twin was my best friend. We shared a womb together, entered this world together, and learned to walk together. When one of us fell down, the other was always there to help. Just because life later dealt us completely opposite hands doesn't mean he isn't hurting, too.

In fact, I know he is. The look in his eyes when he pressed all those cigarettes to my skin was half the reason I stopped fighting and screaming. It broke something in him, and I felt the snap reverberating in my soul.

"Say something," Rocco urges, gently moving strands of hair from my face. "Anything. Scream at me. Or better yet, take your pain out on me. I can take it, Cara. But I can't stand seeing you like this." His voice takes on a gravelly quality, and I know he's feeling my hurt like it's his own.

"I-I don't know how to s-stop," I hiccup.

The mattress dips as he climbs in behind me, spooning me until I'm no longer shaking with pent-up emotions. He continues to hold me, pressing his lips to my shoulder until I'm able to breathe normally again.

"You were dreaming about your sister again," he says. It's not a question which means I must have called out her name.

"Not a dream," I mutter. "Always a nightmare."

Rocco remains silent, and I know why. He wants to know what it was about, but he doesn't want to ask me. Just like I didn't want to ask him what happened before he lived on the street. I did it anyway, though. Pushed for answers I had no right to.

"You said she was killed in jail by a monster. Was it an inmate?"

I nod.

"Someone she had issues with?"

This time I shake my head. While I was feared and maybe begrudgingly respected, Julietta was actually liked. Despite the different cliques, people showed her kindness and never bothered her. That's the kind of person she was. Somehow, she always brought the best out in the people around her.

"No," I croak. "In fact, she loved her killer very much."

I feel the exact moment Rocco figures the truth out for himself. His hold on me tightens as he rasps, "Fucking hell. No wonder you're trapped in that nightmare. Why did you do it?"

Fighting more tears I squeeze my eyes shut. "It was my gift to her. Julietta's spirit was slowly dying. She'd been through so much... and... and..." I swallow down the lump in my throat. "The fucker she was married to broke her, and she wanted to die. But she asked me to do it."

Rocco exhales audibly, but remains quiet.

"At first I said no, but then I realized that was selfish of me. She wasn't happy, and I don't think she could ever find happiness again."

"Why didn't she do it herself?" As soon as he's asked the question, Rocco curses. "Fuck, I shouldn't have asked that."

I place my hand on top of his to let him know I understand. "Even though I already knew the answer, I asked her the same thing. Julietta was religious and believed that she couldn't get into heaven if she committed suicide."

My hand closes around the cross dangling from my necklace. It makes me feel closer to her when I touch it, like I can almost imagine hearing her voice.

"One of the women agreed to help me, and she fashioned a shiv. Two stood guard as Julietta and I went into the... the..."

"You don't have to say it."

Ignoring Rocco, I finish. "Shower."

"Fuck," he hisses. "And I locked you in the bathroom. I literally fucking locked you in your worst nightmare."

The irony that we've both made the other suffer their personal nightmare isn't lost on me. Yeah, Rocco locked me in the bathroom, but I also took his choice from him and lost my virginity on his cock without his input.

Yet, we're still here. Still together, and I like the change he's brought out in me. Through his actions, he's showing me a life I never even dared to dream of—one where I matter and have a voice.

"And I took something from you," I remind him as shame burns through me.

Fuck. I still can't believe I did that.

Okay, the thing I'm having the hardest time coming to terms with is that I don't fully regret it. Because that was the moment things changed between us, which has brought us here. To the moment where I realize I need Rocco's help.

"Rocco," I say, turning in his hold so we're face-to-face. "Will you help with something?" Nerves make my voice sound formal like I'm about to pitch a business proposal rather than ask him to try something with me.

"Of course, Killer," he replies immediately. "Name it."

The eagerness in his tone makes my heart skip a beat and my breath hitches. "Rocco."

Unable to express the way he makes me feel, I slant my lips to his. His surprised intake of air spurs me on, and I deepen the kiss as I hoist my leg around his hip and move us so he's on his back and I straddle him.

Rocco's hands immediately seek out my ass, and he isn't gentle in the way he squeezes the globes. "Fuck. Cara," he rasps into my mouth.

As I feel him harden between us, I rock my hips, seeking friction on my clit. My thong and his boxers do nothing to diminish the feel of his cock rubbing against my bundle of nerves.

"Is this what you need help with?" he chuckles when we come up for air.

The words I want to speak stay lodged in my throat, so I whimper and reclaim his lips. Our tongues battle, teeth clashing, and I fucking love every second of it.

Rocco wraps my long hair around his fist and eases my head back. I growl, annoyed he's putting a stop to our kissing.

"Answer me," he demands in a harsh tone.

Shaking my head, I say, "No." Then I lick my lips and take a shuddering breath. "There's something I want to try. But I... I can't do it alone."

His gaze softens. "Anything."

As I look into his dark eyes, I find that I don't just believe him. In my heart I know he's the only one who can help me—the only one I trust and want to help me.

"I want to have another bath," I admit. A shudder runs through me at the mere thought of going back into the tiled bathroom, but I have to try. "Will you come with me?"

To his credit, Rocco doesn't ask any questions. He simply rolls out of bed and goes to fill the bathtub.

My legs feel like lead as I slowly place one foot in front of the other. The small walk to the bathroom feels like miles rather than feet, and when I reach the door, my legs are shaking so badly I can barely stand up.

Leaning against the door frame, I force one foot onto the tiled floor. The towels are still there, but I swear I can feel the tiles beneath them. Rocco looks at me over his shoulder. His brows are furrowed and his lips pressed into a thin line, but he doesn't try to stop me.

Okay, I can do this.

That's what I'm telling myself as I tentatively move my foot further into the dreaded room. The other is still on the threshold and for some reason it makes me feel better to know I literally have a foot in each room.

"You can do it, hermosa," Rocco rasps.

I'm not sure I can.

Yes, I must.

No, I can't.

"I-I..." I bite down on my bottom lip as I trail off.

Tilting my head to the side I try to guestimate the distance between us. It's not as much as my mind keeps telling me, that much I know. Two or three strides, that's it. I can do it.

With a yelp, I kick off the floor and very awkwardly spread my legs as much as possible to make my steps as big as possible.

"One more, Killer," Rocco encourages me.

I look into his dark eyes, and the moment our gazes lock, I no longer feel the tiles under my feet. Instead, I feel the fire in his orbs lick across my skin, making it feel like my body is aflame.

"Rocco," I half-sob as I close the distance between us and jump into his arms.

Not fully ready for me, he stumbles back, and before I know it, we fall into the tub, sloshing the warm water everywhere.

"Oh my God." My voice is caught somewhere between a cry and laughter.

"A little warning next time," Rocco laughs.

Rather than making empty promises, I press my lips to his. It starts out as a slow, close-mouthed kiss, much like the one we shared on our wedding day. Though, this time I welcome it, and I'm intimately familiar with the feeling he stirs in my chest.

"Why aren't I naked yet?" I huff as I pull back.

Rocco quickly rips the shirt from my body. His movements make the fabric tear, and I fucking love that he's as eager for me as I am for him.

Impatiently, I snake my hand into the slit in his boxers, and fist his length. His breath hitches as I apply more pressure than usual, but from the way his eyes roll back in his head I'm not worried.

"Fucking hell, Killer," he growls, the sound tinted with lust.

"I'm still not naked," I gripe.

He nips my bottom lip, continuing to kiss across my cheek to my neck, licking and nipping the skin all the way down to my shoulder. His hands find my heavy tits, squeezing them to the point it hurts. But fuck, it hurts so good.

"Rocco," I moan.

"Patience," he rasps.

I shake my head. "No. Make me feel good. I... oh!" Throwing my head back, I moan as he pinches and rolls my nipples between his thumb and index finger.

Rocco moves his hand between my legs and cups my pussy. "Stand up," he rasps.

Untangling myself from him proves harder than I first thought. We landed sideways in the tub, so we're neither sitting nor standing, but caught somewhere in between.

While giggling in an almost crazed way, I shakily stand up. Rocco is quick to slide my thong down my legs, kissing my thighs as he goes. Once I've stepped out of my underwear and he's flung them to the side, he gets up as well.

Though the tub isn't small, it feels it as we're both standing here.

I frown when Rocco slides his hands under the waistband of his boxers. "I want to do it," I say resolutely, slapping his hands away.

"Have at it," he says, unleashing a devilish smirk.

After lowering myself to my knees, I tug at his black boxers. I moan with anticipation and lick my lips as his cock springs free, almost slapping me on the cheek.

Can a cock be beautiful? If so, Rocco's should win best in show. It's long, thick, and the red head glistens in the light. Probably a mix of the bathwater and pre-cum.

"See something you like?" Rocco rasps.

I nod. "Yes," I say, wrapping my hand around the base. "Can I kiss it?"

The primal growl coming from deep in his throat is all the answer I need. I press my lips to the smooth head. Unsure exactly what to do, I move my hand up and down his length a few times. Then I lick the head, spearing the tip of my tongue into the slit.

"Fuck, Killer," he groans. "Just like that."

Since Rocco's the only guy I've ever been with, I've never done this before. Courtesy of my mom, I technically know what to do. Hers isn't the voice I want in my head though, so I peer up at Rocco through my lashes.

"Tell me what to do," I implore.

Rocco swallows thickly, and I stare transfixed at his Adam's apple as it bobs in his throat. "Wrap your lips around the head," he says, his tone gravelly with lust. "Move your hand up and down and suck."

Doing as he says, I hollow my cheeks, creating suction while I move my hand up and down the shaft. Rocco's raw sounds spur me on, and I let them guide me into finding a rhythm he likes.

Feeling bolder, I move my hands to his ass. I dig my nails in as I take him deeper into my mouth. He stiffens for a moment, and his breathing turns shallow as I part his cheeks.

"Cara," he groans, and it almost sounds like he's in pain.

Shit, I didn't mean to do that. It just... happened.

I let go and pull back, scared I've crossed a line. "I'm sorry," I rush out. "I didn't mean to, and... I'm so sorry."

Leaning down, he cups my jaw, shaking his head. "Do it again," he demands.

I take him back into my mouth and move my hands to his ass again.

"Just like before," he rasps, and I part his cheeks again as I slowly work him further into my mouth.

Rocco's length is no joke, and I can safely say I now know why it's called a blowjob—emphasis on the job.

I look up at him, and I hate the anguish on his face. His eyes are squeezed shut. Wanting to make him feel better, I take him all the way to the back of my throat. I don't pull back until my eyes water and I gag around his dick.

A tremor runs through him, but he still doesn't ask me to remove my hands. Though he hasn't specifically said it, I feel like I know what he wants—maybe even needs. With him, I've faced my fears, and I think that's what he needs right now.

As I gag around him again, I slide my hand into the crevice of his ass, making sure the tips of my fingers graze his opening.

"Cara," he hisses through clenched teeth.

I pause, waiting to see if he's going to tell me to stop. But he doesn't. He gives me a barely perceptible nod, and I take that as permission to do what I think he needs.

My eyes won't leave his face. I'm desperate to capture the look of pain and pleasure flickering across his features as I press a wet finger against his opening. He shudders, but instead of pulling away, he pushes back against me.

Seeing him like this, so tense, and clearly caught in a dark place in his mind is damn near breaking my heart. I don't know if I should stop or continue, only that I can't stand the look on his face.

I pull back until his cock falls from my mouth. "Rocco," I sob, and he finally opens his eyes. "Tell me what you want me to do."

His breath saws out of him, and the look he gives me can only be described as lost. "I don't know," he admits.

I know it's taking a lot for him to be this vulnerable, just like it does for me. But when I've been in his position, he's been the strong one. Guiding me through it until I got to a place where I felt better. I decide that's exactly what I'm going to do for him.

Needing him to relax, I fist his cock, slowly moving my hand up and down as I cup his balls and gently massage them. When I don't go anywhere near his ass, he finally relaxes. Even moans as I stroke his length.

I take him back inside my mouth. With a better idea of what he likes, I swirl my tongue around the head and use my thumb to add pressure to the angry vein on the side of his shaft.

"Fuck. Killer. Fuck." His groans are like music to my ears, and I eagerly keep up the momentum.

I slowly move my hands up his thighs, grazing his skin with my nails. I move all the way up to his toned stomach, where I dig my nails into his skin for good measure.

"Cara," he warns, but it's a warning I don't want to heed.

I want Rocco to lose control instead of being this closed off.

"Give it to me," I moan around his cock.

"What?" he rasps.

I wrap one hand around the base, moving it up and down as fast as I can. "Let go," I murmur. "Let it all fucking go and give it to me."

With a sharp nod, he groans, which I know is his way of answering. He's going to do it, or at the very least, try. That's more than I expected, and it makes me feel special.

"Do you want me to try?" I ask, needing his confirmation.

He nods again.

"Okay," I murmur.

I want to do this. Not just for Rocco, but also for me. I don't like that there's a side of him that isn't mine. I know it makes no sense, and that's okay. It doesn't need to be understood for me to act on it.

Rocco's gaze is burning against my skin, and his shallow breathing is almost like music. But his cock is still hard, telling me he wants this.

I lick my lips and look up at him. "Okay," I repeat, my voice more steadfast this time. "I promise to make it feel good for you."

His gaze softens a little. "I know you will," he rasps. "I trust you."

Rocco wordlessly hands me a bottle of body oil that he grabs from the shelf next to the bath. Done with taking it slow, I squirt some more of the oil into my hand and rub it so it coats all my fingers. Then I take him back into my mouth, alternating between creating suction and licking down the length. Meanwhile, I move my hands back to his ass, and press a slick finger against his puckered hole.

"Fuck!"

This time it isn't pain edged into his features, but pure, barely contained lust.

"Keep going," he rasps, and I do.

I press my finger against the opening until the tip slides inside. When I gag on his cock at the same time, he tangles his fingers into my hair, something it must have taken all his self-control not to do until now.

Tightening his grip on my strands, he begins to fuck my mouth while I slowly slide my finger further into his ass.

"Killer," he growls. "That feels so fucking good."

The admission causes my pussy to throb, and even though this is about him, I wish he was touching me.

I time the thrusts of my finger with his fucking my mouth, and it doesn't take long before he growls out my name and forces his cock all the way to the back of my throat. As I curl the finger in his ass, he lets out a groaned string of curses and throws his head back.

"Yes. Fuck. Cara... so fucking good..." With a throaty groan, he pulls out of my mouth. "But I want to shoot my load deep inside your cunt."

The promise of what's to come has me moaning as I ease my finger out of him.

As I try to stand, Rocco grabs my arm and hauls me up against him. Without a word, he claims my lips. His tongue slides into my mouth, warring with mine.

I'm painfully aware of his hard cock between us, so I shimmy a little, trying to get it angled against my pussy.

Rocco chuckles. "Do you want something, Killer?" he taunts. "Because if you want something, you have to ask for it."

He spins me around so my back is against his chest. I feel his dick nudging against my drenched opening, and I push back against him, but he retreats with a tisk.

"Fuck me," I hiss. Rocco brings his thumb to my clit, circling the needy bud until I'm panting with need. "Please."

"Anything for you," he rasps.

He pushes the tip inside my opening, but instead of slamming all the way inside me, he eases his way. It's infuriatingly slow, and I'm quickly losing patience.

"Fucking do it already," I gripe. "I need you inside me, mi rey."

The endearment which is the same as his last name falls from my lips before I can stop it, but when he finally sheathes himself inside me I'm glad I didn't.

Rocco withdraws almost completely before slamming all the way inside me, fucking me hard while his hands are on my hips in a bruising hold. It's so delicious my eyes flutter closed as pleasure unfurls inside me.

Remembering why we're out here, I force my eyes open, and deliberately look at the tiled floor. Nope, can't do it. I clench my teeth together as my legs begin to shake. It's not from pleasure, but fear.

Is this how Rocco felt when I pushed my finger against his ass? If so, he's a lot stronger than I am, because I'm ready to beg him to carry me out of here.

"Come back to me," Rocco rasps as he moves his hands from my hips to my tits. "Focus on my cock inside you. Can you feel it stretching you?"

I moan. "Yes."

"And feel the way I'm hitting your G-spot?"

How the hell does he know?

"M-maybe... I think so."

Without warning, Rocco pulls me back up and spins me around so we're chest to chest. My nipples rub against his chest with every inhale, and the coarse hair creates a delectable friction.

"Look at me, Killer," he demands on a rasp. "We took care of my trauma, so look at me while I fuck yours out of you."

I want to retort that I don't think it's that simple, but I press my lips into a thin line instead.

"Hold on to my shoulders."

My hands are barely clasped around the muscles before he hoists my leg up, and angles his cock against my drenched opening.

"Eyes on me," he implores.

His eyes are darker than normal, lust making them almost clouded. I feel as though his irises are seeing beyond the flesh and bone, seeing my soul.

"Don't close your eyes," he groans as he thrusts into me. "Keep looking at me."

Every time he pistons his hips it becomes increasingly harder to keep my gaze on him, but I refuse to budge. Even as my orgasm builds, I don't waver. But as I come around him, my pussy squeezing his dick like a vise, my eyes flutter closed.

Rocco pounds into me once, twice, and on the third thrust he roars his release.

I sag against him, feeling beyond spent. Yawning, I move my arms around his neck and kiss him above his heart.

"Thank you," I murmur.

"What for?"

I'm not sure I can put it into words, so I just say, "Everything." I take a deep breath, loving the way his smell lingers in my nostrils. "For trusting me. For helping me, and... just for everything."

How the hell can I ever thank him for everything he's done for me? It's too much to put into words. The Rocco I'm getting to know is the most amazing guy, one I could maybe see myself being married to for longer than I have to be.

We rinse off in the shower, and I watch regretfully as the bathwater disappears down the drain. I did actually want a bath, but that will have to wait until tomorrow. I'm too tired now.

Afterward, Rocco wraps one of his beach towels around me while placing two on the tiled floor. It's such a small gesture, yet it speaks volumes.

As we get into bed, I wonder if the Rocco I know is the same man everyone else sees. Somehow I doubt that they know how he looks when he's vulnerable, or how much he actually allows me to get away with.

Though I can't claim to know much about the guy the others know, I've heard enough to know they respect him, and some even fear him. As I drift off to sleep in his arms, my brain struggles to connect the two. My Rocco, and the world's Rocco are two very different people.

A smile plays on my lips at the thought that I have a version that's just mine, because I think the same can be said about me. Despite fighting him as much as I do, I've also opened up about things I thought I'd take with me to the grave.

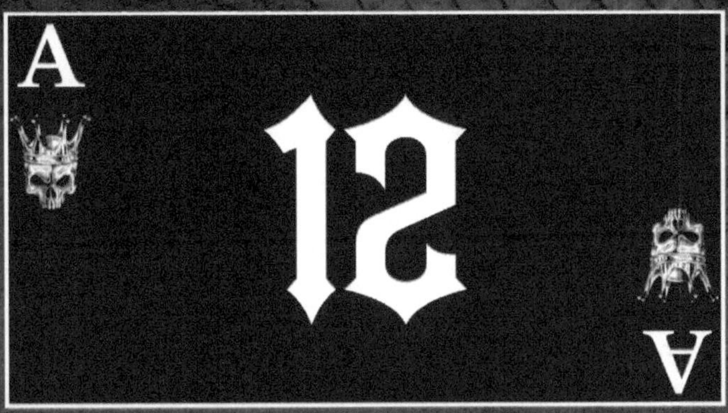

Rocco

Something has shifted inside me over the past few weeks since Cara and I opened up to each other, both emotionally and physically. Cara has turned my life upside down. In a good fucking way. I'd never thought much about actually having a wife other than doing my duty to protect her. But now, it's so much more. She's so much more, and in turn, she's made *me* so much more.

"Make sure your phone is off or on silent, Killer." I remind her, watching her nod and quickly un-pocketing the phone I got her last week so we can communicate when we are apart. She powers it down, shooting me a sinful fucking wink before hiding it away again.

Fuck. She's still affected by our fuck session, and if I'm being honest, so am I. It's hard to switch my mind off to the way she's evolved in the bedroom. She's more assertive. Dominant. Which can be tricky since I'm that way too, but we've worked out a rhythm. Sometimes I make her yield and submit to me, and I make fucking sure she enjoys it, and other times she doesn't back down, so I know it's my turn to let go and give her the control.

Like when I let her slip her fingers into my ass. That takes a lot of fucking effort for me to let go. There's always a moment of panic, but the flashbacks are getting less, and my killer always ensures it feels so good I forget my fucking name.

I made sure we had the opportunity to get lost in each other before we came out on this job tonight. It's going to be a tough one, but I promised her I'd show her what it is we do, aside from run a fucking strip club.

I hope she realizes that when I purchased her, I was actually trying to save her, and maybe after she sees for herself the kind of things we do she might understand that I, we, the Diamond Crew, are the good guys. Or at least, the better of the evils.

Aside from being fucking proud of the vigilante work we do, I've seen into Cara's soul. She's strong. Badass. And she's protective. Just like me. So this world we live in is now *her* world, and I know if she sees what we do, that she'll want to help. Want to be a part of it.

"Ready to get this party started?" Cain asks as he swaggers up like we aren't about to step into a vile, crude scene.

To be fair, he's probably not thinking about anything but the part where he gets to kill.

Woods Lagoon is dotted with moored boats that look like they are floating on a sea of black. There is no moon tonight, which helps us stay out of sight, but also means we can't see shit.

Munroe, an ex-marine, is the only one wearing night vision goggles, and he quietly breaks open the gate that is meant to provide security for the dock.

"You ready, Killer?" I whisper, tugging her to my chest, and she nods frantically, her eyes wide with excitement to see what it is we do.

Quietly, we move into single file, stepping onto the dock. I turn back to Cara and press my finger to my lips, signaling to stay quiet, and she gives me a nod, taking my gestured instruction easily.

Most of the boats at this end of the marina are smaller, except for the one our targets are on.

The vessel sticks out like a sore thumb, owned by a pompous banker from San Francisco. And tonight, he's entertaining two of his old college buddies, while their wives tend to their children back in the city.

If only the pompous banker knew that his wife was on to him after hiring a private investigator. And well, once they figured out the truth, she asked her investigator to take care of it and make sure he suffers.

Naturally, they reached out to us to take care of that part.

Creeping onto the boat at the end of the dock, we move carefully to make sure the vessel doesn't rock too much as we step on and alert them to our presence.

After helping Cara onboard, I keep one hand linked with hers and the other holding my gun as I survey the empty cabin. The lights are off up here, but light filters from below deck, and as soon as I crack open the glass sliding door we hear music, male laughter and female sobbing coming up the stairwell.

"Me and Munroe will go to the bow," Cain whispers, any hint of mischief gone from his face. I nod, knowing after we studied the plans for the boat, that there is below deck access from each end.

Cara shuffles from side to side, most likely from nerves, and once I see Cain and Munroe round the corner at the bow, I nod at Stretch.

"Gun ready," I whisper before turning my sights to Cara. "Stay behind us, and don't do anything unless we give you permission. Got it?"

She nods, cheeks flushed with both excitement and anger at the noises coming from below deck. She's not stupid. She knows those noises. She knows exactly what's being done to that poor girl.

One by one we storm down the stairs, timing it well as Cain and Munroe enter at the other end, and the overweight fuckers with round bellies and not a stitch of clothing, still, like a deer caught in headlights.

The girl, probably no older than fourteen, sobs, her wrists and ankles bound to a daybed, her body completely bare and exposed with one of those sick cunts, who's at least in his fifties, still buried inside her.

"Get out!" he yells, and as I drag my gaze over the three men, he is definitely our intended target.

The other two men are collateral, since we can't leave them alive for this crime.

I hear Cara move before I see her try to barge past me, and I whip my arm out to stop her.

"Don't forget my orders, Killer." I growl low, not wanting to draw attention to her. "You stay behind us until I give you permission."

"Give me permission now." She snarls through clenched teeth, her eyes trained on the scene before us.

"Not yet."

Her heated gaze is locked on the man buried inside the girl, and I get it. She wants to save her. Wants to make this man suffer. And she will, in good time.

"While love bug and his woman argue, how about you sick fuckers tell us who you purchased tonight's entertainment from?" Cain suggests, twirling his shotgun around like he's in a fucking parade twirling a baton.

"None of your business." The old fart slipping his now limp dick from the girl snaps, and even though I shouldn't be looking, I notice the oozing white substance tinged with blood that follows his dick out. "This is my boat, and I demand you leave!"

I chuckle. "Did you hear that Cain? He *demands* we leave."

"I fucking heard it." Cain does a spin on the spot, still fucking twirling his shotgun.

"What do you think, Killer?" I glance down at my wife. "Should we leave because he demanded it?"

"Well, I mean, if he demanded it then..." Cara smirks sinisterly, falling into the role like a fucking queen.

I glance back at our target and let my grin fall from my face. "I don't think so, asshole."

"You have no right to be here." One of his buddies cuts in, and I shake my head.

"Oh, we are definitely trespassing. Maybe you should call the cops. Let them come here and decide who the real criminals are."

The man pales, and number three tries to make a run for it, but Cain slips his foot out, tripping the man, who then face plants with a thud as he cries out.

"Whoops. My bad." Cain shrugs as Munroe fists the man's graying hair and drags him into the center of the room.

The sobbing of the young girl has quieted as she sucks in shuddering breaths, hopefully realizing we aren't here to hurt her.

"I'm ready." Cara hisses, facing me, her hands balled into fists at her sides.

Reaching out, I brush her dark hair back over her ear. "I know you are, but first, can you help get the girl free? I think she will feel more comfortable with you doing that."

Cara nods, as Cain and Stretch scuffle with the other two men, subduing them and forcing the three men to their knees in a line.

Knowing the men can't get to her, Cara darts across the space to untie the poor girl, while Cain binds the assholes' wrists and ankles with zip ties, and throws a few punches into each man's gut before Cara speaks up.

"The girl has something to say."

Turning back, I see that the young girl is now sitting on the daybed, a blanket wrapped around her as she trembles.

"T-these m-men, they b-bought m-me from some other m-men who c-call themselves the C-cali Reapers. They ride m-motorbikes and they k-killed my gran," a loud sob escapes as her face contorts with the internal pain she is suffering from that loss. "A-and when my m-mom tried to save me from them, they beat her up and t-took me."

Fuck. The Cali Reapers again. They are becoming a bigger fucking issue than we originally thought.

"How long have you been with them?" I ask, and her tear-filled eyes shift to me.

"A f-few weeks I g-guess." She shrugs. "When I m-met Tina, I t-thought I'd be okay. That she'd t-try to protect me," she sobs again, but this time, there's anger in it. "But that w-woman is worse than the m-men. She made s-sure I was clean and p-pretty looking, before she brought men i-into the room they kept me in, a-and made me..." She cringes, and a shiver of revulsion makes her shudder. "S-she made me suck t-them. She t-told me it was p-practice for the big event, when I'd m-meet my new owners." She sobs again and Cara turns her glassy eyes to me.

"Tina?" she asks, looking back at the girl. "As in Martina?"

Fuck. Cara's mom.

The girl nods, tugging the blanket tighter around her naked body. "Y-yes. How did you know?"

Cara shakes her head, dropping her chin to her chest briefly as her breathing quickens. I want to step up and hug her and tell her that everything will be okay, but it's not what she needs, and I know I'm right about that a moment later when Cara lifts her head and stands tall before rolling her shoulders back.

There is no sign of the young girl she once was. She's nowhere to be seen. This person in front of me is all woman.

A warrior.

"It doesn't matter how I know." Cara finally answers as she steps toward the girl. "Was the big event tonight?"

The girl starts to sob again, nodding. "Y-yes. They took my v-virginity."

All five of us growl in unison, turning our eyes to the three men who look nowhere near as cocky as they did when we entered before.

"She's of age." The pompous banker pipes up. "Dolly is legal. I have the paperwork to say as such."

I scoff right as the girl screams.

"I am fourteen! And stop calling me Dolly! My name is Rose!"

Cara's top lip twitches with the urge to slay, something I know she needs. Not just to take out her anger on the type of people that she was meant to be sold to, and not just because she knows that her mom is involved, as well as the Reapers.

There's something carnal brewing inside her. It's dark and consuming and something I'm all too familiar with.

She needs to punish.

Unsheathing my blade from my boot, I step up to my wife and offer it to her.

"Make them suffer, Killer."

The courage and resolution in her nod nearly sits me on my ass. She's never done anything like this before, yet she faces it with determination, not letting any fears she has get in the way.

"Little one, you may want to avert your eyes. This ain't gonna be pretty." Cain suggests to Rose, but she shakes her head, refusing to miss the downfall of her abusers.

Standing before the three naked men who are now looking very fucking panicked on their knees, Cara glares at them, taking the time to stare each man in the eye as they look up at their punisher pleadingly. They won't find any mercy from anyone here. Not from me, my men, and certainly, not from Cara.

They should be very fucking scared.

Pacing in front of them, Cara eyes each one before looking at the blade, a frown crinkling her brow.

"Want me to walk you through it, mi pequeño salvaje?" Cain asks, stepping up beside her and she nods.

"If you wouldn't mind."

"It would be an honor." He gives her a bow, before setting his shotgun aside and pulling out his own blade.

Then he starts to instruct her. He goes over what parts of the body hurt the most to be slashed, or stabbed, and before we know it, as red starts to paint the light blue carpet under the men's knees, Cara needs no more instruction as she doles out her first punishment. And fuck, I just know it won't be her last.

The men's cries are drowned out by Cain's singing. It's not even a real song, but something he makes up as he goes, singing about their demise and Cara's reign.

When Cara has had enough of slashing and stabbing, she leans in close to each trembling man, ignoring their sobs and apologies for being scum, as she starts carving something into their chests. One by one, she drags the sharp tip of the knife over each man's flesh, spelling out a word on each.

Rapist.

Paedo.

Pervert.

"Haha yes!" Cain sing-songs, clapping like he's giving a standing ovation at a fucking Broadway show. "A masterpiece if I ever saw it."

"Is it bad that I agree?" Stretch asks, tilting his head to look at the angry bleeding letters.

"Not at all. I think we are all on the same page right now." I admit, feeling my cock stir at the sight of Cara painted in the metallic crimson of their blood.

Turning to me, she looks thoughtful. "Husband, I'm sorry, but I have to do this last part, and if you don't want to see me touch another man's dick, then you should turn away."

My brows shoot up as Cain cheers and Munroe mutters, "Fuck me, we've created a monster."

As much as I never want to see her hand wrapped around another man's cock, this is different.

"I'm not turning around, Killer. Do your worst."

Slowly, her plump lips spread wide, her white teeth flashing as she gives me a nod and turns back to the pleading men, who we all fucking ignore.

Flexing her gloved hand, Cara bends, coming eye to eye with the first old college buddy.

"Say goodbye to your puny dick."

Then she wraps her hand around the limp member and starts sawing the blade through it.

His screams are piercing, and he passes out slumping to the side before she's even halfway through, but she keeps going until it's cut free.

"You look hungry." She tells the unconscious man, stepping over his body to pry his lips apart before shoving his dick in his mouth.

"Fuck. No, please." Old college buddy number two cries with mortification, eyeing his friend in his humiliated state before he starts pissing himself.

"Oh now, that's uncalled for." Cara announces, straightening to glare down at him.

"P-please don't."

Cara turns a raised brow to us, but looks past us men, and focuses on Rose, who is now standing as she watches quietly.

"What do you think, Rose? Should he keep his dick?"

Rose is shaking her head before Cara even finishes.

"Oh well," she turns back to the two men. "Karma's a bitch."

Even as he tries to struggle away, with nowhere to go, Cara wraps her gloved hand around his dick and repeats the process. He too passes out before it's even done, and this time she simply drops his dick to the floor before dicing it up.

Obviously a little squeamish at seeing a dick diced, Stretch sits down looking rather fucking green, but he doesn't stop watching Cara's punishment. None of us can stop watching. It's a sight to behold.

"How m-much?" the pompous guy stammers. "H-how much to p-put an end to t-this? I can h-have the m-money to you within m-minutes."

"Oh, you poor thing." Cara pouts dramatically. "There isn't enough money in existence to end your suffering. Not after the crimes you have committed against children." She punches him in the face then, surprising all of us, before she sets to work on his flaccid dick.

"You're a fool," she sneers as she saws the blade through his flesh. "People like *you* think you won't get caught. And maybe the cops won't get you, which would be a mercy, wouldn't it?" She tilts her head, sneering in his face as he pants and screams. "But what sick fuckers like *you* don't consider, is people like *me*. Like *us*." She gestures her head backward toward us, finally sawing through the last bit of skin. The pompus prick nearly topples backward as blood pisses out everywhere from where his dick once hung. "Because one way or another," she slaps him across the face with his own dick, "I'm gonna get ya."

And fuck me, as she rains down her wrath, carving them up until each man no longer breaths, I swear I hear the song in my head.

One way or another.

I've never been fucking prouder.

Turning to me with wide excited eyes, I can see Cara's desire thrumming through her veins.

Fuck. She's beautiful. Stunning. And she needs to fuck bad.

"Shower." I insist, pointing to the door off to the side where a small bathroom is attached.

"But—"

"No buts." I shake my head, hardening my gaze as I stare at her so she understands that right now, I am still in fucking charge. "Shower. Dump your clothes on the floor in the middle of this room while we prepare the boat for a good old fashion cremation ceremony."

"But I have nothing else to put on." She frowns, and I grin.

"All you need is a towel, hermosa. And let me fucking tell you, it won't be on for long."

Her nostrils flare, and her breathing increases as we stare each other down.

She wants to fuck right now. I can see it in her eyes. I can feel the fucking *want* radiating off her body, even from the six feet between us.

I wonder if she'd actually do it, if I allowed it. Fuck me in front of my men. Take what she needs despite all the eyes on us.

I have a feeling the answer is yes.

"Go on. We don't have long." I insist, and she nods, handing me her phone before brushing past me and closing herself in the small room.

The floor inside the bathroom doesn't have tiles, so I know she'll be alright, and I turn my attention to what needs to be done now.

Turning to Rose, I offer her a pitying look, hoping she knows she is safe with us.

"Do you have anywhere to go?" I ask. "Back to your mom?"

She shakes her head. "N-no. A-after they beat her u-up, she kinda went nuts trying to find m-me, and the last I heard she got arrested for trying to kill a police officer who she thought was in the Reapers' pocket."

Nodding, the story sounds familiar. Not about the Reapers, but I did catch the news a couple of weeks back where a crazy woman had been arrested for assaulting a police officer.

"Well, Rose. I know we don't seem like the most well-behaved citizens, but we have some girls that work for us at Dirty Diamonds. I'm sure they can take you under their wings and look after you. Unless you'd rather me take you to the police station?"

She shakes her head frantically. "No please, no police. Not after my mom..."

I nod. "Fair enough." I turn to Stretch since he is the least fucking scary of us.

"Stretch will take you back to Dirty Diamonds. It's a strip club, but we won't ever ask you to do that sort of work, okay? The women there are nurturing. They will take care of you."

"Okay." She agrees, still wrapped in the blanket, her eyes landing on Stretch, who gestures to the staircase where they both depart.

"That was a brilliant fucking show mi pequeño salvaje gave." Cain snickers and I glare at him. I don't know why, but it pisses me off when he calls her his little savage. Cain grins like he knows how much it annoys me, shouldering past me in a playful way. "Now, if you will excuse me, Munroe and I have a dance to perform."

"It's not a fucking dance." Munroe complains, throwing his arms up like this has been something they have been arguing about for a while.

"Oh really? Just watch me then."

And just like that, Cain dances around, phone in hand as he snaps pictures as requested by the pompous banker's wife, before he drags Munroe up the stairs, going in search of Gunner and Grayson.

They are only sixteen, so we try not to involve them too much in the gruesome part of what we do. That will come in a couple of years, but for now, they are our lookouts, and have the job of torching the boat and keeping watch from a distance to see which authorities turn up so we know who to pay off, and who we are going to have trouble with.

Grayson and Gunner work silently as they douse the interior of the boat with accelerant, dumping a heap on the three bodies, and when Cara steps out of the bathroom, clothes balled up and only a towel wrapped around her, I have to smack both Gray and Gunner for fucking ogling her.

"Eyes fucking off." I snap, pointing to the floor for Cara to dump the clothes. "Just here, Killer. The boys will make sure they burn."

"You wouldn't survive a night with me." Cara shoots Gray and Gunner a sly smile before shooting me a sinful fucking wink.

She's calmed a little from before. I can see she's not on edge ready to pounce on me at any second.

"Are you ready?" I ask, and she bites her plump lip, nodding.

Taking her hand, I start leading her up the stairs, glancing back to see Gunner dousing Cara's clothes before the two boys follow behind.

Moving quietly off the boat and up the dock, I lead Cara up to my truck, opening the door and helping her in since she's only wrapped in a towel.

"Will they be alright?" she asks, looking over my shoulder to where Grayson and Gunner lurk near the boat.

"Yep." I nod. "They are good at this part."

I close the door as a sinister smile spreads across her face, and through the glass of the window, I see her skin light up with an orange glow, as I hear the whoosh of the fire engulfing the boat behind me.

After a quick word with my men, I get in my truck and drive us away, heading toward the main beach.

Cara is quiet as I drive, but she shifts in her seat a few times, and I can tell she's rubbing her legs together. She's so fucking horny right now, which is good, because my dick is fucking hard as stone.

"You okay over there?" I ask, and she groans, tipping her head back and squeezing her eyes shut.

"I'm not sure. Is it wrong that I'm so... so..."

"Horny?" I ask and her lids snap open before she glances at me.

"Yes. I shouldn't be right? That's... sick."

My hands grip the steering wheel as I shake my head.

"Hell fucking no, it's not sick. You're riding a high from your kills. It's not about the blood and gore of it. It's about the power you held while doing it, and now, you need a release."

Without being able to help it, she moans and presses both hands to the towel, parting her legs to hit the right spot.

"Cara. Not yet."

"But... I can't wait." She rubs again, and I hiss.

"Pull your fucking hands away right fucking now."

"But..." she breathes before she moans.

"Stop," I hiss, and she finally drags her hands away.

"I can't wait until we get home." She complains and I chuckle.

"It's a good thing we aren't going home then."

Not that home is far. It's literally a four-minute drive, but I wasn't planning on going home, and when I flick my indicator on, Cara's eyes widen as she looks out the window to see where we are going.

"What are we doing here?" she asks, as I turn into the parking lot of Cowell Beach. "Skinny dipping?"

I chuckle. "Not today, but you will be naked."

She doesn't even hesitate as I park the truck. She gets out, her feet bare with only a towel wrapped around her.

I can't wipe the grin off my face as I quickly get my shoes off before joining Cara and lead her down to the beach. It's dark down here, so I use the flashlight on my phone to guide us until we hit the sand, and then Cara grins sheepishly at me, before she drops the fucking towel and runs off giggling.

"Look out for the crabs." I chuckle, but she has no cares in the world right now, and I fucking love that.

Even though it's dark, I can see enough to see her kicking her feet in the water, like a child that rarely gets to go to the beach.

"Move down this way." I call to her, and she follows my order, kicking the small waves as she skips along toward the wharf until she's finally under the structure trying to kick water at me as she hides behind the posts.

We laugh, and play a bit of tag around the posts under the wharf, splashing in the shallow water until I can't take not having my hands on her any longer, and I catch her before we tumble onto the sand as waves splash over us.

Like magnets, our lips collide, tongues clash, and our hands roam. She's completely fucking naked while I'm still fully dressed, and it's a form of torture having the fabric barrier in the way.

"Get these off." She pants against my lips as she grinds herself over the hard bulge in my jeans.

I make quick work of tearing my shirt off. The moment it's gone her teeth are biting my nipples while we both work on my fucking jeans.

I flip us around in the small waves, surprising my killer before standing and finishing the job at removing my fucking pants, before lowering myself back down to the sand.

Sharp nails dig into my shoulders as I press my aching cock against her heat, and she arches into me, even as she tries to flip us again.

"Uh-uh, hermosa. You've had your control tonight. Now it's my turn."

She doesn't argue, instead answers with her lips against mine as she kisses me hungrily.

The water is cold, but not cold enough to douse the fire burning between us, and I reach down and grip my hard length, before lining it up and surging in.

"Yes." She cries as I fill her cunt, her back arching again as the waves lap at us under the wharf.

"I need to apologize now, for how fucking quick this is going to be." I rasp against her lips as I thrust over and over.

"The boat..." she pants, "was the foreplay," she moans. "I'm already..."

Her words drop off as she starts fucking me right back, two bodies in the sand and waves pistoning together in a frenzy, completely and utterly united as one.

I pound into her as she slams her cunt over me, and even though our hearts are pounding like we've been running a marathon, I know we have only been here connected like this for a matter of minutes.

But it doesn't matter. Nothing fucking matters when I'm with Cara like this. Nothing is even comparable.

"I'm... I'm..." She squeezes around my cock, and a scream rips from her lungs as she comes apart, kneading my dick with her tight walls and milking a dizzying climax from me.

A roar flies from my lips as I surge one last time inside her, the muscles in my back coiling as I go still, feeling the hot spurts of my cum shoot into her tight hot heat.

Cara King, is my fucking paradise.

Rocco

"I've got an hour before the girls pester Lily to call me. So let's get started." Dante orders from across the table as his Aussie mate, Baz, relaxes back in the chair looking like he doesn't have a care in the world.

Since Baz had business over here in the US and Dante was concerned with the increasing Reaper situation, they flew over together from the UK in the Marx family's private jet and got here an hour ago.

The fact that Baz came with Dante to see us is significant. It means there's cause for real concern. Dante may want his advice or even access to his associates, should we need it.

"If they call, let Uncle Cain handle it. They love me." Cain beams from next to me and Dante frowns.

"They don't even fucking know you. They think it's Santa, and the Easter Bunny and whatever else I can come up with to hide who is really sending all the fucking candy and extravagant gifts, half of which I have to fucking send back. You're not fucking taking that call." Dante growls and Cain snickers.

"And why don't they know me? Huh?" Cain raises his brows. "Because you're fucking greedy and won't share them with me. I'm a good uncle, and when I speak to them, you will see how wrong you are."

"Jesus Christ." Dante pinches the bridge of his nose.

"Tell us about the Reapers?" Baz asks, directing the conversation to business.

"The Reapers are a problem, but so is Cara's mom," I tell them, knowing they have already been updated on last night's events.

"So it seems." Dante frowns. "She's been a ghost for so long, but with Cara being released from prison, she's taking risks. Coming out of hiding. It's a good thing because we have a better chance at catching her, but why does she want Cara so bad?"

"At first, I think she originally wanted her because she thought Cara was still a virgin when she got out of prison." I state, hating saying those words about my wife out loud. But I trust these men. They only want what's best.

"I take it by the way you had her pressed against the wall before we came in here that you have taken care of that?" Dante smirks.

"It's been well and truly taken care of." I smirk back, knowing that details aren't required, because that's not the way any of us roll.

Wait.

I take that back.

Cain rolls that way, but the rest of us like to keep our intimate moments to ourselves.

Cara is out in the club, sitting and chatting with Rose while the other Diamonds and Tex prepare for a busy night. I can see Cara feels almost responsible for the poor girl. Not in the blame way, but in the way that Rose is now alone, and Cara wants to make sure she doesn't feel that way, so she is devoting time to the girl, talking her through the assault she endured.

"So what's Cara's appeal to her mom now?" Baz asks and I shrug.

"I assume a big part is so she can have control over her daughter again. When she showed up on my doorstep, there was mention of getting Cara hooked on drugs so that she'll comply and be a high earning whore for them."

"But the Reapers are involved too? Who are these men? Why haven't we heard of them before this?" Dante asks.

"The Reapers are a nomad club, causing havoc everywhere they go. For some reason, they've set their sights on this area after hearing the territory could be up for grabs. They are bad news. Dealing in the skin trade, and probably various other nefarious things." I slam my fist on the tabletop in frustration. "We can't let them take over our area."

Dante and Baz share a look, before Dante speaks.

"Our crew is big, but we are just that. A crew. Not a fucking motorcycle club. Their business dealings are different to ours. Morals too."

I nod, knowing all of this.

"Then what do we do? Just sit by and let them destroy the peace we've brought to the area?" I ask, clenching my fists on the tabletop. "Gang crime is down because of us. Most of them move on over the mountains rather than go up against us. We can't lose that."

"I don't want to lose that either but short of finding another club willing to relocate and take over the area so the Reapers can't, I don't know what to do." Dante admits, and we all fall silent before I speak up.

"They're buying little girls, Dante. Reselling them. Helping Cara's mom keep her fucking sick empire going. We can't sit on this."

"He's right." Baz agrees, sharing another look with Dante. "The only way to keep this region safe is to fill the gap."

"But we aren't a fucking MC." Dante hisses and Baz nods.

"So start one. It's not like you don't have men to spare. Start a fucking MC right here in Santa Cruz. Bid for the territory and keep this place yours."

Dante frowns, staring at the tabletop. "We know nothing about running an MC. They deal with Cartels and Mafia and powerful men with too much money and God complexes." He shrugs.

"Like you?" Cain interjects with a laugh, but Dante ignores him.

"Who would I even get to run a fucking MC?"

"I will," I say before I even realize the words are slipping from my mouth.

Baz grins pleased while Dante continues to frown.

"You're only twenty-two." He tries to use it as an excuse, and I shake my head.

"The same fucking age you were when you started the Diamond Crew, as well as the same fucking age Cain is right now, running the DC over here. Don't you think I can do it? Lead?"

Dante leans closer to the table, staring me straight in the eye.

"I have no fucking doubt you can lead, Rochus. You are a born leader. My reservation comes from losing you."

I relax back in my seat, crossing my arms over my chest. "Are you gonna miss me?"

"Shut the fuck up. I already miss all of you. I hate being so far away from my OG crew." Dante admits and Cain swoons.

"Awww, he loves us."

We all chuckle before falling silent again, deep in thought about the prospect of starting an MC.

Honestly, I had thought about it briefly, but like everything to do with this life, I needed to discuss it with my crew. Baz bringing it up made it easier for two reasons.

The first, because I didn't want Dante to think I'd ever desert him.

And secondly, Baz bringing it up means it's not a ridiculous notion.

Next to me, Cain glances at his phone, reading a message before showing it to me. It's from Gunner.

Gunner: Have you seen Gray? He was gone when I woke up.

"I haven't seen him." I offer, remembering how they checked in at sunrise to give an update on the boat bonfire before going to bed for the day.

"He's probably buried deep in pussy. He's been sniffing around one of the new Diamond recruits lately."

I chuckle. "Well, he deserves a few extra hours off before he starts his shift helping Tex."

Grinning, Cain shoots Gunner a text back and I glance up to see Baz and Dante talking quietly. I sit and wait, wondering if he'll take me seriously.

I know I'm young, but with Cara by my side, and some help from the crew, I have no doubt I can form an MC and make sure the Reapers don't get access to our fucking territory.

"Okay, let's talk more about creating an MC." Dante states, shooting me a look of absolute respect.

Both Cain and I sit taller in our seats, more than ready to have this conversation.

"It'll take a bit of setting up." Dante continues, "You'll need to recruit for the MC. You can take some of the crew with you if they are willing, just don't take them all." Dante grins, and we all chuckle before we sink into a strategy session on how the fuck one starts an outlaw MC.

Cara

I yawn, stretching while I try to make myself more comfortable on the couch I'm sitting on with Rose, Sasha, and Alana.

"Ha! I win again," Rose exclaims, throwing down her cards with a sly smile on her lips.

"What a surprise," Sasha laughs.

"Okay, you have to be cheating. There's no way you keep winning by accident," Alana says with a mock frown.

Both she and Sasha act like they don't know me and Rose are trading cards so she can keep winning. Hell, both of them have discreetly shuffled the deck, so Rose keeps getting winning hands.

"How long do we have to stay here?" Rose asks.

She doesn't sound perturbed or like she wants to leave. In fact, she seems to really enjoy the endless supply of soda and peanuts. Or maybe it's the attention she's enjoying. All I know is that against all odds, Rose seems fine. More than fine.

"Do I get a knife as well?" she asks so suddenly I choke on my water.

"W-what?" I gasp.

She nods eagerly. "You have one. So do I get one as well?"

Sasha throws her head back and laughs. "Savage little thing, aren't you?"

My phone lights up with an incoming text, and I bite the inside of my cheek to keep my smile at bay.

> *Rocco: I don't know how long this is going to take.*

> *Me: Take your time, mi rey. I'll be waiting for you.*

> *Rocco: I'm your king?*

> *Me: Well, it's your last name, isn't it?*

Took him long enough to work that one out. I know he probably used an online translator rather than just ask Cain or any of the others that speak Spanish around here. That's Rocco, stubborn, proud, and so mine.

> *Rocco: I want you to say it again while I'm fucking you. Hard.*

My breath hitches as I read the message.

> *Me: Hurry the fuck up then!*

"What did Rocco want?" Alana asks with a knowing smirk, and I flip her off.

"None of your business," I grin as I pick up my cigarettes and get off of the couch. "I'm going out for a cigarette."

Technically, I can smoke inside if I want to. But I like the fresh air, and I don't really want to accidentally blow smoke into Rose's face.

As I lean against the wall outside, I can't stop thinking about the girl. Rose. She's the epitome of strength. She isn't cowering, crying, or anything like that. Instead, she seems to have moved on. I don't know whether to applaud it or dread it, since I know better than most that trauma isn't something you can just shirk off.

Now that I've seen Rocco in action, I want to be part of what they do. I want to punish the guilty and help the innocent. While it sounds like the slogan of do-gooders united, that's not what it's about.

I want to do my part to ensure people like Rose, like Julietta, and, yes, like me, can have a normal childhood—whatever that is. But mostly, I want to feel the rush from yesterday, again. The exhilaration of punishing those men was all-consuming, addictive even.

My phone rings, and I smile as I accept the call without checking the number.

"Rocco," I breathe. "Are you already done?"

The voice that greets me isn't who I expected. "Cara Rodríguez?"

I frown and look at the caller ID. Unknown number.

"Yes, that's me," I say hesitantly after putting the phone back to my ear.

"Listen up, cunt," the voice barks, and my back becomes ramrod straight. "You took someone that belongs to us, so we took someone who belongs to you."

"W-what?"

Without missing a beat, the guy on the other end carries on. "In two minutes, a white van is going to park outside Dirty Diamonds. If you don't get inside without warning any of your friends, Grayson Black is going to pay the price."

Before I can ask any questions, the stranger ends the call.

Shit, what the fuck do I do?

After we left the boat yesterday, Gray and Gunner burned it the fuck down. Cain told them both to stay low, and not return to Dirty Diamonds until tonight. So how the hell do I know if he's really missing, or if the caller is bluffing?

My phone pings with an incoming text, and as though the stranger has a direct line to my thoughts, there's a picture of Gray bound and gagged. His left eye is swollen, and there's blood at the corner of his mouth.

Fuck. Okay, so the threat isn't empty.

My phone beeps again, but this time it isn't a picture of Gray, it's of... "Mateo," I gasp as I look at the picture of my twin, who looks just as bad as Gray.

Scratch that, there's a cut on his forehead and another on his cheek, so he looks worse. A lot worse.

I shake so hard I drop my phone, but before I can pick it up, the van arrives. I can barely believe it's only been two minutes, because to me, it feels like a lifetime.

I look between the two doors I have to choose between. One will take me to safety, to backup—to Rocco. The other to uncertainty, but probably pain, and possibly even my death.

A guy with a black mask opens the van door and points at me, making it clear they're here for me. I swallow, and before I'm aware I've decided, my feet carry me to the vehicle.

"Blindfold the cunt," I guy spits as soon as I reach them.

"And don't fucking forget to tie her up. I can still feel her fucking kick."

Someone laughs at that, and scathingly teases him about being soft if he thinks I can hurt them. Though it's hard, I bite down on my bottom lip to stop myself from retorting.

Another guy, also wearing a mask, hauls me into the back of the van and slams the door closed. The tires screech as we speed away. The guy back here with me, fastens my hands behind my back before he ties my legs together. I sit still through it all. Then he forces a blindfold over my eyes. I don't know why he bothers when I can't see their faces, and there aren't any windows in the back.

I don't put up a fight, I just sit there as we drive. With each swing or turn in the road, I'm thrown against the van, much to the amusement of the guy watching me. I bare my teeth and hiss at him, not that it does me any good. If anything, it makes him laugh harder.

"Think Tina is going to let me fuck this one once she's done with her?" one of the guys asks.

My blood runs cold as I realize they're taking me to my mom.

The words from the call reverberate in my brain. *"You took someone that belongs to us."*

Rose... we took Rose and killed the men.

Even though I know it's horror-movie stupid that I gave myself over to the men, I don't regret my decision. Gray's started to turn his life around, and he's less angry. He deserves another chance at life. And Mateo... fuck. My tortured twin, I can't turn my back on him either.

The van comes to a crashing halt, which makes one guy grumble about the driver's abilities. As they get out, I listen intently, trying to pick up on any clues as to where we are. But all I can hear are their muttered voices, and the gravel they walk on.

"Get her inside. Tina said she wants her in the basement."

I hate the way my heart sinks and my hands tremble at my back at the mention of coming face-to-face with my mom. Fuck, since she showed up on Rocco's doorstep, I've regretted that I didn't kill her all those years ago.

Back then, I mistakenly thought her to be pathetic, weak even. Now, I'm pretty fucking sure I had everything backwards. I'm not saying my dad was innocent, and I never will. But I am questioning who really pulled the strings behind the scenes.

I startle, letting out a yelp as someone picks me up and throws me over their shoulder.

"Did you hear that?" he chuckles. "The cunt is finally making some noise." He slaps my ass, hard.

As the sounds of gravel stop, I'm hit in the head with a wall of cold air. I realize we must be inside, a place where the AC is working overtime.

The room, or whatever we're in, smells dank. And the smells don't get better as we get further into the building. The air is heavy with the stench of piss, vomit, and... blood.

"Why the fuck does Tina want this one, anyway?" one asks. "She isn't even that pretty. And I doubt she's untouched after living with that Diamond Crew fucker."

I swallow down a whimper as I'm jostled, and the guy's shoulder digs into my ribcage.

Wait... what did he just say? Well, it wasn't as much what he said as it was the way. Do these guys not know Martina is my mom?

Their chatter turns to what they want to do to me, so I tune out their vile words, instead preparing myself for a range of scenarios. One being that Gray and Mateo are already dead. Another being that my mom tries to force me to be with Gray, which would be just as wrong as if it was my actual brother.

I already know that whatever she has in store for me won't be good, and... fuck, I might as well stop guessing. It won't do me any good. And even if I somehow magically guess her plan, I'm not in any position to stop it.

Doors open and close around us, and I no longer feel the cold air blasting me in my face. As the guy carrying me unceremoniously drops me to the floor, I let out an oomph and pain shoots up my ankle as I land. With my hands and legs still tied, there was no way for me to soften the blow, and now it seems my poor ankle is paying for it.

The sound of struggles and metal clanking intensifies, and even though I'm still blindfolded, I instinctively swing my head in all directions as I try to hone in on the sound. Wait... it's coming from two places. That and the... it sounds like muffled cries or shouts.

"Gray," I gasp. "Mateo... is that you?"

The muffled noises grow louder but not clearer.

Heels sound on the concrete floor, click-clacking their way to me. Then the blindfold is ripped from my face. The luminescent light seems much too bright, and I squint against it.

"Welcome home my dear daughter." My mom's words are followed by a cackle. "It's been so long."

"Daughter?" one of the men wonders out loud. "Fucking hell. She's your daughter?"

My mom tilts her head to the side and looks up at the man who spoke. "Got a problem with that?"

He immediately shakes his head, though he can't hide the disgust on his face.

"Are you sure?" mom asks, and I'm pretty sure she noticed his grimace as well. "Don't be shy. If you have any problem, all you have to do is say so."

The guy looks to the others, and if I were to guess, I'd say these are the men from the van. "Nope," he confirms. "No problem at all."

Mom nods. "That's what I thought."

He may not have anything else to say, but I have plenty. It's physically hurting me to stop myself from hurling insults and accusations at the woman who birthed me. But I can't succumb to my fears, hatred, and anger. Not when I don't see Gray and Mateo.

As soon as I think that, my mom moves the light, so it's not shining right into my face. I blink a few times, and as soon as my vision clears, I see them. The two men are bound and gagged, but otherwise they look just like they did in the pictures I received.

Thank God they haven't been harmed further!

"Now, daughter," my mom taunts as she pats Gray's cheek. Then she walks over to Mateo, repeating the motion. "You have a choice to make."

No! She can't mean...

My blood turns to ice, and my eyes widen as a gasp slips past my lips.

"Oh, yes." Her laugh is a deranged sound. "The look on your face is priceless. Exactly what I wanted. It's nice to see you're not always a disappointment."

"You can't be serious." It's hard forcing the words out. There's a lump in my throat, and my eyes burn with unshed tears. "You want me to choose which one you kill?" My voice is barely audible.

"No, no, no," she laughs coquettishly. "You misunderstand me, dear daughter."

Her eyes are filled with mirth as she walks over to me, swinging her hips in a way that makes her look more ridiculous than powerful. It's only now, when it's too late, that I realize the costume my mom has worn so much it's basically a part of her.

All my life she's been acting meek, even asked me not to piss off my dad. I've seen the bruises he left on her body in the past. Except... maybe he was never the one to hurt her. Or, if he did, maybe she wanted it. After all, it helped perfect the façade she's hidden behind.

"It hurts me that you think so little of me," my mom says with a pout.

"I-I..." There are no words to describe what I want to say, so instead of trying, I simply stop without finishing the sentence.

My eyes trail to Gray, who's slumping against the guy holding him up. His eyes are open, and I don't like the look in them. He looks resigned, like he's given up. Mateo, on the other hand, has a fire in his eyes I recognize from looking in the mirror. He hasn't given up at all, he's ready to fight.

Mom snaps her fingers in my face. "Here's the thing," she says when I finally look at her. "You deserve to be punished, mija. You're an insolent, ungrateful, and hateful cunt. It's like you've been raised by a pack of wolves and not a loving family."

Shock reverberates through me, and my jaw becomes slack as I glare at her. Is she for fucking real? Ungrateful? Loving family? What world is she living in?

"You can't be serious," I snap.

Mom makes a tsking sound before she slaps me across the face. Despite the sound following, I know her hit wasn't meant to hurt, but to silence and belittle me.

"Always with the interruptions," she says. "Watch your temper, mija. I won't let you spoil my fun again. Do you know how hard it's been to establish myself without your dad?"

"You never cared about him, did you? Just like it wasn't him that wanted this life. It's always been you, hasn't it?"

She shakes her head. "That's the thing with you, Cara. You think you know the truth, but you never care to ask the right questions. So let me give you the answers you really want."

What the hell does that even mean?

"Your dad bought me. Not as his wife, but as his entertainment for the weekend."

I unthinkingly look at Mateo, who just nods. I guess this isn't news to him.

"Do you know how hard it was to convince your dad to keep me around? To see me as anything more than his whore? In time, I succeeded, of course. He made me his wife, and I helped him expand his business."

The woman in front of me is cold, completely void of all emotions. Her eyes are like an abyss, there's nothing there.

"Your dad never could see the big picture, but I could. So I used my body to garner favors and influence with the right people. When Julietta was born, her future husband was the first to hold her. And—"

Unable to stop myself, I interrupt her. "And let me guess, it was the same for me?"

I already know that can't be true. Not only is Rocco only three years older than me, but I also know that the Diamond Crew aren't the kind of people who play the long game. They intercede as soon as possible, because they don't want people to suffer unnecessarily.

Besides, I know in my heart that Rocco would never do anything that vile. To hold a baby, claiming it as your future wife, or cum dumpster, is a special kind of evil.

"What about the auction?" I ask, confused as to why there even was an auction for Julietta if she was already sold.

My mom waves her hand in the air. "Julietta's auction was... necessary."

"Necessary?" I ask, horrified.

She nods. "Yes, mija. Julietta's intended died when she was twelve. At the time, it seemed like a stroke of luck really. And I convinced your dad that we should allow people to buy her for the night. It was a good way to have a steady income."

"Why did she get married then?" I ask, not able to make sense of it at all.

Mom turns and looks at Mateo. "Your brother is soft," she sneers before turning back to me. "He convinced your dad that it was best to find another husband for Julietta. *My* darling husband bought your twin's reasoning, but I knew better. I knew he only came up with the idea to save her from having new men all the time."

My stomach churns, and acidic bile creeps up the back of my throat.

"Since your sister wasn't a virgin, we didn't get much for her. It was laughable, really. At least we got it right with you. Even if your husband turned out to be a soft bastard unworthy of one of my kids, you still earned me a lot of money."

Anger lances through me. "How the fuck can you even get those words across your lips? What the fuck's the matter with you?" I scream as I pull against my restraints.

Mom taps a finger against her chin, narrowing her eyes as she studies me like I'm a fucking exotic animal at the zoo. "That husband of yours really doesn't know how to handle you, does he? The mouth you have on you now shows how weak he is."

Before I can stop myself, I throw up. I lean to the side, but I still throw up over myself. As I retch, mom barks orders to one guy, who's quick to get a bucket of water that he throws at me.

"The fuck," I shout as the ice-cold liquid hits me.

"Get her some clean clothes as well," my mom snaps. Then she turns her icy-glare on me. "Disgusting."

My teeth chatter and my entire body shakes as cold seeps through my bones and all the way into my marrow. Chunks of my last meal are stuck in my hair, and the burning smell assaults my nostrils.

"Now, where was I? Oh yeah." Mom snaps her fingers. "Really, all you need to know is that your dad was weak, and so is your brother. You and Julietta were my best hopes, but you took her from me. I know it was you who killed her. So it's only fair you work for the both of you."

My head is spinning with the overload of information. Some of it I knew, or suspected. But mostly, she's ripped the carpet from under me, and now I'm not sure of anything. Maybe I heard her wrong, or maybe some of the things I've been told while growing up were lies.

It doesn't matter, though. All that matters is that we're here, and I need to find a way to kill her.

The guy who went to get me some clothes returns, but I don't get a chance to see what he's carrying before another comes closer. There's a black hose in his hand, and I know what's coming a second before water spurts out. The pressure is cruel, and it hurts as he points it straight at me.

"Make sure she's clean," mom says, coldly. "I have plans for her, and I can't have her smell and look like she's been living on the street."

I scream as the hose is pointed at my face. It feels like I'm being attacked with ice, making it nearly impossible to breathe.

The guy lowers the hose and grunts something to another guy. I can't hear the words, but as he walks right up to me and cuts my clothes from my body, it doesn't matter. The knife knicks me a few times, and every time he sneers at me to keep still, which is fucking impossible with the way I'm shivering.

Once I'm naked, he cuts the binds from my hands and legs. He wraps his arms around me, holding me tight against him as I'm hosed down once more. I don't know which is the biggest torture, the icy blast of water, or the erection digging into my back.

I scream and thrash, to no avail. All it does is make my mom laugh scornfully, repeating what a pathetic disappointment I am.

A grunt has me looking up from the floor, and I notice Mateo and Gray now standing next to each other. Both of them try to break free from the person holding them, but they don't fare any better than I do.

"Stop!" I cry out when the guy holding Gray punches him in the stomach.

Mom rolls her eyes and throws a towel at me. I do my best to cover my body while drying, but it's a waste, really. Everyone in the room has seen my naked body, so why worry about it now.

Once I'm as dry as I can get, mom hands me a black, see-through babydoll dress. "Here. Put it on," she commands.

I arch my brow. "No underwear?"

"No," she says, shaking her head. "You haven't earned that privilege."

I swallow down more bile, and hurry to put on the dress that covers absolutely nothing.

"Now, where were we?" mom says, sounding way too eager for my liking. "Yes. I asked you to choose, and you thought I was asking you to pick who I'll kill. But that's not exactly right. I won't be doing the killing, mija. You will."

"W-what?" I stammer, sure I didn't hear her correctly.

"That's right," she says gleefully. "Who will you kill? Your brother or this Gray guy?"

My eyes fill with tears again as I look between the two men. How can I ever pick between them? Gray is... Gray is my kin—we may not share blood, but that doesn't matter. I recognize the darkness inside him. Mateo is my relative, and my twin. How the fuck can I pick?

The longer I look between them, the more it feels like I'm choosing between my future and my past. Gray belongs in my future, hopefully. But Mateo can only ever be part of my past. Even if I save him, there's too much bad blood between us to have any kind of relationship in the future.

I'm barely aware that one of the goons presses a gun into my trembling hands, but it's there. I feel the steel. He stays at my back, and his hands are hovering just over mine. The message is clear; don't do anything stupid like aim the firearm at my mom.

Fuck!

"Choose," my mom sing-songs.

I take a shuddering breath. "N-no."

She nods like my answer is exactly what she expected. "If you don't, I will kill them both. This is your chance for one of them to live."

As I look into Mateo's gray eyes, I feel like our twin-bond snaps back into place. I feel the pain, anguish, and regret I see in his orbs. It slams into me like a wrecking ball.

Unable to look at him any longer, I meet Gray's dark gaze. He nods, and I know he's telling me it's okay to kill him. There's understanding in his eyes, and it breaks my heart that this guy is willing to sacrifice himself.

Fuck, I've only just gotten to know him, yet he's in my heart. There's a bond between us, one I couldn't shake even if I wanted to.

"Choose, daughter." My mom's cold voice rings out again. "Now," she demands.

I look back at my brother and mouth, 'I forgive you.' Then I look at Gray, and mouth, 'I'm sorry.'

My heart breaks, the shattered pieces are jagged, and I can feel them cutting my insides. Tears make my eyes blurry, and my hand is shaking so hard it's difficult to hold the gun.

"Please," I beg, not caring about being strong. "Please don't make me do this. I'll do anything you want. Just... not this..." I want to keep begging, but hiccups steal my voice.

Mom laughs, and it's a hard and cruel sound that hurts my ears. "You'll do anything I want soon enough, daughter. This was your test. A chance for me to see if you were strong enough to one day be my equal, but you're not."

She isn't wrong. If she views what she's doing as being strong, I want to be so weak the wind can blow me away. I want no part in this sick game. Apart from... I want to be the one to end it.

While chanting those words over and over in my head, I lift the gun, aim, and pull the trigger.

Rocco

A scream from out in the club has us out of our seats before Tex has a chance to come barging in, and we nearly crash into him as we go to inspect what the fuck is happening now.

"Help!" The scream comes from the entrance, and my gun is in my hand in an instant as I quickly survey the area in search of Cara.

Where the fuck is she?

"It's Grayson!" Sasha comes charging in looking frantic, blood smeared across her palms. "Help him! Someone help him!"

I push past her, flying out the door before skidding to a stop at the body laying on the ground before us.

"Fuck." I hiss, momentarily stunned.

"The fuck!" Dante roars barging past, kicking me in motion.

"Gray!" I shout, dropping to my knees by the sixteen-year-old kid. Or who I think is Grayson.

"Gray!" Gunner's voice comes from behind us, and I hear Tex stop him.

"Hold back, kid. Let them check him."

Accessing the battered boy, I can see past the blood and swelling that it is Gray. It fucking is him.

"Who the fuck did this!" I roar as my eyes spot something sticking out of the pocket in his shirt.

"Call a fucking ambulance!" Dante calls to anyone who will listen as he kneels on Grayson's other side.

"Already on it." Baz informs him while I tug what looks like a photo from Gray's pocket.

"Fuck," I whisper as I wipe the blood smeared on it to see familiar gray eyes. "FUCK!" I roar, shooting to my feet.

"What is it?" Dante asks with urgency, snatching the photo from my hand.

"Where the fuck is Cara?!" I roar, pushing through the wall of people as I go back inside the club, in search of my wife. "CARA!"

"She's not in h-here." Rose cowers as my angry glare shoots her way. "S-she went out for a smoke b-before and never came back in."

"WHY THE FUCK DIDN'T ANYONE SAY ANY-THING?!"

"Rocco, man. Calm down." Dante's hand clasps my shoulder from behind, but I wrench myself away.

"Calm down? Are you fucking serious? My wife goes fucking missing, and no one thinks to go fucking looking for her or fuck, at least tell me?"

Sobs sound from nearby and I snarl at Rose's tear-stained face.

"There's a message on the back of the photo." Baz hurries to me and shows me the back.

IF YOU WANT YOUR PRECIOUS WIFE BACK THEN COME AND GET HER MOTHERFUCKER!

Warehouse 7 – Industrial Road.

"Ahhhhhhh!" I scream, turning and flipping the closest table over.

Pain slices through my chest like someone has cranked my chest cavity open and is attempting to pull my heart out.

I heave, anger controlling each fucking breath as I look down at the photo again.

Cara is in the middle of a few Reapers, her hair dripping, and her body barely covered as one Reaper grabs her fucking tit, and another Reaper is in the frozen motion of wanking, his cock angled toward my wife.

By Cara's feet are two people. One is her brother. He lies lifeless, a bullet wound right in the center of his forehead, his eyes open but they're nothing but cold pits of emptiness, and next to him, on her haunches, is Martina Rodríguez.

Smiling.

Fucking cunt!

I glance at Cara again and notice the gun in her hand by her side, and my fucking gut twists.

Did she kill her brother?

Even as I think it, I know it to be true by the look in her eyes.

She's done.

Not with life. Not that sort of done.

It's the sort of done when tolerating people, or being treated a certain way, is no longer possible.

She's the sort of done that her mom is in no way prepared for, and all I know is that I have to go to her, and make sure she finishes this. Today.

As the siren of the ambulance distracts everyone, I spin on my heel and go to the elevator. I rarely go down to the basement level. It's like a fucking bunker down there, and I prefer to see the motherfucking sky, but today, it holds what I need.

"Rocco," Cain calls, rushing to my side. "What are we doing?"

"I don't know about you, but I'm going to get my wife."

"I was hoping you would say something like that." He grins as my eyes dart to him.

Why is this fucking elevator taking so long to arrive?

"You don't have to risk your life, Cain. She's my wife. I can't ask you to risk yourself."

He scoffs. "You think she only belongs to you? My man, you are mistaken. Mi pequeño salvaje is mine too. She may not be my betrothed, but she's my family. And we fight for our family, no matter what."

"Exactly."

The voice comes from behind me, and I glance over my shoulder as the elevator doors open to see Dante, Baz, Munroe, Stretch, and Tex.

Fuck. My eyes burn. I can't cry in front of these fuckers... can I?

"Let's weapon up." Dante nods at me, stepping past and onto the elevator, and each of them do the same."

"Who's with Grayson?" I ask as I step in the elevator too and the doors close.

"Gunner and the Diamonds. They will stay with him and keep us posted." Dante advises and I nod, staring at the numbers as they descend to the basement where we load and strap as many guns, bullets and knives as we can onto our bodies before piling into two trucks and heading to the warehouse.

I drive like a crazy motherfucker through the streets, Cain holding on and laughing as he bounces in the seat like he's on a fucking ride.

"Take the next right." Baz directs, looking down at his phone map, trying to get us there quicker.

"Hold on," I hiss, giving them a warning as I yank the wheel and we slide in a loud screech around the corner.

"You're going to kill yourself before you even get there!" Dante's voice comes through the speaker, our open line still connected as him and Baz talk attack strategies.

"Nothing will stop me from getting to my wife!" I snap, and Cain claps.

"I like this version of you. I'd fuck you if I were gay." He admits, and I frown, shooting him a confused look. "You know what. I'd legit just fuck you, anyway. You're so sexy when you're angry." He purrs the last part and I shake my fucking head.

"Touch me and my wife will dice you up."

He bounces in his seat again. "Ohhhh she'll make it hurt so good."

"Left!" Baz barks, and again, I jerk on the wheel, the back end of my truck snaking out and nearly taking out a parked car.

"We are approaching from the north. You'll get there before us, but we won't be far. Just go in guns blazing. They are likely waiting," Dante informs.

"Do not kill Martina Rodríguez!" I yell, just having her name fall from my lips sending me into a red fucking rage. "Subdue her but leave her for Cara. Martina is *her* kill."

"Noted." Dante agrees and I relax a little.

That bitch is going to wish she was never fucking born.

"Industrial Road is your next left." Baz notifies me, and I nod, my hands gripping the wheel tighter as nervous energy pulses through me.

I need to get to Cara.

I need to keep her safe.

Our next left isn't as fucking violent as the others before it, finally turning onto the dark street and looking at the warehouse numbers.

"There it is!" Cain yells and points as he jigs around in his seat like he has fucking ants in his pants.

Killing the headlights and slowing the truck, I veer off the road and up the short driveway, bursting through the wire gates that were closed but not locked.

As soon as we are through, bullets start spraying my truck, and while Baz ducks in the back seat because that's the fucking smart thing to do, Cain lets out a war cry, puts the window down and starts firing back.

"You're gonna get yourself killed," I hiss, and he laughs.

"I am invincible!"

"Jesus Christ." Baz mutters from the back, as I slow the truck, looking for the entrance.

There's a small entrance door, and there's a garage type of roller door.

I choose the roller door.

"Hold on!" I yell, planting my foot down before my truck shoots forward toward the warehouse.

"Oh fuck." Baz hisses as Cain laughs manically.

I love my truck. I worked hard to earn money to get it. But it's expendable, and my wife isn't.

We all yell, vicious sounding roars right before we slam into the door, the hard body of my old truck stronger than the door, peeling it open like a can opener.

Coming to a bumpy abrupt stop as my truck slams into the back of a white van, we are thrown forward, and I brace for pain, but it never comes.

"Onward we ride!" Cain cries, shoving his door open and leaping from the truck even as he sprays bullets toward a group of men running in the other direction.

"Why the fuck did Dante leave that guy in charge?" Baz mutters and I chuckle.

"Don't be fooled by the craziness. He's the smartest man you'll ever meet, and always the guy you want watching your back." I check my gun and open my door too.

As gunfire pierces the air, a masculine whimper draws my attention to a stack of crates next to my truck, and with my gun raised, I round the stack to find a guy, probably not even in his twenties yet, curled in on himself, trying to hide.

I press the barrel of my gun to his head.

"Are you ready to die?" I ask him, and he stiffens, lifting his head from his arms to stare wide eyed at me. A quick glance down and I see he's wearing a leather vest. A cut. And the badge on it says Prospect.

His trembling body quivers, but the shake of his head is clear enough, so I kneel down to get eye level with him.

"You have two choices here. The first is, you can continue to support the Reapers and not cooperate with me, in which case, I will pull the trigger. Or, you can choose to live, tell me where the girl is that they brought in not long ago, and I'll let you go, but you have to leave this behind," I fist his cut, and his nostrils flare as he heaves in panicked breaths, "and choose a new fucking path in life."

"She-she's down in the b-basement level."

"Show me." I snarl and he balks.

"B-but you said if I t-tell you where she is t-that you'll let me go."

"I will let you go. Once I have my wife."

"Your w-wife?" His brows shoot high. "N-no one said s-she was married."

With my fist still in his cut, I drag him closer. Nose to nose.

"That's because you are taking orders from motherfuckers who only care about money. And even if she wasn't married, it still wouldn't be alright!" I scream the last part of my sentence in his face, and the smell of piss meets my nose.

"Get the fuck up and take me to her." I hiss, dragging him up before shoving him deeper into the warehouse.

As Cain covers us, Baz follows behind me, watching my back, as I force the kid to lead the way. He hurries along. Not wanting to drag it out, which I'm fucking grateful for, because every fucking second that I'm not with my wife, is a second too long that they are with Cara, possibly doing heinous things to her.

As we walk, Baz shoots anyone trying to come at us from behind, and I end about three Reapers on the first level, and another two on the lower level, before we reach the basement steps.

"They are down there." The kid trembles at the top of the steps, and for a moment, I feel fucking guilty for what I'm about to do.

Shooting Baz a look over my shoulder, I prepare to shut my morals down, knowing the only way I can get to Cara is by leaving them up here.

"I have to do what I have to do," I tell Baz, and his eyes dart to the kid before meeting mine again.

He nods. "I'll follow your lead."

Nodding, I turn my eyes to the stairs and suck in a deep breath before grabbing the boy by the scruff of his neck.

"Hey. What are you doing?" he cries, but I ignore it.

"Move." I demand, shoving him forward, but not letting go of him as we start our descent.

The kid whimpers as we hurry down the steps, and at the bottom, we turn into a room, and are immediately assaulted by gunfire.

Holding the kid in front of me, I use him as a shield, wrapping an arm around him as I point and shoot with my other hand. His body is peppered with bullets, and his limbs fall lifeless as I hold him up, moving further into the room as I shoot two of the Reapers, and Baz takes care of another two.

"Come back!" a woman screams in frustration as we move deeper in the room, her eyes trained on an open door in the back corner.

"They've run like cowards," I tell Martina, gaining her cold glare. "I hope you weren't paying them too much. It's a pity you won't be alive to ask for a refund."

"You son of a bitch!" she snarls, storming closer to me. "You've ruined everything!"

I chuckle dryly. "If you didn't want me showing up here, then why send the photo with the address on the back when you had Grayson dumped at our doorstep?"

Her brows shoot up. "What? There was an address on the back of the photo?"

This time it's my eyes that shoot up. "You didn't ask them to do that?"

"No," she hisses. "They were meant to dump the boy with the photo only, to show you that you lost."

"That's what you get for hiring thugs," Baz tells her, strolling past her to the door on the side wall and gesturing his head to it. "Is she in there?"

"Get the fuck away from there!" Martina cries, lunging for Baz, who raises a lazy brow and clocks her in the head with the butt of his gun, sending her crashing to the floor.

"Watch her," I tell Baz, marching past him as the gunfire above increases, and I know Dante and the others have arrived.

The heavy metal door is latched shut from this side, so I jimmy the lock until it pops free, and then heave the door open.

My breath catches as I come face to face with my wife, but by the dark expression she's wearing, I don't make an attempt to move into the room.

"Move."

Her tone is laced with dark intent, and I know the killer in her is here with me right now. The punisher.

Giving her a curt nod, I step aside, allowing her the space she needs, and her sinister gaze scans the area as she steps out of the room where her dead brother still lies in a pool of blood.

"Cara." Martina pleads. "You know I only did it because I love you. I just wanted the best for you."

Slowly stalking toward her mother, Cara scoffs. "What a crock of shit. You wanted me to make money for you. End of discussion. There's nothing more to it." As she moves closer, Martina tries to scurry backward, still on the floor. "There was never any love involved."

Holding her hand out, Cara demands. "Knife." Even while her eyes remain locked on her mom.

I unsheathe my knife, stepping up behind her and placing it in her open palm, and Martina starts to shriek.

"What are you doing?" She springs to her feet, but she has nowhere to go.

On one side Baz blocks her path, and I block the other. And since her daughter is directly in front of her and there's a wall at her back, she realizes she's trapped.

"Please, mija. Don't do this."

"I should have done this three years ago." Cara snarls before lunging forward and slamming her mom hard against the wall, the blade at her throat. "Julietta and Mateo were mercy killings. Because of what you put Julietta through, she wanted an end to her suffering, so I gave her that. I granted her wish. Let her leave this life on her terms." Cara knicks the skin at her mom's neck, making Martina hiss in a breath. "Mateo was different. His suffering was never going to end, so I put him out of his misery."

Cara pushes off her mom and slams the blade into her shoulder. Martina screams like a banshee, the noise echoing off the metal walls, blocking out the sounds of war from above.

"You and dad, however." Cara reefs the blade free, and Martina nearly collapses to the ground, but somehow manages to stay standing. "There is no mercy for you. You and he were, are, monsters. The absolute scum of the earth. There's nothing you can ever do to make up for the vile things you've done to me, to Mateo, to Julietta, to Rose..." She slams the blade into her mom's gut this time, and Martina collapses with a cry. Standing over her, Cara presses her bare foot to her mom's hand when she tries to reach for the handle of the knife protruding from her abdomen. "Or to the countless other girls you have abused over the years."

"C-Cara... p-please." Martina gargles in pain, but her daughter doesn't falter. Not even for a millisecond.

Dropping to her knees, Cara tugs the knife free, holding it up over her mom's face.

"Look at your blood. You're dying mom. Your life source is oozing out of you, and you're going to die here on this filthy floor of this shitty room, knowing you were betrayed by the men you hired for protection. How does that make you feel?"

Martina whimpers, and Cara shrugs. "Not that I care. I hope this is excruciating for you. I hope you suffer as you watch my face, knowing I'm the one who killed you, because you're nothing but a fucking oxygen thief."

"C-Ca—"

"Don't say my fucking name!" Cara roars, slamming the blade back into her mom's gut. "You are not fucking worthy!"

And then, as Martina watches the monster she created at work, my beautiful killer starts stabbing her mom over and over as she screams.

Blood sprays and splatters as Cara plunges the knife repeatedly into her mother's torso, before she moves to her face, her mom already gone, and she stabs her face until she's unrecognizable.

A rumble from above snaps me and Baz from our hypnotized state, and while he moves, gun raised to check the stairwell, I approach my wife like she's a wild lioness.

"Killer." I rasp from next to her, my voice snapping her attention to me, and I gesture my head to Baz. "We have to go, hermosa. I need to get you to safety."

With her chest heaving from her explosive assault on her mom, Cara slowly stands, knife still in hand and gives me a nod.

"We have to go." Baz calls out, and we hurry forward, as we step over the dead Reapers, and the kid that I sacrificed, and make our way back up the stairs.

All the action is still happening on ground level, so when we step out, we see a couple of Reapers with their backs to us, firing into the main space where I abandoned my truck.

With swift and fluid action, Baz shoots the two Reapers with precision, and we keep moving.

As we step out into the foray, a body slams into me, and we roll, crashing into the wall as Cara cries out.

"You fucking cunts! You have ruined everything!" The asshole snarls in my face as he presses his forearm to my throat. His brown eyes are wild, and his sparse beard is singed, and as I buck him off successfully, the fight turns to fists.

We roll around, grunting and punching, and I can't take my fucking eyes off him for a second to see where Cara is and if she's okay.

My fist lands a crunching blow into his nose, blood spraying out everywhere as he lurches away, and I see the patch on his vest says President, with the name Rusty underneath.

A cry from my left snaps my attention in time to see Cara in a fucking knife fight with a Reaper.

Pain explodes down my cheek before warm blood rushes over my skin.

Shocked, my gaze catches back onto the Reapers' President, and the shard of glass in his hand.

"Did you just fucking cut me?" I snarl and he grins.

"I fucking did. What the fuck are you gonna do about it?"

I lurch for him, copping another slash on my arm, but the shard tumbles from his hand as we thud to the ground, and I start laying blow after blow into him.

A loud explosion booms through the warehouse, throwing me off the Reaper, my hearing vanishing momentarily before it's replaced with yelling and fucking annoying ringing.

"Come on, let's go!" Dante's voice bounces off the walls as he pulls me up off the ground, but I try to pull out of his grip.

"Cara!" I yell, and Dante slaps my chest.

"Over here, man." When I turn to him, he points to a man running out of the warehouse carrying a woman. "Cain has her."

"Cara!" I yell, pushing past Dante as he and Baz run at my heels, and we manage to get outside right before the structure collapses in on my fucking truck.

"That was close." Baz mutters, and I want to agree, but my mind is on my wife.

Cain was carrying her.

Is she hurt?

"Cara!" I yell, needing to have my hands on her. See if she's fucking okay.

Did I fail to protect her?

Am I even worthy of being her husband if I can't fucking do that?

"Mi rey!"

Her voice, so strong and determined, snaps my head to the side, to see her running for me.

"My queen!" I yell back, closing the distance in time to catch her as she leaps on me and wraps her legs around my waist.

Our lips slam together, our fingers claw each other like we can't get close enough.

"Nothing to see here." Cain chuckles as he walks by, and we both grin against each other's lips.

"Fuck. I thought I'd lost you." I admit against her lips, and she squeezes me tighter.

"Nothing on this earth can keep me away from you," she mumbles back before deepening the kiss.

Our tongues clash with want, the metallic salt of blood mixed in as our bodies stay glued together, and I wish there was no one around right now so I could strip my wife bare and claim her right fucking here.

"They got away." Munroe pants from nearby, and I break the kiss to glance at Dante and Baz talking with the men.

"How many got away? Do we know?" Dante asks and Stretch answers as he swipes the sweat from his brow.

"There were at least six. Maybe eight. The rest are dead."

"Did their President get away?" I ask, stepping toward their huddle while I carry Cara. I'm not fucking letting her go. It's okay, though, because she makes no move to get down, and I feel her gaze on me as I await a response.

"Yeah it looked like they were protecting him as they went. They had a truck, and some motorcycles stashed in the tree line at the back of the yard." Munroe offers and Dante curses.

"It would have been an end to our MC problem if we had killed them all."

"Until the next club tries to bid for the territory." Baz points out and Dante nods.

"You're right. There's still a gap there that needs to be filled."

Turning his eyes to me I give him a nod.

"I'm still prepared to do that. Especially with this one by my side." I give Cara's ass a squeeze but then realize it's hanging out the bottom of that skimpy bit of fabric her mother had her dressed in. "Shit." I try to cover her and the guys chuckle before Dante tears off his shirt and tosses it at us, and I make quick work of tugging it over her head and helping her into it, covering her up better.

"Does that mean Cara will be your Old Lady or whatever it is a President of an MC calls their woman?" Cain asks and Cara's eyes go wide.

She's shaking her head before I can even respond.

"No fucking way am I being an Old Lady. I'm your fucking wife."

The men laugh and I grin, looking into her fiery gray eyes.

"Of course, Killer. I wouldn't want it any other way."

She grips my jaw roughly and bares her teeth. "I'm glad we are on the same page."

I chuckle and try to kiss her, but she pulls back, still glaring.

"Who did that to your face?"

My brows shoot up, and like she's flipped a switch, I feel the throbbing pain that runs down my face.

"The Reapers' President."

I tell her, and her brows knit.

"I'm not sure if I should thank him or sever his dick."

"What?" I laugh and I watch as her eyes travel the length of the gash on my face. "Why would you thank him?"

"Well, it looks kinda badass." She grins wickedly and leans in closer, "It's kinda making me wet."

I growl low, squeezing her ass again and grinding my hard length between her legs to let her know I'm right there with her.

"I think it's very befitting of a President of a motorcycle club." She grins and my brows shoot up.

"How do you know?"

She rolls her eyes. "I'm not stupid. I have ears. I listen, and I'm pretty sure that's what you and them," she gestures her head back toward Dante and the others who are still talking shop, "were talking about."

"So you're on board with it?" I ask, hope filling my gut at the prospect of this actually working.

"Hell yes. But I do hope you will involve me in more than just being the pussy you go home to at night. If you do this, I want to do it with you. We have the opportunity to create something great. Fill a gap for more than one reason."

I smile down at my fierce wife, "I meant what I said before. I want you by my side, Cara. I can't do this without you."

She grins and agrees, "I'll be right there with you."

"Fuck." I press my forehead to hers, my eyes locked onto her gray pools as I squeeze her impossibly close. "I fucking love you."

Those gray eyes, normally so confident, and well, angry, soften as they turn glassy. "I love you too, mi rey."

"You do?" I ask as my heart does a fucking triple somersault in my chest.

"Yes. I really do."

Our lips slam together again, claiming each other in the wake of our declarations, and I know without a doubt that although there's a tough road ahead of us, we will navigate it together and come out the other side so much fucking stronger.

Cara

1.5 years later

Life is a strange and unpredictable thing. It's wild and raw. It's tough and infuriatingly imperfect—and for the first time in my twenty something years, I am loving every minute of it.

Since killing my mom, I've felt like a weight has been lifted off my shoulders. My smiles and laughs are genuine. I no longer have nightmares, and I know I've found the place I belong. Not only am I the motherfucking queen to my king, but I feel like I've found a new family with the people closest to Rocco.

Gray and Gunner have become great friends, and, at times, despite only being three years younger than me, almost like fucking pseudo kids. Especially the former who's really pulled himself together, but is still way too cocky for his own good. Fuck, he struts around like everyone is here for his entertainment. At least he tries. And when I can be bothered, I like to remind him of his place and the fact I can still kick his ass.

Since I don't want to stroke his ego, I never tell him that it's getting harder to beat him when we spar. If it wasn't for Cain and Rocco training me, I wouldn't stand a chance. But so far, so good.

Gunner is so different. While he's as cocky as his pal, he's more shy but also genuinely wants to make people happy. It's one of the reasons I love seeing him with Rose, who hangs on his every word, practically worshiping him in silence.

"Are you ready?" Rocco asks, taking my hand and pulling me to my feet.

I pout and frown. "Now? I almost beat Gunner—"

"Like fuck you did," Gunner laughs, his eyes crinkling. "I think you meant to say you almost beat Gray."

Gunner quickly ducks out of the way as Gray tries to slap the back of his pal's head.

Rose lets out an exasperated sigh. "I almost have you all beat, so shut up." Then she looks up at me. "If you leave, do I get your chips?"

"Nuh-uh," Gunner says, shaking his head. "That's fucking cheating."

Laughing, I follow Rocco, and we're almost at the door when I look over my shoulder and yell, "Rose can have my chips and my Royal Flush."

Ignoring the curses and giggles, I lean against Rocco, who wraps his arm around my shoulders.

"Nervous?" he asks.

The scar on his face moves every time he speaks, and I don't mind saying it's sexy as fuck. Though it's been a year and a half, I'm still mesmerized by it. Or more accurately, knowing he suffered that to set me free, that's the real turn on.

"Why would I be nervous?" I ask. "It's just a meeting."

He chuckles. "With Dante, Baz, and Cain."

Yeah, when he puts it like that, I'm not exactly thrilled. Don't get me wrong, I adore Cain, and I always will. Baz and Dante are another story, though. They're nice enough, but every time they're around, it's like their presence sucks all the air from the room. Without them even uttering a word, you know you're looking at people who are willing to go to great lengths to get what they want.

Luckily, what they want is justice. They just prefer to dole it out themselves rather than put their trust in a broken justice system. I swear, there's a story there I haven't heard yet.

"I'll be fine," I say.

We walk the rest of the way to Dante's office in silence. When we get there, Rocco holds the door open and ushers me inside first. It's such a small gesture, yet it makes my heart fucking swell.

"Such a gentleman," I teasingly whisper. Then I wave at Cain. "Hi loco."

He grins and lights up a cigarette. "Mi pequeño salvaje," he greets. "Are you ready to leave Rocco and run away with me yet?"

I laugh and Rocco lets out a growl that's anything but playful. "I told you to fucking stop that."

Cain shrugs. "And I told you I wouldn't."

Baz gives me a nod. "Cara." That's the extent of his greeting.

"Can we get started? I have shit I need to do so I can get back to the UK," Dante gripes.

As I take a seat next to Rocco, Cain turns to Dante. "I still don't know what the hell is wrong with the Christmas presents I bought for the girls. They'll need to learn to defend themselves eventually, and I even bought the knives in girly colors and had them engraved."

Dante pinches the bridge of his nose, while Baz coughs to hide his laugh.

I cock my eyebrow at Cain because, as far as I know, the girls are only kids. So I can see how knives might not be appropriate.

But I'm thankful that Cain was interrupting the awkward hellos. Not that I'd ever admit it out loud, but I think I might be on Baz's and Dante's shit lists.

The first time I met them wasn't the day we killed my mom, that's just when I found out who they really are. During my three years in lockup, I saw them at least four times a year. Each time, they wanted me to say my killing was under duress, which I promptly refused.

I'm not sure why, but it was important to me that everyone knew I stood by my action, and I might have used colorful language and made a few suggestions of where they could shove their scheming.

If I'd known who the two men were, I might have held back on the insults. Then again, it's possible I wouldn't have. Even when I didn't know their names and places in the Santa Cruz criminal world, I knew they were somebody. Especially since they were allowed to show up with presents that the guards didn't search for, and we were always alone with no cameras on.

"Let's get down to it," Baz says, looking straight at Dante. "Call the fucking vote."

Dante turns his head to Rocco. "You're sure? It's not too late to change your mind."

I place my hand on Rocco's thigh and squeeze, silently giving him my support. This is the first meeting I'm attending, and he made it clear I'm only here because he wants me to be a part of it, which I get.

"I'm sure," Rocco says. "So let's vote."

"All those in favor of Rocco expanding the Diamond Crew by creating an MC to take over here in Santa Cruz."

Baz, Dante, and Rocco immediately say yes. The only one not speaking up is Cain. He leans back in his chair, crossing his arms over his chest.

"No."

I can't help laughing at how predictable that is.

"W-what?" Rocco sputters. "Why the fuck not?"

For fuck's sake, sometimes my husband really is fucking clueless.

"It has to be unanimous," Dante says. "So let's hear your misgivings."

Cain just shrugs. "I don't want to."

And there it is, the thing these men are too stupid to see. Cain doesn't want to lose Rocco, and I'm apparently the only one who saw it coming a mile away.

I squeeze Rocco's thigh harder and murmur, "Talk to him."

My husband looks quizzically at me, but I'm not going to spell it out for him. If he wants this, he needs to convince Cain. If he can't, how the hell can he lead an MC?

It's not like I have doubts. I know Rocco can do it, just as I know he's the right man for the job. But that doesn't mean he can skate through it. As a leader, he should have known Cain was going to object—and more importantly, why.

"What the fuck, Cain?" Rocco thunders, sounding equal parts confused and annoyed. "What exactly is your problem?"

I bite down on my lip and run my hand up Rocco's thigh, very deliberately grazing his junk. If he wasn't wearing jeans, I might even have had some fun here at the table. But alas, that's not happening.

Cain slaps his hands onto the table and stands so abruptly his chair falls over. "I said I don't want to. And we all know I don't do anything unless I feel like it."

As Rocco leaps to his feet as well, Baz and Dante snicker, and I roll my eyes because that's both the truth and a lie all in one. Cain has a knack for finding a reason to want something, and as he says, if he doesn't, then he... well, then that's just not happening.

Like when Rose, Alana, Gray, and Gunner made a bet with him to dye his hair green and have it like that for a job. If Cain hadn't wanted that, it wouldn't have happened. The crazy fucker had a lot of fun with it, though.

When Rocco hurls an insult across the table and Cain just shrugs it off, I can't keep my mouth shut any longer.

"Have you tried asking him nicely?" I ask Rocco as I study my nails. "Without swearing?"

Baz chuckles. "I'd pay good money to see that."

Dante grins at his pal. "I have a feeling Cara's about to give us the show for fucking free."

As I look at them, they both wink and smile in my direction. Huh, okay, so maybe I'm not on their shit lists after all.

Rocco takes a deep breath and runs a hand down his face. The tips of his fingers almost caress the scar, and my pussy throbs.

"Why don't you want to?" he asks. This time he sounds genuinely perplexed.

Cain throws his hands up in the air. "Everyone is fucking leaving. Dante's fucking playing full-time nanny across the big ocean, and now you want to tinker with bikes. No."

And there's part of the reason Cain's refused any involvement and leaves the room whenever Rocco talks about the MC.

Dante nods thoughtfully. "That's not the entire reason."

"Of course not," Rocco barks. "What else?"

"You're bloody blind," Baz says with an exasperated sigh, and I nod in agreement.

Looking at Cain, I say, "You're running the Diamond Crew when Dante isn't around, right?"

He nods.

"And if Rocco's leading the MC you two will need to work on your communication issues."

Both Dante and Baz murmur their agreement, and Dante reminds us once again that he has things to do. Something with needing to find a specific pair of shoes or Caitlin will never forgive him. Brat.

"Cain," Dante prompts, but his second in command just shakes his head.

Having had enough, I speak up. "Rocco, why the hell did you never ask Cain to join you?"

My husband looks at me like I've grown a second head. "Because Dante would fucking kill me."

"He could try," I mutter as I palm the knife strapped to my thigh. Then I look up at Rocco. "You could still ask and let it be Cain's choice."

"Is that what this is about?" Rocco asks Cain. "You want a fucking invitation?"

Men!

When Cain just shrugs looking at Rocco, like he wants to fucking pummel him, I sigh. "Am I going to run the MC with you if you get their approval?" I ask as I gesture between the other three.

"Of course," Rocco answers immediately.

"Cain." I wait until he looks at me. "Do you want to join the MC with us?"

He beams at me. "Why, Cara, thank you so much for asking. But no. I have no interest in riding bikes and getting oil all over my clothes."

I open my mouth, ready to give Cain a smart ass reply, but Dante beats me to it. "Can we do another vote now?"

Once Rocco and Cain are seated, Dante calls for another vote. Like before, he and Baz are quick to say yes.

"Fine," Cain mumbles, still sounding put out. "But I want a fucking open invitation."

"That was never a fucking question you idiot," Rocco retorts. "You're not getting rid of us that easily."

Though he does his best to hide it, Cain looks relieved.

Now that Rocco and I officially have the Diamond Crew's blessing, we leave and head back to our beach shack.

"Are you ever going to let me ride that thing?" I ask Rocco when I get off his bike.

The look of horror on his face is priceless, and I still can't tell if it's real or not.

"Absolutely not. You'd ruin her within seconds."

I cock my brow. "Her? You're telling me the bike is a she?"

He grins and takes my hand as we walk into our house.

"Home sweet home," I call out.

It's hard to believe how much I love this place now, but I can't imagine living anywhere else. I know that I have to once we get the MC going, but I'm secretly hoping it isn't anytime soon. I'm not ready to share what we have here with other people.

"Don't get too comfortable," Rocco says as he walks into the bathroom and starts running the tap while picking up his razor.

We have another job tonight, and at the mere mention of it, I'm itching to dole out punishment to the fuckers. These aren't the main players, so Rocco says it's going to be a quick in and out. I say the bastards deserve to scream for hours.

I walk over to the bathroom and lean against the door frame. "I know," I say.

Looking around, I'm again reminded of the weeks Rocco slaved away. He pulled out all the tiles and redid the entire floor with vinyl.

If that doesn't say love, I don't know what does.

"We have time to get dirty first." Wiggling my eyebrows, I slowly walk backward. "Unless you can't catch me."

Rocco drops his razor and lets out a playful growl that goes straight to my clit. "You better run fucking fast, Killer."

I squeal and spin around, running for the back door. But before I can reach it, Rocco wraps his arm around me and hauls me back against his hard body.

"Finders keepers," he rasps.

Not in the mood to delay my gratification by fighting him, I arch my back and glide my ass over his cock. He growls and moves his hand to my bare thigh, sliding it up under my skirt.

He chuckles as he skims the knife. "I should have known you had it hidden here." Then he continues, trailing his fingers up my inner thigh so slow I can barely stand it.

"Hurry up," I hiss. "I want you inside me."

The moment I show my impatience, Rocco stops moving. "Beg me," he demands.

I shake my head.

"That's okay," he rasps. "I can wait."

It's frustratingly true. Rocco is way too patient for my liking, especially when it comes to denying me. Last year there was a time I thought I could outwait him, but after two days I admitted defeat and begged him to finally let me come. While it was the best orgasm I've ever had, I'm not sure it was worth it.

"But I can't," I retort. I bite down on my lip to stop myself from letting my temper get the better of me. "Please touch me again, mi rey."

Rocco groans and thrusts his cock against my ass before pulling me into the living room, where he immediately sits down on the couch.

"Strip for me, Killer."

The heat in his eyes has me gasping, and wetness spreads between my folds. Fuck, how can he turn me on with his look alone?

When I nod, he pulls his phone out of his back pocket and puts some music on. As the sensual tones reach my ears, I sway my hips to the beat.

The leather crop top I'm wearing has a zipper between my tits, and I reach for it. Slowly lowering it until my breasts spill out.

"No bra," Rocco rasps, licking his lips as he undoes his jeans.

I'm so transfixed by watching him lift his ass and pull his pants and boxers down that I forget to breathe. His cock juts out proudly from his body, bobbing as he pulls his shirt over his head.

"Fuck," I breathe when he stands completely naked in front of me.

"Not yet," he smarts, sitting back down. He wraps his hand around his length, stroking it slowly. "And not at all if you keep me waiting." His husky tone causes a shiver to work its way down my spine.

I close my eyes, centering myself as I become one with the music. I palm my tits, pinching the nipples before sliding my hands down my flat stomach, all the way to my skirt. Rocco's eyes stay on mine as I unfasten the skirt, letting it pool at my feet.

After stepping out of the fabric, I turn around so my back's to Rocco. I bend all the way until my palms meet the floor. Then I pick up the skirt, doing it slower than I need to so I can taunt him with the view.

"Keep the boots on," Rocco rasps. He loves my thigh-high stiletto boots almost as much as I do.

I throw the skirt to the side and drop to my haunches. My hands go to the soft globes of my ass, and I spread them as the sound of Rocco jerking off becomes louder.

"Mi rey," I moan. "Come play with me."

I barely have time to breathe before he's behind me, wrapping my long hair around his fist.

"Get on all fours. Now."

Moving while he holds my hair like that isn't easy, but I manage. And I'm rewarded with his fingers sliding between my folds.

"Rocco!" I cry out as he moves two digits inside me.

He picks up the pace, fucking me so good with his fingers. As he curls them inside me, I begin to shake, unable to hold back.

"Come on my fucking hand, Killer," he demands, and I do.

As the orgasm tears through me, Rocco replaces his fingers with his cock, sheathing himself in one, hard thrust.

I'm fucking soaring. Instead of coming down from my orgasm, it feels like his movements build on it. I move one hand between my legs, eagerly finding and rolling my clit.

Rocco moves his free hand to my shoulder, holding me in place as he fucks me with long, hard strokes. He pulls almost out before slamming back inside me.

"Your pussy feels so fucking good, Killer," he groans. He pulls on my hair and uses the other hand to pull me up so my back is to his front and I'm almost sitting in his lap. "Ride me until your pussy squeezes the cum from me."

My breath hitches and I begin to move. Rocco nuzzles against the crook of my neck, nibbling and licking the skin. My body is hot, and I'm covered in a sheen of sweat.

I'm close, so fucking close I can practically taste it. I cry out his name over and over, until I come again, and my pussy squeezes him.

"That's it, Killer," he growls. "Cara... so... oh fuck."

My legs turn to jelly and I can barely stay in place as he comes deep inside me. Rocco turns my head to the side, and I eagerly kiss him when our lips are only a breath apart. Unlike our fucking, the kiss is soft, his tongue caressing mine with lazy strokes.

Without breaking the kiss, he lifts me up and cradles me against his chest as he takes us into the bathroom. I cling to him as he begins to fill the tub.

"I love getting dirty with you before we clean up," I giggle, feeling so happy I don't know how I'm containing it.

Rocco chuckles and puts me down. "And I love seeing you punish people, which you'll miss out on if we don't hurry up."

"Can't wait," I say enthusiastically.

"Mi castigadora," Rocco rasps, and I raise my brows in surprise at him using Spanish words I haven't taught him.

Especially that one since it means 'my punisher'.

"Tu castigadora," I agree.

Your punisher.

Rocco

1.5 years later

My palms are clammy as I grip the handlebars of my bike. My second love. She's a fucking beauty. Tough as all hell, and fuck, I think the thing I like about her the most is how Cara looks at me when I pull up on it. I hope that look never dies from her eyes.

As me and the guys ride, my heart thrashes in my chest for what I'm about to do.

I glance to my left to see Gray on his bike, and a little behind him is Gunner. The first thing those two did when they had the money was buy a bike, and for now, it works as a chick magnet, but they know that once the club is officially formed, that shit needs to end. In fact, they have both shown great dedication in helping me, and I know having them in the club will be a huge benefit.

Aside from their mad killing skills, which Cain and Dante have allowed since Gray and Gunner turned eighteen, they are like family to me. And to Cara.

Behind them, is Tex, with an excited Cain snuggled up behind him, singing in his ear something about motorbikes and dicks getting the chicks.

Yet another Cain special, conjured up by his unique brain.

Behind Tex are the Long twins. They are our newest additions, joining our fold about six months ago. Nearly identical in looks, the only thing that isn't is the eye patch Slayer wears, like a scary fucking pirate. They both resemble angels of death if you ask me, with their longish black hair, black beards and well, you guessed it, fucking black clothes as well.

Just like you should never judge a book by its cover, their hard exterior, and first impression is a contradiction to their teddy bear demeanor once they are comfortable around you. Of course, they are lethal fucking killers, so approaching with caution is always advised.

Lastly, following in a van, are Stretch and Munroe. I can always rely on them, and they too have shown great dedication in creating a new MC for the Santa Cruz area.

And where are the Reapers? The ones that got away?

Well, they are still around, making themselves known in a tornado of chaos whenever they pass through as they slowly rebuild their club.

They haven't come at us in retaliation yet, but they will. It's only a matter of time.

"Are you ready for this?" Gray yells over the roar of our bikes as we approach the Santa Cruz Wharf, and I fucking grin, mostly reading his lips than hearing his words.

"Am I ever."

Grayson's chuckle fades into the rumbles of our bikes as we slow and make our way up the wharf, the setting sun starting to cast an orange glow across the sky. Any peace and serenity locals just had has vanished as our bikes idle up the strip, and they turn their sights on us to see what we are doing.

We go for daily rides, weaning the community onto our presence. We may not wear a patch or colors yet, but they know who we are.

The wharf is long, but I can see the bend in it up ahead, and I know what lies beyond it, waiting for me.

Cara.

Some local kids run alongside us in front of the shops and restaurants, waving, while a bunch of barely eighteen-year-old girls huddle together, pointing and giggling at Gray and Gunner as we pass.

Rounding the bend, I hear music startup behind us, and I grin, knowing Munroe is holding a speaker out the window of the van. All of Me by John Legend fills the air, and my eyes land on a confused Cara as she stares at us in the middle of the roundabout section up ahead.

Next to her, knowing and giddy, are Sasha, Alana and Rose as they take out zip-loc bags of flower petals and start sprinkling the asphalt around Cara's feet.

"That was my idea." Gray chuckles, and I throw my head back, laughing.

"Why doesn't that surprise me."

Reaching our destination, Stretch pulls the van over while Munroe keeps the music playing, and me and the others ride in circles around Cara.

"What is going on?!" she calls over the noise, but no one answers her.

After a few laps around her, I point sternly. "Stay right there."

Her brows shoot up, but she stays put as we park our bikes off to the side, cutting our engines.

"Would someone tell me what's going on?" Cara giggles in wonder as Alana and Rose dance around her, while Sasha takes photos on her phone.

"Thy highness is getting antsy," Cain sing-songs as we dismount our bikes, before we reach into our saddlebags and pull out a single red Victor Hugo rose each.

"You ready, big guy?" Munroe asks as he and Stretch join us.

"Who the fuck are you calling big guy?" I smirk, looking up at his towering height and he smirks back.

"I guess I am bigger than everyone... in every department."

Gray scoffs as he bumps past him. "Your cock is not bigger than mine."

"Neither's his fucking ego." Stretch laughs and we all join in. Even Gray.

"Okay, guys. You know what to do," I tell them, facing my wife who looks like she's getting impatient.

They all nod and clap me on the shoulder, except for Cain, he slaps a kiss on my cheek, which I'm still wiping off as they fall into a single line in front of me. Gray first, then Gunner, Cain, Tex, Slasher, Slayer, Stretch and finally Munroe. And then there's me.

"What?" Cara giggles, and I peek around Munroe's hulking frame to see Gray bowing to her before he hands her his rose. "What is the rose for?"

"Just go with it." Gray suggests before Gunner does an awkward bow and wave, offering her his rose, before dashing to the side like Cara might attack at any moment.

I mean. She might, since no one is telling her anything.

One by one, each man gives Cara a rose, and it doesn't surprise me when Cain holds his junk and does a spin on the spot worthy of Michael Jackson before thrusting his hips at my fucking wife.

Give me fucking strength.

The closer I step toward my wife, the more nervous I get. What if she thinks this is dumb?

Without another second to prepare myself, Munroe steps to the side and I find myself a couple of steps away from the reason we are here.

"Oh my god, Rochus King, if you don't tell me what's going on right now, I will... will—"

"Will what?" I grin, and she shakes her head, her smile the biggest I've ever seen it.

"I don't know. I hadn't thought that far, but I'm pretty sure it will involve a whip."

"I'll hold you to that, Killer." I promise, taking the last step to close the distance.

Around us, a crowd has gathered, but I ignore them, ignore our friends, our family, and focus entirely on the woman I love.

Reaching out, I hand her the red rose, and she takes it, smiling as she places it in the cradle of her arms on top of the other ones.

Then I drop to one knee.

Her brows knit together, and she looks up briefly, her gaze darting to her friends before coming back to me.

That's when I hold up the small box, crack the lid and reveal the ring. The new ring.

"Rocco," she gasps, her eyes turning glassy as her gaze darts from mine to the ring, and back.

"I know we are technically already married, but I never got to do it the right way. The way you deserve." I swallow the thick lump forming in my throat as Alana steps in and silently takes the bunch of roses from Cara's hold. "Cara. Mi reina. Mi castigadora. Will you do me the honor of re-marrying me?"

A tear spills from Cara's eye, the same one that is marked with the teardrop tattoo, before she nods quickly and lunges for me.

"Yes!"

As I catch her, rising to my feet to claim her lips in a searing kiss, our friends cheer around us, as well as some of the gathered crowd.

Somehow, Cara ends up in my arms, her legs wound around my waist, while she shows me with her lips and tongue how she feels in this moment we share.

When we finally come up for air, we pull apart to see the orange glow of the sunset painting our surroundings, and Gray and Gunner dancing around with Rose and Alana, while Sasha keeps taking photos.

"Did you have any idea?" I ask Cara, and I refocus on her, and she beams, shaking her head.

"None whatsoever. How did the girls keep it a secret?"

I chuckle. "I actually don't know, because it's something we all worked on for a couple of weeks, to pay the right people to keep most of the cars off the wharf."

"Really?" she asks, her dark brows shooting up. "And no one complained about that?"

I shrug. "No one that wasn't easily persuaded."

She giggles and I take the ring out of the box, tugging the old one off her finger, and slipping the new one on.

"So, are we really going to get re-married? Like a wedding ceremony and everything?"

I nod. "Fuck yes. I won't have the day your dad sold you to me as your memory of our wedding. I want you to know I'm marrying you because I love you, and no other woman on this earth will ever walk beside me, than you."

"Well, shit," Cara whispers, emotions getting the better of her. "I really want that too."

"Then let's do it, Killer. Let's get married the way you deserve."

Her smile holds more beauty than a million sunsets in that moment, and as we kiss each other some more, I feel truly excited for our future.

We return to Dirty Diamonds by the time it's completely dark, where everyone celebrates our engagement. Our real engagement despite being married for over six years. And sometime after midnight, Cara and I sneak away to our little house on the water, to get lost in each other.

I know the moment we walk through the door that tonight is my night to submit, something I haven't done since last month when I got a vasectomy. I did that for us since we both agreed we never wanted to be parents. Then again, according to my killer, we'll have our hands full with training and wrangling bikers and girls, so maybe we are parents in a different way.

I will admit, my dominance since then has been about proving my manhood, something she's teased me about, but she isn't holding back anymore.

"Everything off and bend over the bed."

Fuck. I'm instantly hard from her husky demanding tone, and the anticipation of what she has in store for me.

I don't fucking mess around, stripping my clothes as she does the same.

"I thought of a name for the club," I tell her, and our eyes meet across the room as we watch each other for a moment before she nods and points to the bed.

"I said bend over."

I smirk.

Fuck, I love it when she bosses me around like this. I never thought I'd get so comfortable with it. Giving my control over, especially after what happened to me as a kid. But I trust Cara. She makes me feel safe, and while we are in this role, her the dominant and me the submissive, I don't really have to think or worry about anything. She carries that weight for me, makes all the decisions, and I just need to let myself feel.

Moving to the end of the bed, I bend over, parting my legs wide as I press my cheek to the sheets and look at her from the side.

"Tell me the name." She demands, moving to the drawer and rummaging through it.

"The Cruz Kings MC." I tell her, watching for her reaction.

She stops rummaging, glancing up in thought, and then nods. "I like that."

"You do?"

"Hell, yes." She spins around holding a rather large dildo. "It's better than the Santa Cruz Serpents, or the Santa Cruz Devils. They sound more like a basketball team."

I chuckle, already knowing she didn't like those two ideas I came up with a while ago.

"I think we have a winner then." I beam, and she nods, slapping the tip of the dildo into the palm of her hand.

"I think you're right. Have you put any more thought into my proposal?"

I gulp as she holds up the girthy object and squeezes a generous amount of lube on it, before sitting it on top of the drawers.

"I have, but I just need to clarify that your punishments won't be sexual."

She rolls her eyes at me. It's a topic we have discussed on numerous occasions over the last eighteen months since the vote for the club happened. I knew when she came to me with the idea, wanting to play the role as club punisher, that it would be nothing sexual. She has grown into a brutal killer after all. But still, I like to torment her a little. It makes her a little crazy and in turn, she fucks me harder.

"I know what you're doing, and it's totally working. But are you sure you can handle this tonight?" She points to the large dildo glistening with lube as she puts on the strap-on harness.

"Fuck yes." I pant, my ass winking and my dick jerking at the thought of being punished by that thing. "No foreplay, please."

Her brows shoot up. "But foreplay will make it hurt less."

"Maybe it's the pain I'm seeking tonight." I growl and her brows lower again.

"Fine, but don't push yourself too far. Say the damn safe word if you need it."

Nodding, I give my ass a wiggle as I recite the safe word in my head. Bubblegum.

I haven't needed to use it yet.

"So, do we have a deal then about me being the club punisher?" Cara asks.

"Yes." I rasp. "As well as the Mama thing we spoke about."

Moving up behind me, Cara slaps my ass hard, and I hiss in a breath even as my body ignites with arousal.

"I will be the best Mama those women ever had." She declares as a stream of lube is squeezed over my ass, running down the crack, and coating my balls.

My eyes fall to the drawers to notice the dildo no longer there, and I know she's doing the final steps to get that beast of a thing into place, ready to fuck me with it.

Over the past few years, we have researched the dynamics of an MC, plus what and how we want ours to be. There are no steadfast rules that it has to all be the same, but as we researched, we have started a bible of rules, which we add to on occasion.

Cara is very adamant that if we have women in the club, for the men's enjoyment, that we take in women who truly need a family, and that they will be cared for. Not abused.

I couldn't agree more.

"Are you ready?" Cara asks as she runs the tip of the dildo between my cheeks. I can't fucking help it, I push back, fucking hungry to feel her dominate me. To stretch me and fill me in such a way I can't fucking think straight.

"Yes, mi castigadora."

"Open wide."

Her husky tone makes it easy for me to obey, and I relax my ass as she pushes the dildo inside me.

"Fuck." I hiss, loving the pain of it, and the way pleasure follows.

"That's it." Her claw-like nails dig into my hips as she pushes forward. "Take it all."

I moan, letting my lids fall shut as she claims me, her hand sliding around the front to wrap around my dick.

"Oh, mi rey, you're so hard for me."

She squeezes her fist around me, tighter and tighter until it starts to hurt, "now let's see how long you can keep your seed in."

She starts thrusting then, her grip tight on my cock as she uses her free hand to jiggle my balls.

Fuck. I'm not going to last.

She knows my body too fucking well.

Knows exactly how to make me bend to her will.

But fuck, I love that. I love how she claims me, and I feel no embarrassment. No guilt. Just unbridled ecstasy.

Thrust after thrust my wife pounds into my ass, and just when I think I'm going to lose my load, she releases my dick, slaps my ass, and demands, "Roll over!"

I move quickly, nervous about this part, but willing to do it because it's something we've been working on. Me watching her as she fucks me.

"Legs up. Hold behind your knees, nice and wide."

As much as I feel a little nervous about her watching my face when she takes me like this, I soon forget because I also get to watch her face, and fuck, her cheeks are rosy, her pupils blown, and her dark hair pulled into a high pony.

"I want you to come while I watch you," she rasps and I nod, watching as she lines up the big cock, and sinks inside me again.

This position hits differently, and I know it won't be long until I blow.

With her hand tight around my cock again, Cara fucks my ass, her eyes trained on mine, her demeanour radiating dominance.

"You're close, aren't you?" she asks, her nostrils flaring, a telltale sign that she is extremely aroused too and is holding herself back.

"Yes. I'm ready when you let me."

She smiles wickedly. "I should punish you for keeping the proposal a secret."

"Fine. Punish me. But I'm not sorry. It was fucking perfect."

She growls like a tigress and slaps the side of my ass as she pounds faster, her hold on my dick loosening, and she starts to jerk it.

"Fine. I'm only letting you get away with it because it really was perfect." She agrees, moving faster, harder, with both her thrusts and her hand.

"I'm gonna—"

My words lock up as my body does before it detonates in an explosion, cum shooting from my dick as I shatter around the dildo and in her hand.

"That was also perfect." Cara beams, slowly kneading my dick, milking every last drop of cum from it, creating a puddle on my stomach.

"Fuck, Cara. I'll never get enough of you." I admit, and she nods, like she already fucking knows that.

Slowly, she slips the beastly silicone thing from my ass, before climbing up on the bed and standing over me.

"I fucking like this view," I tell her and she waggles her brows as she unfastens the strap-on harness before letting it fall to the bed next to me.

"You mean, this view?" she asks, parting her legs wider and spreading her folds with her fingers.

I growl.

My hands grip the backs of her calves, and she raises a brow.

"Don't forget who's in charge here."

I chuckle. "Then make me suffer."

With a sinister look, she releases her folds and cups her breasts, flicking her thumbs over her nipples. "Oh, I will."

I already know what's coming, and I'm fucking pumped for it. I love it when Cara unleashes herself on me. Gets herself off in a way that has little control.

She moves up the bed, lowering to her knees over my head, and sits on my face.

"Tongue out, and you breathe when I say you can breathe."

I give her a thumbs up, because I can't fucking talk, or breathe, but I've become a master at holding my breath while she fucks my face over the last few years.

I watch her over me, the way her abs coil as she grinds herself on my face. The way she pinches her nipples, and pulls her own hair, using me to get off.

Occasionally, she lets me breathe, and I know from experience it will only be a short breath, so I take in as much air as

I can before she's smothering me again, to the point I nearly pass out.

It's when she braces her hands on the headboard and starts mashing her cunt over my lips, tongue and nose that I know she's close, and moments later she cries out as her juices flow.

I lap at her, desperate to lick up every drop of her slickness until her clit is too sensitive to touch anymore, and she leaps off me, shooting me a grin.

"I should punish you for that."

"Go for it." I urge, but she smiles wide and shakes her head.

"I'm ready to give you aftercare now."

Smiling, I nod, and she walks into the bathroom while I lay on the bed with a puddle of cooling cum on my stomach.

The thing about Cara and aftercare, is I think she loves this part more than the actual fucking. As tough as she is, she can be very nurturing, and I think it makes her feel good that she has that in her, despite her upbringing.

"I've had an idea about what we can call the girls in the MC." She tells me, moving onto the bed next to me and pressing a warm washcloth to my skin, wiping up my puddle of cum.

"The girls under your care?" I ask, and she nods.

"The Cruz Cunts."

"You want to call them cunts?" I ask, a little fucking confused.

"Yes. Cruz Cunts. I want to take power over that word since it was used against me, and probably millions of women across the world, too. I'm taking the power back on the word."

I chuckle. I get where she's coming from, and to be honest, it's a pretty catchy name.

"Okay, Killer. I'll make sure that's included in the final vote when we establish the club."

Grinning, she nods before dragging me up off the bed and into the shower where I get to sink my dick for the first time into my fiancé-wife's heat.

Cara

1.5 years later

"**C**an I come in yet?" Rocco asks, laughter palpable in his tone.

"No." Urgency makes the one word sound like I'm angry. "You know you can't see the dress."

I listen intently as he laughs and walks away from the office door. Once I'm sure he's gone, I turn back to the two mannequins wearing my options. I still can't decide which one to wear.

One is a replica of the one I wore at our original wedding, and I like the idea of wearing it as I say I do again—this time of my own volition, because I love the man who owns my heart.

The other is not really a wedding dress, or a dress at all. It's a sinfully sexy two-piece ensemble. The black leather top has holes and laces in the front, and the skirt is full length with a slit reaching my crotch.

I'm caught between the girl I once was and the woman I've now become. And try as I might, I can't decide, which means

I'll probably end up making a split second decision on the day.

There's a knock on the door, and before I can answer, it cracks open and Cain saunters in.

"Still can't decide?" he asks, cocking his eyebrow in that annoyingly all-knowing way of his.

"No," I mutter.

He nods thoughtfully. "You know Rocco doesn't care, right?"

We've already been over this a million times. Cain knows I'm not making this decision for Rocco, it's for me. I just wish I knew what the fuck I want.

Ever since the vote for the MC, Cain and I have become closer. In fact, I think I might be the only person who knows he has a serious side to him.

"Did you get it done?" I ask, changing the subject.

Fist pumping the air, he grins widely. "I did. And I wouldn't have done it for anyone but you."

My lips turn up as I say, "Well... you did owe me. But now we're square."

Cain sighs theatrically and runs a hand down his face. "Fucking hell, mi pequeño salvaje. I thought you were going to lord that favor over me forever."

With a laugh, I admit, "I was tempted. But no." Then I point at his laptop. "Let's resolve it right now."

I watch as he inputs his password before opening the sheet I'm referring to. With a grin, he clicks on the comment where he said he owed me all those years ago.

"Wait," I say. "Log in to my account instead."

Cain lets out a laugh while doing as I say. "You are thorough, aren't you," he says with a wink.

He isn't wrong. But with how many things are changing, I want this to be done the right way.

Dirty Diamonds no longer uses sheets for their scheduling and internal stuff. They've moved on to other systems that track everything, which is for the better. But Cain kept this one, insisting he wouldn't get rid of it until he repaid my favor.

Hip bumping him out of the way, I take over and resolve the comment that's been open for over three years. "There we go," I grin. "Favor officially repaid."

I don't know why there's a fucking lump in my throat, or why I'm so emotional these days. Despite what Rose, Sasha, and Alana suggest, I know it isn't wedding jitters. Rocco is the one constant I'm sure of, and I'd follow him into the gaping mouth of hell as long as he keeps his promise of me being his equal.

There's another knock on the door.

"Come in," Cain calls out as soon as I've covered both mannequins.

Gunner walks in, his chest is puffed out and his smirk is framed by the beard he's trying to grow. "It's done," he says, giving me a thumbs up.

"You did it?" I ask excitedly.

He nods. "Yep." Looking toward the two mannequins, he cocks an eyebrow. "You still haven't decided on what to wear?" he asks on a drawl as he leans against Cain's desk.

"You just settled it," I say, pointing at the mannequin I want. "This is the winner."

Gunner has worked around the clock to help me get things ready, even putting up with my unreasonable demands and crazy ideas.

Unlike Gray, who's made it clear he only cares because it's me and Rocco, Gunner seems to have a genuine interest. Not just in helping, but he's even helped me plan for the three days Rocco and I are going to spend wrapped around each other after the wedding.

Instead of going away for our honeymoon, we're moving into the house we've found. It's an empty warehouse with a decent amount of property. As soon as we found it, we agreed it was perfect as the clubhouse for the Cruz Kings.

After working out the last few details, I follow Cain and Gunner out of the office. We head into the main room where everyone is already getting rowdy.

"Killer!" Rocco exclaims. Everyone laughs as it takes him two attempts to get out of the corner booth. "I've missed you." I snigger at the slur in his voice.

"I've missed you too," I smile.

Tonight will be the first time we spend apart since I got out of prison, and while it's at my insistence, I'm not entirely happy about it. But it's important to me that we adhere to this one tradition. If for no other reason than because our lives are so crazy that normalcy is like a rare decadence.

Rocco pulls me over to the wall, placing his hands on either side of my face as he cages me in. "Have you changed your mind about spending the night with your Cunts?" he asks with a grin.

I shake my head. "Nope," I say. Then I wrap my arms around his neck and pull him down until his forehead rests against mine. "But I'll miss you, mi rey. A lot."

He lets out a strangled growl. "Why did you have to go and say that, Killer? Now I'll be hard all night while imagining you saying that with my cock in your mouth."

I fuse my lips to his, kissing him with all the love and desire I feel for him. As our tongues tangle, I can't stop thinking about how lucky I am. Even after all these years, he still makes me weak in the knees and makes my heart skip a beat.

"You better get going before I decide to keep you around," Rocco rasps when we pull back.

He squeezes my ass so hard my breath hitches. "See you tomorrow, husband." I place a chaste kiss on his lips before I leave.

After parking Rocco's truck, I make my way into the clubhouse where Sasha, Alana, Rose, Izzy, and Cilla are already having a blast.

The last two only joined us a few months ago, but they're quickly becoming a part of our growing family. Izzy came to us after she'd heard of the Cruz Kings through the grapevine, and Cilla is a friend of the Long twins.

"Cara!" Sasha squeals as soon as she spots me. "About time you got here. We almost thought you'd changed your mind and stayed with Rocco." Her voice barely penetrates the music blaring through the speakers.

"I'm not as ruled by cock as you are," I say with a grin.

"Lies," Rose laughs. "You're the worst one of us." I offer her a shrug because I'm not entirely sure she's wrong.

I look around, taking the room in. The other times I've been here, it's only been me and Rocco. But now, the five women make it feel much more alive. My lips curve upwards in a smile as I ponder what it'll be like when there are more of us.

"You're still not drinking." Alana frowns and looks at me like I've committed a grave faux pas.

"But you are," I dryly observe. "How far behind am I?"

Cilla laughs as she hands me a paper cup filled with tequila. "Not too far to catch up. So get to it," she urges, and I do.

Damn, that's so smooth I bet it's from Dante's or Baz's private stash. While the Cunts look on with excitement written all over their faces, I empty the cup in one go.

"Better?" I ask, raising my brow.

Sasha claps her hands together and whoops, "Now it's a party."

I let Rose and Izzy drag me over to the only table with chairs around it, and we all settle there. The alcohol flows as freely as our conversations, and it doesn't take long before I feel buzzed.

"Where are you going?" I ask when Rose and Alana get up.

"Don't worry about it, Mama," Rose sniggers. "Just wait for us here."

I give up on questioning them when Sasha refills my cup, and insists we toast to me living the rest of my life monogamous to one cock.

"It's a travesty, really," she slurs. "We aren't meant to only have one dick for the rest of our life."

Cilla cackles like a fucking witch. "You only say that because you can barely stick to one per night."

Sasha nods eagerly. "Too damn right. What's the point of having all those lovely looking dicks around if I can't sample them all?"

I burst out laughing, almost falling off the fucking chair that I swear is spinning. "Why keep looking if I've already found the perfect one?"

"Cock or man?" Izzy asks as she looks at me out of the corner of her eyes.

"Both," I giggle. "Rocco is... both."

Did that make sense? Fuck, I don't know, and with the way the room is spinning, I don't really care.

Rose and Alana return, each carrying a plastic bag that they place on the table before retaking their seats. After downing a few shots, they pull a few presents from the bag and shove them in front of me.

"What's this?" I ask, pointing at the wrapped boxes. "I thought I made it clear there'd be no presents."

"They're not from us," Alana sing-songs.

"That's right," Rose nods emphatically. "We didn't wrap ours."

Izzy grins. "And they're not presents," she says with a wink.

"That's right," Cilla interjects. "We're only lending you a few things."

I take a large swig of the tequila as I try to decipher their well-rehearsed speech. "Okay. So these presents aren't from you?"

They all shake their heads, which is all I need to know who they're from.

"Rocco," I breathe.

I reach for the first present and quickly unwrap it. The Cunts laugh like a fucking pack of hyenas when I reveal the black leather collar. Attached to it are two chains and at the end of each chain dangles a blue nipple clamp.

"Something new and blue," I say as soon as it dawns on me what I'm looking at.

My fucking husband.

"Keep going," Izzy encourages.

I frown in confusion as I open the next present. "Purple highlight kit?" I don't know why I'm phrasing it like a question when that's exactly what it is.

"Yep," Sasha says, popping the P.

I keep looking at the hair dye, wondering what that's all about. I don't usually dye my hair, and I haven't since... "Oh," I gasp. "Something to bring back my old look."

Cilla laughs again. "Told you she'd figure it out. Pay up."

I don't pay attention to the money changing hands, all I can think about is my overwhelming need to be with Rocco. To have him with me, tradition be damned.

Before I can decide if I want to interrupt my... bachelorette party, or whatever you call it when you're already married, Sasha and Alana drag me toward the small bathroom.

"Let's get your hair done before we're too drunk," Sasha laughs.

Even after all these years, sweat still runs down my spine and my breathing becomes ragged as I get closer to the tiled room. Fuck, will I ever get rid of this fucking sinking feeling?

"N-no." My voice wavers as I take a step back. "We can do it outside."

"Wait," Alana calls out, letting go of me at the same time.

"Oops," Sasha laughs, not noticing my change in mood.

Shooting me an apologetic grimace, Alana switches the lights on and explains, "Rocco told us to show you the changes before bringing you in here. But we forgot."

The Cunts haven't been told my full story, but they know enough to know tiled rooms freak me out. Well, that's an exaggeration. With Rocco's help it's nothing more than discomfort now. Still, he goes out of his way to make sure I'm as comfortable as possible.

"Oh my God," I gasp. Needing to make sure my eyes aren't deceiving me, I blink rapidly.

The tiles that used to be here are long gone, and I know without a shadow of a doubt that it's Rocco that's replaced it with vinyl. Just like in our bathroom at home.

"Rocco wanted to make sure it was perfect for you," Rose says, as she walks up behind me.

A lump forms in my throat, and I can only nod when Sasha asks if I want to continue. As they work on my hair, I make the decision to call Rocco and ask him to come. I don't know what they're doing tonight, and it doesn't matter. He'll come if I ask him to, and I'm selfish enough to want that.

Since my hair almost reaches my waist, it takes forever to add the purple highlights. But the Cunts are no less enthusiastic when we finish than they were when we started.

"It looks amazing," Cilla whoops once we're done and my hair is dry.

"Thank you," I say, looking at each of them in the mirror. "Not just for this, but for making tonight so amazing."

They nod, and I feel like an understanding settles around us as we look at our reflections. We need no words to cement the bond between us, it runs deeper than that. And I know in my gut that I'll protect these women with my life.

"Right," Sasha says, wiping a tear from her eye. "This is fun and all, but I want to get laid."

I bark out a laugh. "Go," I grin as I turn around to face them. "I want to call Rocco."

"Wait," Izzy interjects. "There's one last thing to take care of."

"Oh, yeah," Cilla says, nodding as she looks at me. "You need something borrowed."

I gape at them. I know the tradition to have something old, new, borrowed, and blue, I just never even considered embracing it and making it part of my second wedding day.

"Here," Sasha says, holding her fist out. She unclenches, releasing something that falls right into my outstretched and waiting hand. "It's all of ours, and we want it back. So take good care of it."

I'm almost scared to look at what it is, but of course, curiosity gets the better of me. "A button?" I ask, feeling like I'm missing something. "You're letting me borrow a fucking button?" There's definitely something I'm not getting here.

The Cunts snigger and share amused glances. I'm just about to demand an answer when Izzy clears her throat. "Remember the jeans you once lent Sasha and didn't want back because of the cum stains?" I nod because you don't easily forget when that happens. "Well, we've all worn them, and all had an orgasm while wearing them. So it seemed fitting that you, the Mama of Cunts, borrow the button."

I run a hand through my newly washed and dried hair, letting out a deep breath. "You're all fucking certifiable," I laugh. "But I love it, and I wouldn't have it any other way."

Waving them all closer, I wrap my arms around Rose and Cilla, pulling them into a hug. Though I can't reach all of my girls, I hope they know how much they mean to me.

After a while, I step back. "Right, I want to call Rocco," I say with a grin.

They exchange knowing glances but don't clue me in on the big secret as they leave the bathroom together.

Once I walk back into the main room, I realize why. Rocco's already here. He's sitting at the table we partied at earlier, and he's looking right at me.

"Sorry," he drawls, not looking sorry at all as he gets to his feet. "Couldn't wait until tomorrow."

Grinning, I run to him and jump into his waiting arms. "Mi rey," I whisper, wrapping my arms and legs around him. "I was just about to call you."

I claim his lips, eagerly letting my tongue trace the seam of his lips as I move my hands into his hair. Rocco's tongue delves into my mouth, stroking mine in a way that sends wetness to my core.

"Cara," he rasps into my mouth.

"Fuck me," I purr.

I don't know if the Cunts are still here or if they've left, and right now I couldn't care less. All I want is Rocco to consume me.

He chuckles darkly. "Not until after you've said I do tomorrow."

I gape, not sure I heard him correctly. "You can't be serious."

"Oh, but I am, Mama." He pinches my ass and rolls his hips so his erection grazes my core.

"Please?" I beg, gyrating my hips to get more of him.

Despite my pleas, Rocco doesn't change his mind and instead carries me into the room he intends to use for church.

When he puts me down, he points at the air mattress on the floor. "But I still want to sleep with you tonight. Emphasis on sleeping, Killer."

Fuck me, Rocco's thought of everything, hasn't he? I guess this tells me that he never had any intention of staying away, and I think I love him even more for that. Both for letting me have my idea, but mostly for knowing what I'd want at the end of the night.

Him. Always him.

"Fine," I grumble as I begin to remove my clothes. "I still want you naked."

He shoots me one of those smiles that makes me weak in the fucking knees as he unashamedly strips out of his clothes before helping me with mine. The tequila still courses through my veins, making my movements... awkward.

As soon as we're both naked, we lie down on the mattress. Rocco lies on his back, and I place my head on top of his heart, letting the steady thumping lull me to sleep.

When I wake up the next morning, Rocco's already awake. "Morning, Killer," he rasps.

I stretch and yawn. "Hi," I say, the remnants of sleep evident in my hoarse voice. "I wasn't sure if you'd still be here."

He gives me a wicked smile. "I wanted to help you with the nipple clamps."

My brows shoot up my forehead, and my lips part on an O as I remember the presents from last night. "Please," I say.

Rocco lifts his pillow and pulls the collar from under there. "Are you okay with the collar?" he rasps.

"Of course," I answer immediately. "I trust you."

The fact that he asks is just one of the many reasons I love Rocco. And while I've made it clear, I'll never be his Old Lady or his property, I'm more than okay with the games we play and his occasional show of dominance.

My breath hitches as he wraps the collar around my neck, fastening it at the back before he reaches for the blue clamps at the end of the chains.

"Are you ready?" he asks on a groan.

At my nod, he pulls the sheet down. My nipples pebble under his heated gaze, and when he closes his mouth around one, I moan loudly.

"Rocco." He pulls back with a chuckle before licking the other, not pulling back until I'm panting. "Fucking tease," I whine.

As he shifts, his hard cock catches my attention, and I lick my lips. His length jerks as though it can feel my attention, and I have to remind myself now isn't the time.

"Here we go," Rocco rasps.

I take a deep breath and hold it as he closes the clamps around my nipples. The sensation that follows is hard to explain. It's too much and also not enough. It hurts while also feeling amazing. My cunt throbs, and I whimper.

"Rocco... I need..." Fuck, I don't know what I'm begging for. Him? A release? Whatever it is, I want it badly.

"This is how I want you, Killer," Rocco says solemnly. "As desperate for me as I am for you. Can you give me that?"

Gritting my teeth, I nod again. "Okay," I agree.

I consider returning the favor and working him up as well, but decide against it. This is what Rocco wants, and I want to give it to him. Besides, I already know it'll be worth it later.

Rocco gets out of the makeshift bed, and hands me my clothes before getting dressed. I follow his lead and get up. Though instead of putting my own clothes on, I snatch his shirt.

"I need this more than you," I snap when he tries to take it back. "Do you know how hard leather is to get into? I'm not putting my clothes on just to take it off in a few minutes."

He relents with a chuckle. "Whatever you say, Killer." Then he pulls his phone from his jeans pocket and looks at the clock. "I have to go."

Laughing at the regret in his tone, I shoo him away with my hand. "Go before I change my mind and pounce on you."

His eyes become hooded, and he lets out a low growl that I know will lead to us being late to our own fucking wedding.

We're interrupted by a knock on the door, and Sasha calling, "Cara?"

"Saved by the Cunts," I grin before answering Sasha. "In here. Give me two minutes."

The words barely leave my mouth before the door is slammed open, and Sasha saunters inside with Rose in tow.

"Nope. Not happening. We know that tone, and we're not letting you distract each other today."

Rose points at Rocco. "Go," she orders, scowling at him.

Throwing his hands up in the air, Rocco huffs. "I just want to—"

"Not happening," Cain drawls as he joins us. Palming Rocco's shoulder, he practically pushes him out of here.

As soon as they're gone, Alana comes into view. "We're waiting for you," she says, and I spring into action.

I forgo the shower I wanted since I don't want to remove the nipple clamps. So instead, I go directly to getting dressed. While I put my outfit on, Sasha explains that all the guys have the cuts with the logo on them.

Gunner helped me design the skull and crown logo befitting of the Cruz Kings. And after he confirmed everything was ready yesterday, he ironed it onto the back of my skirt as well as the cut I'll give Rocco after we say I do.

The Cunts are already wearing their black dresses with the logo on the back.

"The guys are already here," Rose says as she watches me put the last touches on my makeup.

"It's a woman's prerogative to take as long as she needs," Alana grins.

She's right, of course. But since I'm ready, there's no point in waiting longer. "Are Gray and Gunner ready?" I ask, smoothing the skirt.

"Yeah," Sasha answers. "Everyone's ready."

"Go take your places," I say. "And tell everyone I'll be there shortly."

When Rose's about to leave with the rest, I stop her in her tracks. "Hold up," I say. "I want to ask you something." I swallow harshly when my voice sounds like gravel.

"What's up?" Rose asks.

I don't know why I'm so nervous to ask her, but I am, and it makes no fucking sense. "I want to ask you something, and feel free to say no."

"Okay?"

"Rocco's not the only one who's going to need a second in command," I explain, pointing at myself like it's necessary to spell it out for her. "I'll need one too. Will you be me when I'm not around? Help with the duties, and whatever else might be needed?"

Rose's jaw becomes slack, and her eyes take on a glassy quality as she fights her tears. "Really?" she asks.

I nod, determined that it has to be Rose. I can't explain what it is, but there's something about her. I trust her implicitly, and... if I'm honest, I feel a stronger connection to her than to the rest.

"Absolutely," I clarify.

"Then I accept," she croaks, quickly wiping a stray tear from underneath her eye.

As I contemplate hugging her, she mumbles an excuse to go join the others and practically runs away. I get it. We don't do emotional well, and right now, I've made her just that. I take a deep breath, happy with my decision, before I, too, leave.

Gunner and Gray wait for me near the doors leading outside to the unkempt garden. They're both dressed in black jeans, black sleeveless shirts, and the new leather cut with the logo on the back.

"Mama," they grin in unison, and I mock scowl at them for good measure.

"That's going to take some getting used to," I say, referring to my MC title.

"You look amazing," Gray says with a nod.

Gunner whistles under his breath. "Rocco's a lucky guy."

"I know," I laugh.

Then I link my arms with theirs, and follow them to where everyone's gathered.

Rocco stands next to Cain, and to the left are Dante, Baz, Munroe, Tex, Stretch, Slayer, and Slasher. Opposite the men are my Cunts, Alana, Sasha, Rose, Cilla, and Izzy.

"He hasn't seen their backs," Gray assures me just before we reach them.

I smile as my gaze finds Rocco's. Even though it's only been a handful of hours, it's still too long since I last saw him.

"Who gives this married woman away to be married to the same man again?" Cain asks.

"We do," Gunner and Gray answer in unison. Then they kiss my cheeks and while making sure Rocco can't see their backs, they awkwardly walk over to join the other men.

Rocco takes my hand and pulls me to his side. "Killer," he murmurs only loud enough for me to hear.

"Mi rey," I breathe.

"Since I've never ordained shit before, let alone an already married couple, I'm just going to wing it," Cain sing-songs.

A few people chuckle.

"Most of us have no idea what Cara sees in Rocco's ugly face, but here we are," Cain grins.

"It's his cock," Sasha pipes up. "She told us that yesterday."

I burst out laughing as Cain nods like that makes all the sense in the world.

"Can we get on with it?" Rocco growls.

He might sound annoyed, but I know better. He's just eager for us to get married for real. Well, no. That's not it... it's for us to voluntarily say I do to each other.

"Yes, yes," Cain says, waving him off. "So, umm... if you two would like to get married again, please recite your vows."

Rocco takes my hand and turns to look at me. "Cara." He swallows thickly. "When we got married, you were a job. A mission. I never imagined that day could turn into something real, but here we are. I can't wait to spend the rest of my life with you by my side."

I gulp and my eyes become misty. "Rocco..." Blinking rapidly, I try to get rid of the tears gathering behind my lids. "You're everything that's right in this world. I never knew that men like you actually existed, and I definitely never believed I'd be able to love anyone. But you've made me see that there's more to life than what I knew, and that love is worth fighting for."

Some of the Cunts sniff, but I don't turn around to see who. I'm too transfixed on my husband, and the moment we're sharing right now.

Even though our first marriage wasn't what it should have been, it was still kind of perfect. Not at the time, but in hindsight. Because I'm not sure I could have opened my heart to Rocco, or trusted him, if we'd met under different circumstances.

Evil forced us together, but it's love, understanding, and respect that binds us together.

"I love you, Killer," Rocco rasps.

Beaming at him, I say, "And I love you, mi rey."

"By the power vested in me by the almighty internet, I now declare you husband and wife... again," Cain announces. "You may now kiss the fuck out of your wife."

The laugh on my lips dies when Rocco wraps his arm around my middle and dips me. Before I can say anything, he slants his lips to mine in a kiss that has my toes curling. Our guests fade into nothingness, and all that exists is Rocco's mouth and tongue.

I let out a hiss as the corner of his teeth knicks my tongue, and the taste of copper explodes between us. "Rocco," I moan, unashamedly needy for him.

"Killer," he rasps. "Are you still wearing the nipple clamps?"

Now that they're at the forefront of my mind, my nipples pulsate, sending waves of lust through my body. "Yes."

He chuckles darkly before pulling us both upright. "Good."

"You know you didn't have to get ordained to remarry them, right?" Sasha asks Cain who wiggles his eyebrows.

"Oh, I know. But I owed a debt," he answers while winking at me.

Rose clears her throat and points at the small plastic bag at her feet. Oh yeah, I almost forgot about my present for Rocco. At my nod she comes over to me, and I take the bag.

"Husband," I purr, loving the smile stretching across Rocco's handsomely scarred face. "I have a present for you as well."

I give him the bag, and while he pulls the cut from it, I signal for our guests to turn around so their backs face us.

Rocco holds the cut up, nodding thoughtfully. "Our first cut," he says, clearly he hasn't looked at the back yet.

"Turn it around," I encourage impatiently.

He does, and I watch as his jaw becomes slack when he sees the skull with a crown on top. Below it says 'Cruz Kings MC' and below that 'President'.

"This is perfect," he rasps. "We need one for everyone."

"Isn't it?" I beam. Then I point behind him. "Take a look."

He turns his head, and I wish I could see his expression as he takes in their cuts. Of course some of them are just honorary. Dante, Baz, and Cain aren't part of the Cruz Kings, and they'll likely never be. But today, logistics doesn't matter.

"You did all this?" Rocco asks as he turns back to me.

Before I can answer, he pulls me flush against him and crushes his lips to mine in a brutal kiss. Our teeth clash, and this time I bite his lip.

"I did," I moan into his mouth. "My present to you."

When we pull apart, I have to literally point at the Cunts before he notices the skull on their clothing as well. And, lastly, I turn and bend over to show him the one on my ass.

"You're fucking perfect," Rocco growls as he helps me back up.

"And you're fucking mine."

Rocco

1.5 years later

My back slams into the wall as Cara and I fight for dominance, the sounds of the first pre-club orgy well underway as the Cruz Cunts show the future club members just how things will be around here from now on. There's not a stitch of clothing to be seen. Just the flesh of tits, cunts, ass, and well... dicks. Something I'll have to get fucking used to given that a good old-fashioned orgy is a well-known event that happens inside an MC.

"Are you watching them fuck?" Cara hisses her question as she wraps her hand around the base of my nuts and gently squeezes.

"It's like live porn," I observe, and she snickers before grazing her tongue up my neck.

"It is," Cara breathes against my ear. "The Cunts have done their research well, even though it's not required. They aim to please." She releases my balls and fists my cock. "Sasha has even mastered deepthroating. The men will love that."

I growl, squeezing the bare round globes of her ass before giving one side a sharp slap.

She sucks in another hiss, and I growl, spinning us to slam her against the wall this time.

"Look at them." I demand, watching her dark gaze shift from mine to the scene behind me. "Do you like live porn, Killer?"

A slow sensual smirk tugs at her lips before she drags her gaze away from our writhing members.

"I do, in fact. I like watching it. I even like participating in it," her claw-like nails dig into my chin as she grips it forcefully, "but only with you. I will never share you with anyone."

Baring my teeth, I growl like a fucking lion. "And I will never fucking share you either," I declare before slamming my lips into hers.

She meets my kiss with ferocious need, her legs wrapping around me even as I lift her and slam my cock deep into her slick cunt.

She cries out, gripping my shoulders before our bodies fight for dominance again, each thrust met and claimed as we clash in a pounding frenzy.

My feet move, leading us on a wall bumping journey up the hallway, leaving the orgy in full swing before I push through the doors of church, and bend to place my wife on the new, yet old and distressed looking table.

"What are you doing?" Cara pants, not stopping her gyrating thrusts as our position changes. Her dark gaze glances over the room briefly, before a smirk tugs at her lips. "Really?"

I snap my teeth at her as I press my lips to hers before standing taller and looking down over her bouncing tits and flushed skin as I continue to pound into her over and over.

"What's a church altar without a christening?"

Laughing, Cara nods. "You have a point. Let's christen the fuck outta this table."

"My thoughts exactly." I agree before pressing my thumb to her swollen clit.

Cara's back arches off the table, pressing her head into the carved Cruz Kings MC logo in the center, and a primal growl rips from me as I take in the sight of my stunning wife laid out on the table like a feast with the club logo behind her.

"Mine!" I roar, pistoning inside her as my thumb picks up speed on her needy bud.

"I'm-I'm—"

Cara's strangled cry gets cut off as her walls tighten around me, and I speed up, pounding into her hard, hitting her as deep as I can go while mashing my thumb over her clit. I feel the moment when her first orgasm rolls into the next, and that's when I finally let go, a roar ripping from my lungs as I throw my head back and shoot cum deep into her cunt.

I swear, it's the longest climax I've ever fucking had, since Cara's kept rolling and her walls continue to pulse around my hard length until I can't take it anymore and jerk my dick free.

"Fuck, woman. You're going to kill me."

She giggles through her panting breaths, and nods. "Best way to die."

I throw my head back with a laugh at her comment as she props herself up on her elbows to look at me.

"Well, that was something else."

"Yeah." I agree. "Sure fucking was."

We beam at each other for a few beats before my eyes drop to her parted thighs, and the pool of cum oozing from her.

"You're making a mess on the table, Killer."

She shrugs. "It's actually your mess. But like you said, it's a christening."

"Fuck." I chuckle. "You're right. But even so." I lower myself down until I'm eye level with her exposed flesh.

"What are you doing?" Cara's question sounds curious rather than concerned or confused, and I shoot her a wicked grin before I start scooping up the cooling cum with my fingers and push it back inside her.

"This was a gift. Don't waste it."

She giggles and tries to push my hand away. "Since we are never having children, I think your *gift* is wasted."

I shake my head, pushing the last bit in before glancing up at her amused expression.

"The gift is for me."

"For you?"

"Yes." I nod, standing and holding my hand out to her. "I want to see it oozing down your thighs when we go back out there, and I want everyone to fucking see."

Taking my hand, she grins and rolls her eyes. "Of course that's what you want."

I pull her up off the table, flush with my naked flesh as we take a moment to kiss again, then I spin her to face the table and point at the slick sheen left behind.

"You left a mess. Lick it up."

An exasperated glare gets sent my way over her shoulder, so I slap her perky ass and press my lips to her ear.

"I gave you an order, mi reina. Today you obey me."

A shiver runs up her spine, even as she reaches back and grips the top of my thighs with her clawed fingers. "Fine. I'll submit now, but just so you know, you'll be licking up your own cum tomorrow."

"I don't doubt it." I rasp against her ear, and I see a smile lift her cheeks.

Releasing my thighs, Cara slowly, and very fucking sexily, leans down over the table and starts to lick up the mess we left.

I take a moment to step back and get a good look at the glistening lips of her cunt between her legs as she bends, and the trail of my cream starting to seep from inside her already.

"I hate to cut the orgy short," Cain's voice comes from behind me, and I turn to glare at his tilted head as he studies my wife's weeping cunt. "But I have to get back for a crew meeting."

Cain's eyes meet mine then, and any heat that was there a moment ago when he was ogling my wife slips away.

I stand slowly, watching Cain button up his jeans and looking kind of nervous.

"You will always have an open invitation to our orgies," I tell him and fuck, a lump the size of an orange forms in my throat.

I feel Cara shift behind me before she wraps her arms around my middle, resting her head on my arm as she stares between us.

"Thank you," Cain says, and I frown. I was expecting some sort of crude retort, or even a song about orgies, but he says nothing, just stands in the doorway and stares at me.

"Uh." Cara clears her throat, "I'll be right back."

I frown as my wife steps around me, as naked as the day she was born before sauntering past Cain and out into the winding down orgy.

"You sure you have to go?" I ask Cain, my voice cracking a little like I'm a fucking teenager.

"Yeah." He nods. "It's time."

Fuck.

Why is this such a big fucking deal?

Heat pricks at the back of my eyes as I stare at my best friend.

"Are you sure?" I ask, and he nods.

"I'm sure." He clears his throat like he has a fucking lump the size of an orange lodged in there too.

"Here." Cara's voice joins us again as she tosses me my jeans, and I quickly step into them while she slips my t-shirt over her head, covering up.

"Thanks, Killer." I offer her a warm smile, and she gives me a nod, already knowing what's going on here.

"Don't be a stranger." Cara gains Cain's attention as she steps up and gives him a hug, and I don't even care that he holds her tighter than he should or that he lingers longer than is appropriate. He's not trying to be creepy. He genuinely cares about Cara like a sister.

"Same goes for you, mi pequeño salvaje." He rasps, and she pushes back from him.

"Dammit, Cain. You're gonna make me cry. We are literally down the road. This isn't goodbye."

He nods slowly, like he doesn't believe her.

Stepping out of the way, Cara excuses herself, leaving me with Cain again.

"She's right. This isn't goodbye," I tell him and he shrugs.

"Not goodbye, but it's the end of... us." He chokes out, and I can't fucking hold back. I storm over to him and grip his upper arms.

"Never. You and me, we are brothers no matter what. A different club or crew doesn't change that. And we are still fighting on the same side. Just in different units."

Cain's eyes turn glassy, but no tears fall.

"It's been what? Six? Seven years since the idea of forming an MC was discussed?" When I nod, Cain continues, his hands coming to my shoulders in a tight grip. "I thought it would be enough time for me to get used to the idea of not having you by my side. But it wasn't."

"Fuck," I hiss, pulling him in for a manly hug, our bare chests clashing as we each pound a fist on each other's backs. "The invitation for you to join the MC is always open as well. You know you'll always be my right-hand man."

Slowly pulling back, we drop our holds as Cain shakes his head.

"No. It can't be like that anymore. From now on, Gray is your right-hand man." He nods like it's something he's finally accepting. "And from now on, even though we will always be friends, we need to step into the roles of associates."

He's right. I know he is, but it doesn't mean it doesn't hurt. Cain has been on this ride with me for so long. I'm not sure how I will go without seeing him every couple of days.

"Thank you for everything," I say, because I don't know what else to say, and he grins.

"Thank me later when I video call you and show you my big cock sliding into the new Diamonds we recruited to replace the girls you stole."

I roll my eyes. "I didn't fucking steal them. Dante gave them to me."

"Steal. Gave. Same difference." He shrugs.

I chuckle as Cain does a twirl before giving me his back and strutting up the hallway like he's a fucking king. It's fucking hard to tell with that guy.

As soon as he steps out of sight, I turn and face the room, sad that the part of my life with Cain by my side is over, but excited to start the new one with my very own fucking MC.

"Are you ready?" Cara asks, and I turn back to see that she has re-dressed, much to my disappointment before she tosses my t-shirt at me, and I slip it on.

"Have they finished their fuck session?" I ask, referring to the members about to be sworn in.

"They have. They are ready." Cara advises, approaching me with my cut in her hand. "Here you go. Prez."

I snicker, shucking on the cut as Cara beams at me. "I wonder how long it will take for me to get used to that?"

"It won't take you long since I plan on screaming, oh yes, Prez, right there, fuck me good, every time you claim me."

Throwing my head back laughing, I pull my wife to my chest and claim her lips.

"I'll hold you to that." I rasp against her lips before we pull back, and a throat clears.

"Everyone is ready." Gray declares, standing in the doorway, wearing his cut.

"Okay. Everyone can come in."

A meeting of the MC is called church, and normally, only full patch members can attend, but since I am the only official patch member right now, I open the first meeting to everyone who is joining our ranks in one way or another.

As Cara takes my side, one by one, the men and women file in and stand in an arced line at the end of the small room.

"I am Rochus King, the President of the Cruz Kings MC. This MC is the first chapter of the Cruz Kings MC, and will be referred to as the mother charter." I take a breath as Cara hands me the book of bylaws that we have spent the last few years creating. Prior to today, each invited member received a copy of our club rules which included the code of conduct and the code of silence, the latter being one of the most fundamental rules in an MC, ensuring members do not divulge any club secrets to the authorities and outsiders.

Today, they will sign the registry in acknowledgement of these rules, after they are sworn in.

"Each of you has been invited to join our ranks. Everyone has an important role, and as we grow bigger with more members, and more women, we will embrace this club like a family."

Each person standing in line nods, even though they aren't required to, and I feel a sense of pride.

"Will each recruiting patch member please step forward and place your fist over your heart."

The men step forward in the line, several thumps sounding as they do as I ask with fierce determination.

My eyes travel over the men who are here today, in support of me, and what my club represents, and I know that even though these are grown men, I feel like they are my sons. My little brothers.

They all stand tall, like their fist over their hearts is a salute.

"Please swear your allegiance to me, as the founding father of the Cruz Kings MC, and the club and its members, and swear to uphold our values with honor, and protect each other with your life."

Like they've rehearsed it for hours, the men talk in unison, declaring their allegiance.

> *"I swear my allegiance to our founding father, Rochus King, and the Cruz Kings MC and its members, both patch, and pussy. I swear to uphold the club values with honor and protect each member with my life."*

Another fucking lump forms in my throat as I take in each club brother, and the sheer loyalty already confirmed on their expressions.

Moving forward, I open the book of bylaws onto the registration page, and place it on the end of the table as Cara steps up with the patches in her hand.

"When I call your name, please step forward, and accept your patch, and sign your name against your role in the register." I order, feeling a rush of excitement churn inside my chest. This is really happening.

"Grayson Black." I announce, and the homeless looking kid that Dante took in all those years ago resembles a man now, the same age I was when Cara came back to me from prison. He stands tall, his dark waves tousled from the earlier activities, and he holds his chin up with pride.

"Do you accept the Vice President patch?" I ask, and like an obedient soldier, he nods.

"Yes. I accept with honor." Gray's dark eyes meet mine before I hand him his patch, and as he looks down at it, reading the words, Vice President, a small smile tugs at the corner of his mouth.

Gesturing to the book, he leans down and signs his name next to VP in the registry, before shaking my hand and taking a seat at the end of the table, to the right of my throne.

"Rodney Texas," I call, and Tex steps forward, as we repeat the process, and he accepts the Treasurer patch.

"Gary Munroe," I call, and Munroe steps forward, accepting the Secretary patch, again repeating the process.

Next, I call, "Billy O'Shaughnessy."

Everyone glances around for a moment and Stretch chuckles as he steps forward. "People often think my nickname comes from my never-ending dick, but I first got it at school when a teacher said my name stretches so long."

Everyone laughs as he steps up to accept his Road Captain patch before signing the book and taking a seat.

"Eddie Gunn," I call, and Gunner steps forward. He's spent the last few years growing a beard, wanting to represent an MC properly, his words, not mine. I offer him the Sergeant-at-Arms patch, and he accepts, happy to be our enforcer.

"Slasher and Slayer Long," I call, and yes, their mother really called them that, which is fitting to the men they've grown into. I hand them identical badges, and they nod with pride as our Tail Gunners, the men who will ride at the back and ensure if anyone has to stop along our rides, that one of them remains with the member, as we never leave a brother behind.

As I take my seat at the end of the table, I gesture to Cara to proceed, and she turns to face the women left standing.

"Alana, Sasha, Rose, Cilla and Izzy. I am Cara King, the Mama of the Cruz Kings MC. You have been invited to join the ranks as a Cruz Cunt."

I swear I'm about to fucking pound my fists against my chest with primal pride at my woman standing there, being the queen she is.

"Do you swear your allegiance to me, as your Mama C of the Cruz Kings MC, and to the President, Rochus King and his loyal members seated around this table?" Cara gestures to me and the men as we watch on, and each woman nods with enthusiasm.

"I do," they say in unison like they are getting fucking married, and I suppose in a way they are. They are dedicating their lives to us, and in turn, we will protect them.

Cara steps up to each woman, and hands them a necklace. It's nothing more than two letters on a thin silver chain. CC for Cruz Cunts. But it means more than two measly letters. It's their version of a patch, linking them to us.

A couple of the women start crying as they accept the necklaces, all putting them on without question and then Cara asks them to sign the registry under the section marked 'Cruz Cunts'.

Once they are done, they stand in their line at the end of the table looking at the official members of the Cruz Kings MC with huge smiles on their faces. And the biggest belongs to my wife as she stands with them.

It takes me a moment to clear my throat, and that fucking lump that keeps appearing today, but I glance around the table at my new family, ready to get this shit started and officially claim this territory.

"We will no doubt have some challenges ahead of us, but together we will stand, we will fight, and we will win. So my brothers, chant with me."

Pride surges through my veins, as each man joins the chant as listed in the copy of the rules and code of conduct, each of them already knowing the words by heart.

With honor we ride, side by side. Brothers by choice. Brothers by heart. Brothers with pride. In this life and the next, together we fly. We are the Cruz Kings, ride or die.

My eyes find my wife's again, as I announce that the men will spend the afternoon getting the Cruz King death head and name tattooed into their flesh to match mine, and as everyone's attention is focused on me, I pick up the gavel, and close the very first church meeting with a thunderous slam.

WITH HONOR WE RIDE,
SIDE BY SIDE.
BROTHERS BY CHOICE.
BROTHERS BY HEART.
BROTHERS WITH PRIDE.
IN THIS LIFE AND THE NEXT,
TOGETHER WE FLY.
WE ARE THE CRUZ KINGS,
RIDE OR DIE.

www.ingramcontent.com/pod-product-compliance
Lightning Source LLC
Chambersburg PA
CBHW060654190726
48289CB00002B/398